The Future for Curious People

THE FUTURE FOR CURIOUS PEOPLE

a novel by

GREGORY SHERL

ALGONQUIN BOOKS OF CHAPEL HILL   2014

Published by

ALGONQUIN BOOKS OF CHAPEL HILL

Post Office Box 2225

Chapel Hill, North Carolina 27515-2225

a division of

WORKMAN PUBLISHING

225 Varick Street

New York, New York 10014

This is a work of fiction. While, as in all fiction, the literary perceptions and insights are based on experience, all names, characters, places, and incidents either are products of the author's imagination or are used fictitiously.

LIBRARY OF CONGRESS CATALOGING-IN-PUBLICATION DATA

Sherl, Gregory.

  The future for curious people : a novel / by Gregory Sherl.—First edition.

    pages cm

    ISBN 978-1-61620-369-6

    I. Title.

    PS3619.H46375F88 2014

    813'.6—dc23   2014014695

10 9 8 7 6 5 4 3 2 1

First Edition

For Rebecca

✳ ✳ ✳

Life is a series of collisions with the future;
it is not the sum of what we have been,
but what we yearn to be.

—José Ortega y Gasset

The Future for Curious People

Evelyn
THE BREAKUP

I'm breaking up with Adrian on the corner of Charles and Mulberry where he's passing out half-sheet advertisements for his band, the Babymakers. He's pale and weedy-looking, permanently anxious. His cheeks are flushed, his boxy nose red. It's cold and has just started to snow. The snow is partly the reason I've decided that today is the day. The air has taken shape, and everything suddenly seems like it's in motion, full swirl.

He shouts into the wind, "You're breaking up with me because I'm not a successful guitarist and because I seem like I'm just a guy handing out pamphlets on a street corner! You're disgusted." This is why Adrian is disgusted with Adrian and has nothing to do with me. Very little of our relationship has much to do with me, which is one of the *actual* reasons I'm breaking up with him. He loves me but doesn't really understand me—so, in effect, does he really love *me*?

"No. Listen to me!" I circle around him, my wool coat flapping at my knees. "We both need to look forward with new eyes again."

"You want to look forward and see someone else. I get it." Adrian pushes his knit hat back and scratches his forehead. "You know, it's really superficial and judgmental of you to break up with me because I don't meet your standards. I expected more." This isn't about my standards—although should I date Adrian because he meets someone else's standards? But now Adrian has just called me superficial and judgmental. He's not usually the type to throw stones. This attack comes off as desperate. Both kind of embarrassed for a moment, we look off in opposite directions like we're standing at a shoreline. In some ways, his attack is so last ditch that it's really an admission of defeat.

"Seriously," I say softly, "I love you." I do love Adrian. We've been good to each other. There's an undeniable accumulation of tenderness. "But . . ." I breathe into the air not wanting to say the rest. "I think we're just holding on to something that can't endure." And then I whisper. "I've seen what's going to become of us, and . . ."

Adrian looks at me sharply. He knows I'm talking about having seen our future together at Dr. Chin's office. He'd refused to come, calling all of these newfangled romantic-envisioning offices new-agey bourgeois bullshit. But in Chin's office I saw our sad future—the two of us singing "Happy Birthday" to a Chihuahua in a Hawaiian shirt and pointy hat. "Don't." Adrian holds up his flexed hand; he knows I'm about to launch into the session and he hates hearing about it.

For his sake I summarize, "We were old and tattooed and had a rusty space heater, and we sang to that dog in Spanish." Because the dog was a Chihuahua, this last detail feels slightly racist or something. We were also wearing baffling T-shirts, which I assume will be provocative in the future: THE JUSTICE CURE? PARK IT HERE! and another outraged about moped rentals.

Adrian says, "I just don't believe that's our future." He turns away and then back again, turning a full circle. "Even if it is, how do you know we weren't happy, deep down?"

Here's what I know about possible futures: They're limitless, and all potential. They aren't messy like the past and the present. As soon as I was wearing the paper gown and that weird helmet in Chin's office, staring at the screen, I knew that the future *seems* like it has clearly marked forks in the road, but there are forks within forks within forks until each choice—whether to bring an umbrella or stop for a doughnut or break up with Adrian—is a fork. "Most people choose their futures by accident," I say. "They don't even know they're making choices. They don't even know that there are forks in the road—much less forks within forks. The future no longer has to be messy. It can be tested out. It can be *known*."

Adrian has a measure of professionalism, I'll give him that. A swarm of commuters charges the intersection, and he's shoving wind-flipped half sheets at their chests. "The Babymakers," he says. "Get your ass off your sofa on Saturday night and live a little." He goes largely ignored.

And then there's a lull. "Almost two years we've been together!" he says to me. "A total waste!"

"It hasn't been a waste," I say. "Time isn't something you put in hoping for a return on an investment. It's experiencing life—both good and bad and occasionally tragic. It's the tragic I'm trying to avoid."

"There are worse tragedies than a Chihuahua in a Hawaiian

shirt, having his birthday celebrated!" Adrian says. "At least we know some Spanish in the future!"

A woman pushing a stroller has stalled, reading the half sheet. She might want to ask a question. The baby is wearing a drawstring hood that cinches up its face, which is placid except for darting eyes. Adrian is glancing at the woman expectantly.

"I'm trying to do what's best," I tell him. "I don't want to end up two hateful old people who fight about cheese."

"How many times do I have to tell you that I won't fight about cheese?" During the Chihuahua's birthday party, we squabble about whether or not melted brie is uppity.

"The cheese is a metaphor for minutiae," I say. "It's just an example of how we will become bitter."

The woman with the stroller looks at us with some obvious pity and walks away.

Adrian sighs and puts his hands on his skinny hips. "Are you being instigated by your mother?"

Both of my parents seem to dislike Adrian, but at the same time, I get the feeling they think he's too good for me, which is the kind of contradiction they're practiced in. "My relationship with my parents is based on reading a language of passive-aggressive sighing. I don't know what they think about me—much less you."

"Dot doesn't like me either." He sighs. "She's a weird bird."

My best friend, Dot, is a little odd and steals things, a nervous habit, really; she just wants me to be with someone who's right for me. "I'm a grown-up, Adrian. Come on. I make my own decisions."

Adrian starts jostling between commuters again, lunging at them, one after another. I look up at the sky, growing dark. The snow is light and dizzying—and new. That's the thing about snow. It's all about promise. It's nature's do-over.

Suddenly Adrian is standing right in front of me. He looks a little teary. Maybe it's just the cold wind. He's so close I feel his warm breath; this is possibly the most exercise he's gotten in weeks. I imagine his ribs, rising and falling, after sex. I'll miss his hands on me and the way he says I'm the best goddamn librarian in the world, even though he's never understood what I do at the library exactly. There's something sweet about how he loves me without knowing me—a blind love, which is almost like an unconditional love but not quite.

He hands me a half sheet and says in his rough voice, "Get your ass off your sofa and live a little, Evelyn Shriner." He nods, a series of jerky chin-up nods, meaning *I'm saying one thing, but I mean something bigger.*

And he means *I'm letting you go.*

I look at the half sheet—THE BABYMAKERS in bold letters and beneath that GET YOUR ASS OFF THE SOFA AND LIVE A LITTLE.

I fold the flyer and put it in my coat pocket. For a split second, I try to memorize everything—the rattle of his papers, the cold shock of wind cutting the thread of my stockings, the exhaust rolling up from idling traffic, and Adrian's wind-chapped cheeks. I'm going to lose him. I feel a pang of panic and remorse. I miss him already. I start to tear up but refuse to cry. I have to stand my ground. I hold the lapel of Adrian's peacoat, curling my hand under the itchy wool. "Adrian," I whisper so softly I'm not sure he can even hear me.

"Evelyn?" he says, tilting forward like he wants something from me, something important.

And I think of my sister—I don't know why. She died a year and a half before I was born; I was conceived as her replacement. But what's worse is that I never met the original. I never smelled my sister's hair after a wash or whispered with her in a tent made of bedsheets or talked to her on the phone. I know I should be over this. There are things that grown-ups must put behind them, but here it is—a loss.

I've never told Adrian about my sister, and I think of telling him now. Is this what he wants? Is it my fault that I feel like he loves me without really understanding me? Because I never confided this, he never had to rise to the occasion of what a secret, especially a sad secret, demands.

It's too late now, much too late.

I say, "Tell your mom and dad to call me." This is a segue that only makes sense in my own head; I never was the child my parents wanted, so I keep trying to create other families to slip into. Adrian's parents still belong to a bowling league and eat popovers.

"They're my parents, Evelyn. I get full custody."

Right, of course. I'll miss our Thanksgivings. "I'll miss you, Adrian."

He touches my face gently with his fingertips and says, "You can't fire me. I quit." But he says it in the saddest voice possible and I love him with a flash that's deep and unmistakable. Each person you love leaves his or her own stain, and the way you remember him is like a smell, a taste, a color—indescribable but distinct.

I almost lean forward to kiss him, but I turn and start walking fast.

Still, I expect him to run after me. Adrian would never run after me. Inexplicably, I put my hands in my coat pockets and both of my elbows are waiting to be the handle that Adrian will use to spin me around, and then he'll kiss me, and say, "Don't go."

This doesn't happen. My elbows just poking out at angles, I walk on. Because Adrian is the kind of guy who lets you go, it's best that he lets me go.

I ball my fists in my pockets, feel the crinkle of the half sheet, and I'm saying no to one fork. I'm doubling back and choosing another forked path. And what will I find down this forked path? I don't know, not yet.

Godfrey
THE PROPOSAL

I find myself walking around the four pinched aisles of Fontana's Super Mart and Pawn Shop twice before stopping in front of the smeary plate glass of the deli meats not far from the cash register. Mrs. Fontana is perched on a nearby stool, stuffing quarters into stiff brown paper sleeves from the bank, her fat fingers disappearing up the tubes with the resignation of a bitter proctologist. And Mr. Fontana, a narrow-headed man with blunt features, is hovering next to her, wiping his hands on his apron.

"What can I do for you?" Mr. Fontana asks. He knows my girl-friend Madge and me but has never given the impression that he likes us. I don't have a cart. It's a Tuesday night in January. Aside from Mr. and Mrs. Fontana and me, the place is empty, which is normal for a Tuesday night in January. The lights flicker.

"I don't know," I tell him. "I was really just out for a walk around the block. I got cold." Mr. Fontana looks at my mittens, the ones

Madge bought me last Christmas. I already feel idiotic in them, like a four-year-old. They're attached by some ancient device that Madge found on an antiquities website—rusty clips connected by yarn that bite the mittens, stringing them together. Wearing them is a romantic concession. Madge presented them as a joke in front of our friends at Bart and Amy's Christmas party. *Godfrey loses things—ha, ha, ha—like his wallet, like his girlfriends.* I guess that's true enough. For a year now, I've had a hard time keeping track of wallets, and there'd been a spate of ugly breakups just before Madge that became part of my *charm.* At the Christmas party, Madge grabbed my coat off a chair and laced the mittens through my sleeves. *He won't lose me,* she said, and she unclipped one of the mittens, attaching it to her own sleeve, and fell drunkenly onto my lap. Madge is a weighty drunk—always hefting herself around. I often wonder where all that weight goes when she's not drinking. When sober, she's thin and light as balsa wood. That doesn't sound as loving as it should. Truth is, I love Madge drunk and weighty because her face goes soft, her lips are fuller, sweeter, and I love Madge sober because her mind is quick and she looks at me sometimes like she sees some great unfinished work of art, my potential, something to live up to.

"You using up my heat? That's gotta be worth something to you. What are you going to buy?" Mr. Fontana says.

I want to tell Fontana to lay off and to confess that I'm a man on the verge of proposing! Seriously, it's a fact that a man about to propose is cuter than a basket of kittens or a squirrel Jet Skiing in an aboveground pool. (Why am I proposing now? Does it have to do with the fact that Bart and Amy—at the aforementioned Christmas party—announced the details of their envisioning session in which they are destined to be rich boat owners? Maybe that was the start of it, a wake-up call. Their announcement's subtext seemed to say, *The future is out there—and are you and Madge going to face it together?*)

I don't know why I want the Fontanas to like me. It's got to be a character flaw on my part. But I'm not confessing to the Fontanas. They're both the type to make a sad joke, sour the whole thing. "Okay, okay," I tell him. "I'll get something."

I glance down at the racks—mini-flashlight key rings, Chap-Stick, Life Savers, Bubblicious. Sometimes it hits me that this is what the world's made up of—the little crap that binds the seams of the universe together. Without this stuff, surely the universe would come unglued and we'd glide off in bits and parts into dark, infinite space. That's how fragile it all seems; maybe I think of this now because what if Madge shoots me down? Only a vulnerable man would think that Bubblicious and ChapStick keep the universe glued, right?

I pull off a mitten, letting it dangle, and put my hand in my pocket just to double-check on the velvet box. It's still there. It's been sitting inside a dress sock in the back of my underwear drawer, the same spot where I used to hide my weed as a teenager.

I pick up a pack of Certs, set them on the glass counter. Beneath the glass, there's a variety of secondhand weapons and jewelry—the Pawn Shop part of Fontana's—and it's a little disconcerting how many hocked engagement rings there are on display.

"You sure I can't interest you in a little something more?" he says, tapping the glass. "Other people's desperation makes for good deals."

"No thanks," I say. "I'm good on weaponry and gems." I pull my mitten back on.

Mr. Fontana rings up my stuff and shoves the mints at me—no bag—rips the receipt from the register, and slides it across the counter with two double-jointed fingers.

"Maybe you're a winner," Mrs. Fontana pipes up.

This is the part that I've come to hate. Fontana has recently started up a Lucky Receipt promotional. One out of every ten receipts has "You're a winner" printed on the bottom, giving you a 20 percent discount on your next food purchase—but the other nine have "You're a loser" printed on the bottom, which has always been included with my purchases.

I pinch the receipt through the mittens and read the faded print: *You're a loser.* I look up at Fontana.

"Well?" Mr. Fontana asks.

"You know," I say, still pinching the receipt, "this might not be good for business. You might want to word the loser sentiment a little more gently. Maybe something like 'This receipt is not a winner.'"

Mr. Fontana rubs his nose, a little angry gesture. "Hey, the cash register calls 'em as it sees 'em."

I want to reach over the counter and shove Fontana in his chest or at least make him give me a shopping bag for my package of Certs. Instead, I let it go, give him a smile, and think, *Poor fucking Fontana, penned up in that shop all day with his pruned wife.* But honestly it's not comforting to pity that dickwad even though I've been taught that that's the right thing to do.

I ball up the receipt and put it in my pocket with the Certs. I walk out of the store, bell jangling, and slowly head up the side-walk. Walking by the storefronts I catch glimpses of myself in the windows. My pants, my jacket—they already appear rumpled. I'm not sure why I rumple so quickly. My mother and father both often look rumpled. Since retirement, my father has always worn wrin-kled button-downs. My mother wears wrinkly silky puffed sleeve shirts, and her mascara always daubs off with each blink, leaving little smudges around her eyes. By the end of the day, she always looks like a fatigued musketeer. They're an exhausted rumpled pair. Maybe it's a permanent condition: the Burkes family curse, rumpling.

And then for no reason I think of the weekend just last summer when they met Madge for the first time. They were wearing terry-cloth bathrobes, drinking cocktails by the pool. I was doing laps when my father said, "There's a golf game on the mini-TV. Come watch." But I said, "No, thank you," and dipped down underwater. Madge was sitting on the pool's edge. I could see her thick ankles, blurred by chlorinated pool water, kicking back and forth. I hate these little memories. Why do certain ones pop back up?

And now I feel a little wheeze inside of my chest cavity—the inching in of a cold, pneumonia, something tubercular? Can the heart wheeze? I remind myself, as I'm slowing down, that I also have great memories of Madge—like how we met. It was in this little coffee shop. I was waiting for a blind date, drawing pastries in the margins of my notebook. Madge walked past me then doubled back and stopped in front of me. She said, "Vaginas?" and pointed to my pastries.

"No. They're pastries."

"Really, Freud? So you're telling me that this little bit here is like a cherry? Look again."

Some did have cherries—and they were all clearly vaginas.

"Vaginas in the margins," Madge said. "I guess that would be vaginalia."

"Nope, they're pastries," I said, trying to stick it out. "This is obviously pastrianalia."

"You're Godfrey," she said then.

"If I'm Godfrey, then you're Madge." And that was that.

She tilted her head and sighed at me as if seeing a current failure of some kind but one with promise. And, in that moment, my pencil mid-clitoris, I don't know if I fell in love with her, but I know I wanted her to take me on. I wanted to fulfill that promise. I loved the tilt of her head and her sigh and the fact that she called me on my bullshit. I needed Madge and that was the start of love. I think that's how it sometimes goes.

Home now. In front of the fourth floor walk-up I've been sharing with Madge for nearly six months. I raise my arms over my head. Coach used to suggest this for cramps. I bend over, stick my head between my knees. I try to count slowly to twenty-five, but I keep losing my place around twelve. I look up, directly at our fourth-floor window, but I only see blinds, blips of light peeking through. Why isn't Madge looking for me? Is anyone thinking about me right now? If not, do I exist just a little less?

A woman walks by pushing a stroller. She's staring at my hands as if looking for what I might be holding. *Just bulky mittens with mitten clips that are more appropriate for a four-year-old in the 1950s!* I want to tell her. I nod politely, look into the stroller. The baby is so packed in that I can barely make out a face squinched up in the puffy drawstring hood. All babies are just pudge until they're not. It's a disturbed little face, so red and puffed it could be choking, but then the face twists and begins to wail. I flinch. My heart stutters. *This is just the kind of thing that happens to all men before they propose,* I tell myself. But then, for a moment, I'm sure I'm dying. This is it, I know, squeezing my eyes shut.

A second later, I'm not dead. Fifteen seconds later, still not dead. My heart still beats. My lips still inch open to let air in. The moment passes. Another moment passes.

"Why are you standing out in the cold?" It's Madge's loud voice, which carries like a soccer coach. She's overhead. Her hair is blowing around her beautiful face; her whole upper body is sticking out the window. Some women's breasts can remind you of the singular term *bosom* but not Madge's. She has great breasts, ample and buoyant, and independent of each other.

I've been expecting her, wishing for her, but I didn't realize how not ready I was for the reality of her. This is going to be my wife. Wife! It's disorienting.

I look away at the gargoyles perched on the corners. One is stuck in an indiscreet position—is he scratching his balls or protecting them? You can never be too sure. The sky is a gusty gray. It snowed earlier and might snow again.

"Godfrey!" Madge yells again.

I'm stuck on the idea of proposing outside. It strikes me that I might pick Madge up and spin her around—if she says yes—that I might actually yawp. I look up and down the street, shout back, "I'm not sure why I'm out here still! Are you ready?"

"I'll be down!" She sighs. It's a gusty sigh, the kind you give a child, and slams the window shut. Standing there in my mittens, I shift my weight from one foot to the other, feeling tall and ga-lumphing. I'm on the tall side; nice Little League coaches told my parents that one day I'd grow into my body and become suddenly coordinated. That never happened.

I shouldn't have worn the mittens. I should feel more manly right now.

But here's something I love about Madge: she's quick to get angry but also quick to get over it. When she appears on the stoop in her red coat, she's over being annoyed with me, and she looks fantastic. She's wearing frosty lipstick, as if she's just kissed a cake. Madge is good to me. She really is. She once made homemade matzo ball soup for me when I was sick and she's not even Jewish. She looked it up online.

I want to yell out, *Madge! I! Love! You!* I am happy. There's so much blood in my head, I'm top heavy. She walks up and kisses me on the mouth. Right there, full mouth. Her lips are warm. Her lips are a heater, and when I hug her, perfume gusts up from her coat. This has been my problem since I've started growing hair where there never used to be hair: I love women. I should stand in the middle of a group of men sitting in chairs shaped in a circle: *My name is Godfrey and I love women.* I'm completely susceptible to them. It's a difficult way to go through life, constantly falling in love. I don't wear love very well. And, because of my weaknesses, I'm dangerous. I have to keep myself in check, always. Madge helps keep me in check mainly because she's enough. Madge is so full of life, so vigorously alive, that I'm rapt every time she walks into a room—or out of a building to meet me.

"Why were you lurking?" Madge asks jokingly. "You shouldn't

lurk. People will think you're a serial killer. Are we going to the sushi place? It's my turn, you know."

And that's how quickly it changes. Taking turns. This is my future. Life doled out simply: Madge's turn. Then: my turn. Everything in this moment seems suddenly permanent. Everything in this moment *is* permanent.

Fact: I hate sushi. Rolls too big for your mouth, but you don't dare cut them with a fork. I don't trust raw fish. Normally I might say, "I only eat sushi that's well done." Or I might say, "I'm not feeling suicidal enough for sushi today." But this would encourage Madge to give me a speech on living life to the fullest, and I'm never in the mood for that, much less now, on the brink of such emotional risk. My hands feel too hot for the mittens, and now I'm thinking of the wallets I've lost and the girlfriends I've lost, too—Tina Whooten, Liz Chase, the Ellis twins. I look up at the buildings around us, hundreds of windows. How many women are in there? How many could I fall in love with? How many would let me fall in love with them? Am I choosing the right one? Does it mean something to even be thinking this?

"Why are you just standing there, Godfrey?" I stop and look at Madge. "Why are you looking at me like that?"

Jesus, I'm just standing here, looking at her like that. To be honest, I'm not really sure what *that* is. "I'm sorry," I say, glancing at my shoes. How is it possible that my *shoes* look rumpled? If I were holding an ironing board, that would probably look rumpled, too. "You know," I tell Madge, "if we ever had kids, they'd have a fifty percent chance of rumpledness." I look back at Madge.

"Are you okay?" she asks. "You aren't making a lot of sense. Are you drunk or something?"

"I mean," I say, "I'm sorry about not having a better job. I should have paid better attention in college, taken harder classes. You know, really hunkered down with something like premed." Madge talked me out of being an elementary-school teacher, explaining how much money they make when they hit their salary ceiling.

"Are you going to throw up? You look that same way you did on the subway that time."

"Just listen," I say, trying not to raise my voice. "I'm not going to throw up." Now that I say it, though, I'm not so sure. I feel shaky. I finally take off the mittens. They dangle on the strings. Slowly, I reach into my pocket. "Madge." My chest tightens. I feel a fiery heat, a certain lightheadedness. "Look, I mean . . ." I manage to say. "Here." I hand her the box.

Madge opens the box and then shuts it. She's smiling.

"I was planning on picking you up and spinning you around." I want to tell her, *Sometimes I wish I could reverse time and start over, from the very beginning—my first wail.* "I feel like passing out." I sit on the stoop.

"Godfrey," she says, "listen." She sits down next to me. "I think we should look into this. Go forward carefully." She draws out the *carefully,* all three syllables. "You know?"

"Is that a yes?"

"It's a yes, kind of. A slow, careful, looking-into-it yes."

"Okay."

Madge smiles and puts her arm around my shoulder like a fellow sailor. We are out at sea together, hunting our dinner: giant whales, kraken. Maybe we are in a submarine, sitting on tons and tons of nuclear warheads. Madge finally says, "I thought you'd say no. Funny, huh?"

I am baffled. "Say no? To what exactly? I mean, *I* asked *you*."

"To looking into it first."

"Looking into what?"

"Well, I don't think we should use the same envisionist. It's like sharing a therapist or something. I've heard a lot of good stuff about Dr. Plotnik and you should see Dr. Chin. I hear he's very good at giving the total experience. I almost made appointments but decided I should at least wait until you asked first."

Madge hasn't put on the ring. It's still in the box. The box is pretty, but nothing should *stay* in the box. "You're talking about *envisionists*?" There's a billboard on the beltway: DR. CHIN'S ENVISIONING SERVICES. NOW OFFERING: THE FUTURE—FOR CURIOUS PEOPLE. At the bottom it says, "It's easier to choose the future, when you've seen the options." And that actor who does all that sci-fi stuff has started doing commercials for some conglomerate that offers discount rates. "No. No way."

"What? You just said yes!"   •

"I didn't know you meant going to envisionists!"

"It's actual science. You know that, right?" And then Madge napalms me with data. She's got an incredible ability to memorize stuff. There's nothing I can do but sit back and take it. "Each human being has vast untapped mental abilities. Our eyes take in some twelve million pieces of information every second while in that same second, our ears are processing one million pieces of information, touch is bringing in five hundred thousand data points per second, smell is only bringing in seventy bits of information and taste is only registering about fifteen info bits per second, but look, Godfrey, do you know how many pieces of sensory information that is per second?"

"You know I don't know," I say. Does she think I've been running a mental calculator? Are we still even talking about marriage?

"That's approximately thirteen million five hundred thousand eighty-five pieces of sensory information per second. And those are just the senses alone. There's also all the deep tissue of long-term memory and the chemical processing of short-term data and the processing of intangible information as each of these senses is synthesized to produce thought, action, reaction."

"That's a lot of knowledge." If I agree with her, maybe I can reroute the conversation back to marriage more quickly.

"And then that Scandinavian researcher figured out that if we could process information without the interference of the subconscious's absurdism and emotion—vengefulness, greed, hope, faith, hatred, and most of all *love,* which blurs *everything* we perceive"— she seems really annoyed by the blurriness caused by love—"and add that to what we know from the past, we could predict our own future outcomes, in minute detail."

"Uh-huh," I say, feeling a little like crying.

"We know," she says. "Our brains know so much more than we ever let them!"

"I get it." I barely get it.

"The drug cocktail that Percel created puts the patient into a short kind of awake-REM state, cuts out the white noise of emotions, and allows the person to predict a specific potential future. And then, this is the best part, Godfrey. Are you listening?"

"Yes," I say, a little defensively.

"This guy named Bacon figured out how to digitize that dream-like state—capturing the synapses—for viewing. See how perfect it is? It's a real tool, but it doesn't come from out there, Godfrey." She straightens her arms and waves her hands at the world. "It comes from in here." She taps her forehead and then my forehead. "Each of us is brilliant, Godfrey. See? So don't sell yourself short."

"I'm not selling myself short! I asked you to *marry* me. Remember?"

"Look. This is my one request. Envisionists. It's the only smart thing to do."

"If people can really tell the future, why do they muck around with people's relationships? Call the next Super Bowl! Put a fix on the stock market!"

"Godfrey, envisioning is overseen by the FCC. Do you really think that they'd let people broadcast futures that would infringe on commerce? There are tons of regulations."

"Really. The FCC." I didn't know this.

"They only have the matchmaking software at this point, but they're working on the regulatory issues around other futures, like career paths. They worry it might have unforeseen ramifications on the economy if everyone suddenly decides to ditch med school and go into investment banking for the cushy lifestyle."

"Right. Investment banking. I probably should have considered that more closely. And we need doctors, too. I mean, who will outfit the investment bankers with pacemakers when their tickers start to fail."

"Don't be caustic."

"I'm not being caustic! Doctors are important! Pacemakers save lives!"

"Well, it really worked out great for Bart and Amy! You can't deny that. They both saw fantastic futures. Incredible. I mean, I don't know how they come up with all that money. I told my parents and my father was like, wow, you should invite them to the cabin." Madge's parents own a ski-in, ski-out cabin in Colorado I've yet to be invited to.

"Like I want to hear about Bart and Amy right now." I've already heard all of this from Bart. Their future entails tennis whites and healthy grandchildren, plus a thick head of white hair for Bart. Before I met Madge, Bart met Amy and now my Bart is gone. I love Bart and I always will, but sometimes I worry he's turned into a gossip who sometimes wears various kinds of facial hair—with irony. I shake my head. "I *proposed* to you. Doesn't that mean something?"

"Don't get all heated up," Madge says.

"Don't get all heated up?" I squeeze my head with both hands. "I asked you to marry me, and you want to look into it first? Look into it first?" Everything's sinking in.

"You're the one with a father who isn't your biological father because your biological father was a married man at the time he and your mom—"

"I don't want to drag Mart Thigpen into this." This is no secret. At age eleven, my mother sat me down and told me that my real father was not Aldo Burkes, the father I'd known all my life, but this other man named Mart Thigpen. A married man. A married man who was a connoisseur of thighs, who had sex with many women, including my mother, but always went back to his wife, which meant he left my mother high and dry! "High and dry, Godfrey!" she said, and I imagined her on a hill in the desert in a boat. She warned me that I was doomed to become a man like Mart Thigpen— a man I've never met. I'm his son, his animal son, and that I had to fight against it.

My mother now rescues bunnies that people drop off at animal shelters. She has a yard full of hutches hand built by the Amish. Her saving once-loved pet bunnies that have been abandoned is an obvious metaphor for Gloria Burkes saving Gloria Burkeses.

"You bring up your dark fear of your animal nature all the time!" Madge says.

This is true, if overstated a little. I do have this fear that I might become an alcoholic who might even do cocaine in a public rest-room, which is one small detail that my mother told me about Mart Thigpen. Lord God, how many years did I have a fear of public restrooms because of my weak predilection for cocaine? How many months did I spend as a sophomore in high school, practicing rolling single dollar bills my mom gave me for morning milk into sniffable straws because I figured I should prepare for the inevitable! "Is that why you're afraid to say yes? Because you're afraid of what I might become?"

Madge smiles. "Oh, Godfrey. How many times do I have to tell you that I'm not afraid that you're going to turn into a wildly lustful seducer of women? You're no animal. You're no Mart Thigpen."

"Thanks," I say. I know Madge is mocking me, but truth is, I can trust Madge's opinion which is important because I can't trust my own—half Thigpen that I am. "This is about you and me. Marriage is a leap of faith. Don't you believe in leaps of faith?" I ask.

Madge shakes her head. "I love you. You know that."

"And I love you, too, Madge." Here are more things I love about Madge: the way she talks with her hands as if carving air and laughs so hard she snorts and believes in helping others hence her job at the downtown clinic and how she knows all the lyrics to the Kinks and talked me out of a bad tattoo.

"We love each other," she says. "We can survive taking our time."

"You're not going to put the ring on, are you? This is conditional. That's what you're saying. I do it your way or it doesn't happen." I swing my arms around angrily and the mittens come flapping after them. I try to pull the mittens off, but the clips seem permanently clenched. I use the voice I usually reserve for customer service personnel. It's the only way I can stop myself from further losing it. "If you aren't going to put the ring on, you should give it back. That's customary, isn't it?"

She tightens her grip on the box and refuses to look at me. She looks at everything but me.

"Do you know how ridiculous we look right now?" I am saying this, but my mouth is barely moving.

She doesn't answer, doesn't move.

"What? Do you want me to wrestle that box from you?" I'm trying to joke now, but it's not going over.

Madge is breathing hard. The steam is rising from her mouth into the cold air. It is her pre-cry panting. I am softening or melting or both. *Don't cry. Don't cry.* Once when Madge's parents were in town, they pulled me aside and her mother said, "Madge has had a very affirmed childhood. We want her to spend her life with someone who truly appreciates everything about her. Everything."

"Everything?" I said.

Her father then said, "Madge's affirmed childhood was her mother's idea. It makes her a force of nature. All that affirmation and no real failure for her to apply it to? Well, it's all bottled up. It's a force field, Godfrey. Good luck."

I don't want to give in. I stiffen up and try to sound definitive. If

I had a necktie on, I'd straighten the shit out of it. "I'm not going to look into our future, Madge. I'm not. It goes against everything I believe in."

She looks up at me. "You have a belief system?"

I nod weakly. "I think I do." I look around the street, the row of trees buckling the sidewalk. "I'm pretty sure I do."

Evelyn
SAVING GATSBY

My boss, Mr. Gupta, walks over to me behind the desk in Youth Services. He's typically bookish. His shoulders slope toward a doughy center. The fuzz of his sweaters seems to have molded to his body. And of course he's wearing bifocals. He was raised in India and therefore has no tolerance for whining of any kind—even the completely valid inner-city Baltimore variety. Much less if you try to tell Gupta that you don't want people eating out of the take-out box you put in the communal fridge for lunch on the grounds that it's unsanitary to co-eat from take-out boxes, he'll say, "Oh, please. Afraid of a few germs? In India people just die on the streets. You step over bodies. It's just how it is!"

But today he doesn't have his normal bravado. "Evelyn Shriner," he says, as he often refers to me by my full name. "The woman in the bathroom on the third floor is dying her hair in the sink." Fadra is a homeless woman who's been living in the library—for all intents and purposes—for a couple of years. She has the strange habit of bringing up the fine art of taxidermy at certain moments when she feels attacked and with a glint in her eye that makes me feel like a muskrat about to be stuffed and boxed in a small display case. "I just feel like dying your hair is really bold," Gupta says. "A new *level* of bold. I need you to go talk to her." Gupta shrugs apologetically and then makes a shooing motion with his hands, flipping them forward on the hinges of his wrists.

"Mr. Gupta," I say politely. "Wouldn't that be Cherelle's area?" The library is a carefully organized landscape of territories drawn by a group of carefully organized human beings. I reside in Youth Services. (I should note that I'm the whitey minority in this library, which means I sometimes don't get the jokes.) It's as if the third floor is an arctic region clearly out of my domain. Plus, I'd like to pawn this off on Cherelle because I'm scared of Fadra. This is why Gupta himself isn't going in after her.

Gupta shakes his head vehemently. "There was the incident," Gupta says, pushing up his glasses, "as you well know. And Cherelle has become a little nervous, you know. I'll never understand it, but she can no longer confront others. Personally, it strikes me as an American privilege to suddenly claim your nerves are shaken. Still, I have to be *sensitive* or they will send me back for another training session. I deplore sensitivity training sessions, Evelyn Shriner. They make me completely insensitive!"

A few weeks ago, Cherelle, who grew up in this area of Baltimore—which isn't the safest part of town—is very tough and officious woman, but she accidentally aided and abetted a criminal who'd just held up a liquor store and was looking for the best way to catch a bus to Philly. Cherelle was exceedingly thorough, the man was truly grateful, and she'd felt good about the whole thing until the cops showed up.

I look around at my little protected area of the library—my nest of Youth Services. I point to the group of teenagers, a brilliant group of kids, all in all—the oddballs that gather, as I once did and then stayed on . . . "I can't leave now. We're about to start the book club meeting," I say. This is actually a ways off. "Right, Keisha? You need me to be here, correct?"

Keisha says, "If it weren't for you, I'd be doing meth in an IHOP bathroom. Of course we need you here."

I wasn't expecting this. I feel all warm in my heart. "Really?" I say.

"No, of course not," Keisha says. "That shit short-circuits the pleasure part of your brain, but it's the thought that counts, right?"

I turn to Gupta. "It *is* the thought that counts. Clearly." I lower my voice. "And she probably read about the bad effects of meth here in the Youth Services area of the library."

"This is a beautiful moment," Gupta says, just lightly laced with sarcasm. "I'm choked up."

"Can't Chuck go?" Chuck is our deputy sheriff, a sweet man with an overly large head. He has to special order his cop caps. His young offspring are similarly large-headed.

"He and I would both go, but it is the *women's* room," Gupta says. "Look, I will stand here while your book club starts to talk about the book and you won't be gone long."

"Okay, okay," I say, feeling screwed over by my own gender.

Gupta smiles, chin to chest. "May the force be with you, Evelyn Shriner."

I head to the elevators, wringing my hands. This wasn't what I thought my job would entail when I first went into library studies, but I love my job. I truly do.

Libraries are my homeland. So, yes, I tried to make Adrian's family my own—one popover at a time—and his family wasn't the first, but I also chose a career that would land me in a place I could call home. When you grow up in the deadened air of loss, you get used to quiet, but you never get used to the loneliness of living with parents who are despairing. As a kid, I went to the library because, in books, there were people really living lives, and *un*like my parents, they talked to me about important things. My own house was austere, hushed, and dusty like a library, but once you understand that each book on the shelf has a heartbeat, then you'll want to stay. I don't tend dead things—paper, ink, glue bindings. I tend books the way someone in an aviary tends birds.

Bookstores, on the other hand, can make me nervous. All those books and I can't possibly buy them all and tend to them properly, love them enough, give them the eyes they deserve. But, here, at the library, the patrons take the books out as a kind of foster care program—into the world and back again.

If they don't come back? Well, some books are meant to live in the wilds. There's not much you can do about that.

But nowadays libraries are in many ways the last public space. Robert Frost defined home as "the place where, when you have to go there, / They have to take you in." Ditto public libraries. Our doors are open—to everyone. In the summer, kids are dropped off here to spend the entire day. Some really little ones manage a city bus route. They don't have anywhere else to go. It's sometimes overwhelmingly sad, and yet they're here. They aren't on the streets.

Just this morning, I got to help an old woman trying to find a book that she'd read in her childhood. She didn't remember the title or the author, but knew it was about a panda. When I showed her the cover on my screen, she said, "Yes, yes, that's it! My father read it to me once and cried at the end. It was the only time I'd ever seen him cry." Books can break a man open, even ones about a panda, maybe especially so.

I love the smell of books, the dust motes spiraling in sun. I love shelves and order. I love the carts and metal stools on wheels. I love the quiet carrels and the study rooms. I love the strobing of copy machines, the video and audio bins. I love the Saturday morning read-alouds for kids and how they try to hush when they come in; all these books can still demand a bit of awe. I love the teen reading groups, clutching books to their chests, little shields protecting them from the world's assaults—those are my people. I even love the homeless shuffling in—it's warm here with running water, safe—and the couples who make out in the stacks. I don't blame them: books are sexy after all.

If Chin's office did, in fact, bring in career envisioning, I wouldn't need it. I'm happy here. One day, I could have Gupta's job, overseeing the place—like head zookeeper of all the bookish heartbeats.

As the elevator sends me up, I imagine Fadra as an auntie of mine—the eccentric kind that my family doesn't possess.

I pause in front of the women's room door on the third floor. I hear the hand blower going and Fadra singing what sounds like Janis Joplin. Was Fadra a hippy at some point? I steel myself, brush back my bangs, and walk in.

Fadra is in the final stage of the process, her bright red hair flipped upside down under the hand blower, which she must have pushed on many, many times because the entire bathroom is warm.

She doesn't hear me walk in. Her hair dye box and latex gloves are in one of the sinks, its basin tinged a pinkish red.

"Fadra!" I call out.

Her head snaps around and then she flips it over. It's impossible to tell how old she is. Her face looks old and her teeth make her look ancient. Her new brash hair color makes her face, by contrast, look older still. But her body moves quickly, like her bones are young.

"What?" she says innocently.

"You can't dye your hair in here."

"That's not written down anywhere."

"I think that's because no one ever thought that someone would dye their hair in here."

"People dye their hair at the bus station bathroom."

"This isn't the bus station bathroom."

"Well, I can do it!" Fadra says. "I already did it."

"I'm not saying you don't have the ability to dye your hair in here. Obviously, you've proven you can. I'm saying you're not allowed—in the future, okay?"

"I don't like it when you talk to me like this." She curls her hands in and looks at her fingernails and I know what's coming.

"Don't," I say. "Don't go to your dark place."

"I used to have bone-cutter forceps and ear openers and goose-neck hide stretchers and—"

"I'm serious, Fadra! I do not want to hear about your previous life in the world of taxidermy!"

"I once created a little scene of Canadian squirrels having sex in a little handmade canopy bed," she says, which strikes me as oddly tender for Fadra, borderline sentimental. "Taxidermy is Greek for arrangement of skin."

"I know. You've told me this before. And I don't like the way you talk about taxidermy because I think you're purposefully giving the impression that you want to kill me and stuff me and stitch me up and put me in some weird display. It gives off a very creepy vibe and it feels like bullying." We talk about bullying all the time in Youth Services and I can't help that it pops out of my mouth, but as soon as I see Fadra's reaction, I know I've gone too far.

"You're going to kick me out. Aren't you?"

"No, I'm not kicking you out." We had to kick her out once. She had a screaming fit in the audio section, in which she told Gupta that she'd stuff his "Gandhi ass." Gupta did not like the reference to his ass looking like Gandhi's.

"I don't touch the books, you know," Fadra shouts. "I never do! I never mess with your stuff!"

"You're supposed to touch the books, Fadra. We've been over this. This is a library."

"I don't like to read because it takes me to other places. I'm trying to just be where I am. Inside my own self." I can appreciate this in a Buddhist kind of way. "You can't *make me* read the books!"

"You have to clean up in here. Okay? And don't do it again. Gupta really wasn't happy about it."

"Gupta can poop in a hole!"

"No, let's not rev up again, Fadra. Okay? Just calm it down."

"Okay, okay," she says, "but I'm going to be me. You know that. Nothing anyone can do. I'm going to be me. You're going to be you. Gupta's going to be Gupta."

This feels like a compromise that I can accept—like the terms of some abstract peace accord. I say, "Agreed!" and I'm about to leave because there's not much more I can do here, but then I stop. "Question: Do you think that our nature defines us or is it just our circumstances? Or is it something else? I mean, what did you mean that each of us is going to be ourselves?"

She looks at me like I'm a child. "All I got is who I am. You have any more than that?"

I think of José Ortega y Gasset, a Spanish philosopher. "This famous thinker once said, 'Life is a series of collisions with the future; it is not the sum of what we have been, but what we yearn to be.'"

"Ha!" Fadra says, looking at me sharply. "Are you still yearning? I thought you'd grown up already."

Is that what it means to grow up? Is the payment for adulthood an end to yearning? I'm flustered suddenly. It's like someone's lifted up the dirty wall-to-wall carpeting of life and revealed some ugly truth. "Uh, just don't dye your hair in here anymore," I say.

"I'll try not to," she says, but, she is who she's going to be, I guess. "And no more taxidermy talk, okay?"

She stares at me. This she can't promise, and I have to respect that.

"Okay," I say. As soon as the bathroom door swings shut behind me, I hear the hand blower rev up.

I'VE SIGNED UP TO volunteer to record books for the blind in the back room of Special Collections. After my shift ends, this is where I'm headed.

The visitors to Special Collections are as rare as the collections themselves: boxes of African American sheet music, war posters, rare books sheathed in protective wrappings, and my favorite—postcards, thirty-three boxes full of them, taking up twelve linear feet of shelving, most of them inscribed by the dead to the dead.

I have to borrow a key to get into the Special Collections room by Jason Binter, who's only here as a sub because Rita fell in love and joined the Peace Corps. Binter's no genius, and how he ended up in library work is a ponderous mystery. But he has a lightly aged frat-boy look—without the date-rape vibe—and I'm eyeing him for a future.

He sits in the sign-in room in Special Collections—a little glass room—as if Binter himself is the true rarity on display. I knock on the glass and he looks up a little dumbfounded. Is it because he was deep in thought or surprised to find himself in his surroundings, as if his life is a process of finding himself places he doesn't expect to be? Hard to say.

I smile and wave the apologetic sorry-to-interrupt half-hand crumple wave.

He nods and waves me in.

"Hi," I say. "I'm here to volunteer. You know. Recording for the blind." I lift my digital recorder and paperback as proof. I'm not going to lie: I want the points that come along with being the type of person who volunteers to record books for the blind.

"You're a good citizen," Binter says, and it strikes me as the kind of thing that might only be a hot come-on to a communist, speaking in a boozy Russian accent. Could this be Binter's attempt at flirtation? I know, I know, this is a stretch, but librarian flirtation can be very subtle. He pulls a key from a desk drawer, unlocks the door for me.

"Zank you, comrade," I say, in a pseudo Russian accent, even though the Russian thing is something that only existed in my head.

"Comrade?" he says curiously. I duck my head and shuffle past him and close the door.

I sit at a desk, find my place in the book, and take a moment to collect myself. I'm supposed to pick books that haven't been masterfully recorded already, but I always end up recording another version of a classic. Look, I'm a volunteer so I figure I should be allowed to read what I want. Today I'm working on *The Great Gatsby*.

I'm reading about Mrs. Wilson at the party, after she changes her dress and how she seems to almost balloon into a different person. She expands and the room shrinks until it's like she's "revolving on a noisy, creaking pivot through the smoky air."

I stop the recording right there. My hand shaking a little because I know she's going to die. She's going to be hit by a car. And then Gatsby's going to be shot to death in his swimming pool.

And, again, I think of my sister on her bicycle with its banana seat. Megan. A twelve-year-old girl I'll never know. I imagine the car, though I don't know what kind it was. I imagine a large bulky automobile, something that's slow to start, slow to stop. It careens toward her. Her death will kill something inside of my parents. Figuratively, they'll float like two dead bodies in a swimming pool. My birth, my childhood, my being are meant to revive them. But I know I'm a failure at this. It's too much to ask of a little kid—of anyone.

I hear Helen Keller whispering in my head, "Although the world is full of suffering, it is also full of the overcoming of it." My parents tried to overcome suffering. I'm the result. Why am I thinking of my sister so often these days? Is it that I now believe that the tragedies that await us can be avoided, if fully envisioned?

Maybe the classics are chock-full of tragedy because the world is full of tragedy. Maybe they're full of tragedy so they can also be about overcoming tragedy. But that's not the case, really, is it? So many classics end tragically, with no overcoming at all. Why does that have to be the case, again and again? If we can pick futures with envisioning, why does literature have to remain fixed?

I know that it's a terrible thought. You can't change classics. One small bit of erosion could bring down the pillars of literature, which are the pillars of culture.

I push the paperback open, feel the slight give deep in the binding.

And I know what I'm going to do, and I know that it's wrong. But just this once, just this one tiny recording . . . I'm going to change the ending of *The Great Gatsby.* Myrtle Wilson will have quicker feet. It doesn't matter who was driving the car—Myrtle will be out of the way before Gatsby's car is even close. In fact, they'll wave. Daisy will put down the window, and they'll have one of those awkward hugs where the driver half leans out the window. Myrtle likes Daisy's dress and Gatsby will agree.

It's not easy to put away the past even when you're making up the future—your own or Gatsby's. But right now, I think of Adrian and his boxy nose and I miss him so much I could cry like Daisy over a bunch of shirts.

I try to remain positive about some future. It's hard, especially at home when it's quiet and my bed is empty. So it's better to be here, with twelve linear feet of postcards, reading about Myrtle Wilson who is *not* doomed, reading about Gatsby who will *not* float in a swimming pool amid ribbons of his own blood.

I read some more, and as I do, I feel a quickening. I'm going back, I decide. I'm going back to all the other classics I've read—and

I've read plenty—and rerecording the endings and uploading them again to the volunteer site. I feel powerful and helium light.

At just this moment, the doorknob jiggles. Binter peeks his head in and says, "Someone's here to look for 'Kiss Me, Honey, Do.'" He nods toward the African American sheet music.

"I can save Anna Karenina," I tell Binter, and then I start counting on my fingers. "Plus Beth, Piggy, Madame Bovary, and Charlotte."

"Um," Binter says. "'Kiss Me Honey Do' is kind of urgent right now so . . ."

"Oh, you want me to leave?"

"Well, that or you'll have to just sit there and not be, you know, weird."

"Right," I say. "I can do not-weird, short term."

"Good."

"Good-good."

He frowns at me because that was slightly weird.

Binter walks into the room with a tall pale scholarly man, his bald pate shining. As he and Binter discuss sheet music, I walk to one of the boxes of postcards. I can't be noisy—or weird—but I'm allowed to rummage.

I pick up a postcard from Wildwood, New Jersey's boardwalk. The date is June 3, 1931. It's written to a Helen. The sign off reads, *I'll only miss you more tomorrow.*

As soon as I read it, I know I've memorized it. It seems like a definition of love.

Godfrey
THE FIRST APPOINTMENT

My appointment at Dr. Chin's office is at eleven, just like Madge's appointment at Plotnik's. We're hoping to have a celebratory lunch together at the Rib Shack before heading back to work.

But I'm still sitting in my cubicle. The Department of Unclaimed Goods is lodged in a grim building with an old-world heavy-on-the-asbestos vibe. Bart and I sit in adjoining cubicles and spend our days discussing our ruination while eating stiff vending-machine sandwiches. I can't tell Bart that Madge has talked me into seeing an envisionist. I don't want to hear all the gloating—tennis whites, boating, full hair, and so on. My ruination has gotten lonesomer. I work as a labeler at the Department of Unclaimed Goods. My fingers have grown numb from the constant rummaging through of abandoned safe deposit boxes. "One day I'll no longer have fingerprints," I say to Bart. "Like a mobster."

I don't like the job. In fact, I can feel it chewing at my soul. But if I move up and one day take over that prick Chapman's job, the pay is actually decent. It's a war of attrition really. Each of us in the general pool, combing safe deposit boxes, battling the sheer boredom, it's a last man standing kind of promotional system.

Inside the current box: some faded bonds, a dowdy pear-shaped brooch, a silver dollar. This box was registered in 1927 by a man named Wickham Purdy. Sometimes the contents of abandoned safe deposit boxes are so lifeless and sad that they make me feel like my heart is small and coated in enamel. I pick up the brooch. Was it Wickham Purdy's mother's? His wife's? And suddenly I remember a dream from the night before. I was at work, sifting through the contents of a deposit box—it's cruel that the brain sometimes makes you dream about what you don't enjoy doing all day long—when I found a baby tooth. With a surge of necessity, I tried to fit the tooth into a gap in the back of my gum line because I had a feeling that I'd lost this tooth. The tooth fit perfectly, and I knew that this was my own deposit box. I found the velvet box that I'd given Madge. I opened it and it was empty. I saw a folded-up note, too. I unfolded it and, in boxy letters, read, *I love you more than you love me, Doug.* I don't know a Doug, not really. I woke up with a jolt, feeling disoriented.

I forgot about the dream until now, this brooch.

What if the envisionist supplies a pale, grudging future that looks like the contents of this box? I see my parents in my mind so clearly; they are eating breakfast—their whole-grain porridge—as silently as two people ice fishing in separate shacks. Even if it's bad like that, I'm going because I love Madge. She's strong and sharp-tongued and she sees in me something I can't even see in myself. She loves some unseen quality—a better Godfrey—and she makes me want to live up to it. When she's disappointed in me, it's only because she believes in me with such conviction. No one has ever believed in me the way Madge does—no Little League coach, no Boy Scout troop leader, no friend, no enemy, no teacher, not even my parents. God, it feels good to be around someone who knows you can do better, be better. With Madge, I *am* better—or at least getting there.

I look up Wickham Purdy in a nationwide database of obituaries and, sure enough, he's dead. In fact, he died the year I was born. He was married to a woman named Netta, who'd died two years earlier. No survivors. His name will be announced on our public records website, and after a sixty-day waiting period, his belongings will be confiscated by the U.S. government.

I press my oversized UNCLAIMED: HOLD stamp into the red ink pad. I can hear Bart stamping away. Lately I've grown suspicious of Bart's stamping speed. Does he really investigate the goods for clues, or is he a blind stamper, just assuming that no one is coming for this stuff?

I check the time. "I have to cut out for a bit," I tell Bart.

His face pops out from behind the partition. Bart was a great golfer at one point, but he gave it up because it made him nauseous to putt in front of people. He looks like a golfer still—athletic with a paunch, mostly ordinary. "What for?" he asks.

I pick something below the waist, figuring it's private enough not to beg questions. "Um, I may have something wrong with my gallbladder."

"Really? My family's full of gallbladder issues. What's the problem?" Bart looks at me like a concerned physician.

Perfect. "What? You're a gallbladder expert all of a sudden?"

"Like I said, it runs in the family. That's all."

"Well, I'd prefer not to discuss it." I shove my arms into my coat sleeves, hoping the gesture ends the conversation.

"I was just asking what kind. There are many different types of problems." Bart is reaching around my cubicle, picking up my can of soda, still mostly full. He takes a sip. "I was just expressing my sincere . . ."

"Don't do that," I interrupt.

"What?"

"Don't drink my soda. That's disgusting." I'm trying to knock Bart off topic.

"What? Since when is that a big deal?"

I glare at him before walking angrily out of the office. Now I'm the asshole who gets pissed off over soda.

I FIND DR. CHIN's office in the center of a strip mall, wedged between a Bagel Hut and a Nail-A-Rama. I sit in my car, the motor still running, and stare at the plate-glass storefront window. Its drawn red velvet curtains make me think of prostitution. I've never been with a prostitute and suddenly that seems short-sighted. I can't now. I'm almost engaged—Madge still hasn't put the ring on, but she is still in possession of it. I think this means we're more engaged than not engaged, but I'm not sure.

Chin's placard reads:

Dr. Chin, PhD, MD, ESQ, CPA
Now Offering:
The Future—For Curious People

(Also inquire about minor surgeries, overseas adoptions, mail-order bride services, pet euthanasia, notarization, and medicinal herbage.)

This is all very disconcerting, though I'm intrigued by "medicinal herbage." Chin used to be a lawyer *and* an accountant? What's the PhD in, anyway? Home decor or psychiatry? What kinds of minor surgeries? And is that "curious people" a play on words—curious as in full of questions or just plain weird? *Is he messing with us?* I am trying to make a mental list of things to ask him but the list is getting too big, and Madge still hasn't put the ring on.

With the motor still running, I contemplate slamming into reverse, driving home and just standing up to Madge. I could tell her I simply refused to go. I still don't buy that my participation is necessary. Madge explained, in great detail, how even though the future is only slightly malleable, we might have two very different perspectives about whether it's positive or negative. In bed last night, she said, "I could see two old farts on a beach with metal detectors, and think, 'How dismal.' And you could see two old farts on a beach with metal detectors and think, 'Wow, we finally made it!'" I didn't like my portrayal in her example, but we'd just had sex and I wasn't thinking straight enough to get into a fight. Fighting with Madge requires top form, and even at that, I'm used to losing or, at the very least, coming out humbled. Sometimes I think people date too long before they get married. We end up being old married couples before we ever say "I do." It's not our fault. It's generational. Sometimes I wish Madge and I had gotten married two weeks after the whole vaginalia conversation, on a tide of optimism that might have really buoyed us for a long time. Why can't I just say what I already feel sure of: my future without Madge is messy and depressed, like a dinghy boat at sea.

I lean forward, flip up the sun visor, and squint at the plate glass more intently. I see a glint of something there—red paint melting into the backdrop of red curtains. Is it a dragon? Is there faded lettering overhead?

In what seems like slow motion, I cut the engine, climb out of the car, and walk up to the window. I can now make out the chipped lettering over the dragon: CHIN'S CHINESE TAKEOUT. "Shit," I am saying to no one, but I still say it. "Shit on this."

If envisionists had existed when I was a kid, like four or five or whatever, I could have seen this exact moment—me, standing in the cold, in front of Dr. Chin's ex-take-out restaurant, bullied by my fiancée-to-be, and wouldn't I have been disappointed in my-self? I would've punched myself in the fucking face. "Where's the highest ledge?" I would've asked anyone who would talk to me. The envisionist could have shown my parents their awful future of detachment interrupted by bickering. If envisionists existed before my parents got married, they may have decided against it. And if my mother had been warned by an envisioning session that Mart Thigpen would knock her up and leave her "high and dry," I wouldn't exist at all. Maybe that's a big part of why this whole thing doesn't make any sense. It's tampering with the notions of my own existence, and the flimsy, dubious imaginary existence of my own offspring.

But, really, it's bullshit. Why didn't Madge just put on the ring? "Madge," I say to no one. "Shit on Madge." Will we one day be two old farts on a beach with metal detectors? The possibility of lost buffalo nickels, wrinkles under more wrinkles? Fuck that. Chin is a failed Chinese take-out guy and a failed lawyer and a failed accountant and a failed PhD in who the fuck knows. Why couldn't I do what Chin does? Hell, I haven't failed at anything, really. I know this is directly related to the fact that I've never really tried to succeed at much of anything, but it's easy not to think about that. I want to give Madge a big speech about love, true love, and the way you have to have enough faith in it to say yes to the unknown future of your life with someone. Or maybe Chin will fail so obviously that I will return to Madge with proof of just how stupid all of this is. That's why I'm out of the car and walking into Chin's office, opening the door, jangling some bells strung to the interior handle. But the bells are the same type of bells as the ones on the front door of Fontana's Super Mart and all I can think of is the faded lettering on the bottom of my receipt: *You are a loser.*

DR. CHIN'S WAITING ROOM is small and packed, much like the greening, overstocked fish tank in the corner where slow fish do laps. I hang my coat on one of the last available hooks.

The good news is that there's nothing very weird (or curious) about the people waiting. They look a little curdled, maybe, definitely bored, a little downtrodden, bruised, slightly repulsive. But aside from one woman singing, a little teary-eyed, to an aged, wheezing schnauzer in her lap, they're unremarkable. The other patients wear poly blends, flip through magazines. An elderly man dozes. I wonder what each of them is here for. Notary seals on mortgages? Root canals or to see if their moles are cancerous? A mail-order bride or child from a third-world country? A bag of pot? Or, plain and simple, a glimpse into the future? In any case, their ordinariness is comforting.

The office smells like Chinese takeout and incense—a combination that reminds me that I probably got stoned too much when I was younger. The incense is so sweet, though, I can't find any heartfelt regret. Those were fine days. I find the sudden onslaught of nostalgia frustrating. I don't want to lose my edge. I don't trust Dr. Chin or the incense or the overpopulated fish tank or even the ordinariness of everything around me.

At the frosted receptionist window where you check in, I get in line behind a woman about my age. She's frantically rummaging through her pocketbook, which looks cavernous. She's saying, "Hold on just a sec. It's in here." She turns to me without looking at me. "Hold this, will you?"

"Um, okay," I say.

She hands me her wallet and a tube of lipstick and a pocket-sized Chinese-English dictionary, which I can only take as a bad sign—does Dr. Chin even speak English?—and some crumpled bills. Noticing, with a quick glance, that she's completely filled my hands, she puts a small stack of things—a train ticket, some business cards and receipts—between her lips.

The receptionist is highly annoyed. She's Asian. Her name tag says Lisa. Her eyebrows are pierced with dainty hoops. I'm expecting a foreign accent, but hers is more Paramus, New Jersey. "Could you sit down? There are other people to check in."

The woman stops and looks at the receptionist and then at me.

The phone rings. The receptionist picks up. "Dr. Chin's now offering the future for curious people," she says, and then firmly states policy. "Chin only does notaries before nine a.m."

The woman tries to say something, but it comes out all *m*'s and tiny *b*'s, what with the things she's holding in her mouth. It's only now I notice that she's completely beautiful—unruly hair, deep brown eyes, skin the color of sun, and those pretty lips clamped around a few flimsy scraps of her identity.

"What are you looking for?" I ask her.

"Her license," the receptionist says. "You'll need yours, too, sir. What's your name?" Clearly she wants to move the line along.

"Godfrey Burkes," I say, eyeing the small stack of paperwork in the woman's mouth. I dip down and look underneath. I think I see the license—a bit of laminated stuff sticking out from behind a receipt. "Here," I say, pouring her stuff back into her pocketbook. I point to the stack. "May I?"

She nods her head, her eyes roving around the room as if she's suddenly realized that she's in public. I pinch the stack, and she opens her mouth a little. "Right here," I say, showing her the license.

She smiles. There's a fine gap between her two front teeth. I am immediately enamored by the gap and everything below and above it. "That's such a bad photo," she says, her eyes pointing to the license. It's surprising how clearly she speaks when she has full use of her mouth.

I hand it to the receptionist, who's finishing up a call. "Try the balm," the receptionist is saying into the phone. "If it doesn't clear up in two weeks, he'll lance it."

"See," the woman says to the receptionist, "I told you it was right here."

The receptionist rolls her eyes and hangs up the phone. She looks at the ID. "Thank you, Evelyn," she says sarcastically.

I step back behind the woman in line. I'm waiting for her to turn around and thank me, but she doesn't. She's trying to get an appointment and she hasn't called ahead. "I'm looking for someone," she says. "That's all."

"You think they aren't all looking for someone." The receptionist nods wearily at the waiting room. "Take a seat. If there's an opening, Dr. Chin will call you back. Sometimes he takes a special interest. You can't predict these things."

This seems funny to hear that you can't predict things in an envisionist's office. I raise my eyebrows—as part of this little interior conversation—and pull out my own wallet, found, just days before, by a gas station attendant.

The woman smiles apologetically at some of the other patients in the waiting room then sits down next to the woman with the elderly schnauzer and starts reading her Chinese-English dictionary.

"Next!"

I FILL OUT THE forms—checking the box "Romantic Future," the only option, though one day, as Madge explained, Americans of the future will all be day traders. And soon I'm asked back to one of the seven examination rooms. I change into a paper dressing gown, which seems unnecessary and humiliating, but what part of this whole thing hasn't been? And I sit on the edge of the examination table, the gown crinkling each time I shift my weight.

There's a television in one corner, sitting on a shelving unit on wheels. It reminds me of the ancient AV equipment from high school and the small arthritic nun in charge of it. There's a cable box on one of the shelves, too. I haven't seen a cable box since I was a kid. None of this inspires confidence, but what's truly unnerving is the metal helmet overhead. It's attached to hinged legs that spring outward, spiderlike, and then rejoin at a dome on the ceiling. Red and blue wires reach from the dome to a metal box on the counter and then the wires swoop up to the back of the television. It's all old-world cartoon—the kind of thing used to transfer brain waves from the hero to the villain.

I try not to dwell on it. Instead, I pick up the information sheet and start to read. I'm most curious about the first paragraph: *Addictions to envisioning are rare but have been known to happen. In case of addiction, you will be denied further treatment and asked to seek professional help. A list of providers is available upon request. Please respect our personnel, premises, and equipment. Breaching our policies may result in a restraining order, legal action, and imprisonment.* If Chin can produce the future—which I highly doubt—could someone get addicted to it?

Farther down, there is an offer to try alternating alternate futures—*Rotation Service: See price list.* There is no price list attached. My visit is only thirty dollars with my insurance copay. Evidently, my insurance company has never seen Chin's flaky storefront takeout paint job.

One clause states that if you don't actually believe you have a shot at being with someone in the future, romantically, your brain won't either. It's a sad bastard who tries to envision a future he can't even envision. There's mention of friend and family envisioning sessions, which I glide right past, but my eyes catch on the final sentence. *Look, if your pet is dead, it's dead.*

Madge had been right on one point, no. 6: *Because of the highly supportive and biased work of an envisionist—who is working toward the best possible future for* you—*we suggest that couples go to separate envisionists to avoid a conflict of interest.* I like that someone would be on my side, for once.

No. 8 is easily the most interesting: *If a couple is not headed for a bright future, we will only allow three sessions of future envisionings—between which they can try to influence the future. Three is the MAX-IMUM. Studies show that more sessions have proven futile. It is better to move on. We offer follow-up counseling to assist you toward a better future.*

And no. 10 is the shortest: *In the case of true love, there can be system failures.*

I'm in a supposed doctor's office where there's a mention of true love? This strikes me as simply embarrassing, an affront to science, really.

And then there's a long paragraph of disclaimers as well. *We do not guarantee clear pictures of your future. In fact, images of lovers in the future are often blocked and/or blurred, as are brand-name items. Usually patients report that they can see themselves clearly, however.* And: *If you are having problems with listlessness, blurry vision, recurring unwanted guests in your dream life, or nausea, please report it to a health care professional. If you are prone to seizures, envisioning may not be the right choice for you. Consult your doctor.* But Chin is a doctor, right?

I've always believed that the future was ultimately my own. I haven't really taken advantage of this way of thinking, of course. I've been pretty passive. I mean, I found out that Madge had been the one to pursue me. She'd found me through Amy, had heard Bart talking about me and requested the coffee shop set up. I had gone grudgingly to get Bart and Amy off my back, but when I met Madge I understood that she could save me. Save me from what? A life of lonesomeness. A life where I'd have a one-night stand and feel really awful about it. *Bad, Thigpen. Bad.* But Madge, with her glowing smile and her upward mobility and her affirmed childhood, well, I could glom onto that and ride—for a lifetime. She's prettier than I am handsome by more than just simple gradations. She even tells me I could be really good-looking if I owned my curly hair and awkward height and bulky shoulders. And sometimes, when I'm with Madge, I have moments when I do almost own it all, almost. Bart and Amy know Madge saved me. And they've been smug about introducing us ever since. I'm uncomfortable with the idea that there are set futures all locked up in front of me, a maze with multiple endings, a video game I can never beat.

Sometimes I just want to pause myself.

There's a brief knock on the door before it swings open.

"I'm Dr. Chin," the man says, but I'm not sure I believe him. Briefly, I wonder if someone is playing a joke on me.

A. He isn't Asian. He has graying blond hair, a small sporty build, and a slight tan. He looks windblown and smart but not too smart—like an Ivy League football player.

B. He isn't earthy or herb-y. There's even a chance he's church-going—albeit something liberal, maybe Unitarian.

C. He's wearing slippers and has a newspaper folded up under one arm, as if he's just done his morning business on the can. This casualness gives him an air of confidence I find disturbing. Still, I can't help but like the guy. It's as if Chin was designed to be liked—not loved, not hated, just liked. But thoroughly liked, someone you'd be pleasantly surprised to run into at the supermarket.

I glance around for hidden pranksters, a camera in the corner of the room.

"And you're"—he looks at his chart—"Godfrey Burkes." He says my name with such authority that I have to assume, at least for now, that this is the real Dr. Chin.

He shakes my hand. He smells old-school medical—like tongue depressors and rubbing alcohol. I don't want to give into him too easily. "You don't look like a Dr. Chin."

"You know," he says with a laugh, "a lot of people say that." He's staring at my chart. "I was adopted."

This answer doesn't quite satisfy me, however, so I continue to press him. "Didn't this place used to be a Chinese takeout by the name of Chin's?"

"I lease this place from my brother, Earl Chin. It's too bad the restaurant went under. Best damn egg rolls I've ever tasted."

"Really," I say. I can still smell the egg rolls.

"You're here to look into your romantic future. Correct?"

I nod. "Are you also a lawyer and a CPA with a PhD in something?"

"I've packed many lives into one life," Dr. Chin says, and suddenly he seems wise in a particularly Asian way. "It's a nice way to go through, if you ask me. I recommend it. But you're here to make a choice of some kind. Correct? Have you ever done this before?"

I shake my head and stare at Dr. Chin's slippers.

"Okay, then. I see you've chosen the Single Future Glimpse. You've written in the name Madge Hedgeworth. You want to see your future with her. Correct?"

I nod and point at his slippers. "Did you just wake up?"

"I have corns. Listen," he says, and then he takes a deep sigh and, with ultimate patience, says, "I'm adopted. I lease the place from my brother. I've worked in a number of fields and I have painful corns. Is all of that okay with you? You seem nervous. Are there any other questions I can answer?"

I glance at the newspaper still tucked under his arm. "Nope," I tell him. "Nothing else."

Dr. Chin reaches in his pants pocket and pulls out a handful of change. He sorts through them, picking out quarters and feeding them into the slot on the metal box.

"Is that coin-op?" I ask.

"Don't worry," Chin says. "All of it is deducted straight from your insurance." This does not address my concern.

Chin pulls a lever, and the spiderlike helmet lowers from the ceiling. "This is all based on neuroscience—our brains' vast under-utilized capacities, but it's got a foot in physics. I mean theories of alternate realities. The world's future iterations are endless. Am I right?"

"You're the doctor, Doctor."

He turns on the television. It snaps and buzzes to life, but the picture is filled with snow. He starts pressing buttons on the ancient cable box. Finally, he gets a black screen. "There we go. You're on station sixteen. That's rare."

"Is it?" I ask. "What does that mean?"

"Nothing really. It's just rare." Dr. Chin places the helmet onto my head and then attaches leather chin straps. I think of my mother tying a winter hat under my chin. I think of Madge's woolen mittens.

With his back to me, he messes around with some pill bottles, then hands me a Dixie cup with three little pills in it. "How far into the future would you like to go? Ten, fifteen, forty years?"

"I'm not sure. I mean, I think beyond fifteen would be greedy, don't you?"

There's a pause as Dr. Chin seems to contemplate this. "Not for me to judge. Let's go with fifteen. Okay?"

"Okay."

He fills another Dixie cup with water and puts it on a tray beside me. "You and Madge Hedgeworth." He types into the computer, mumbling to himself. "Fifteen years."

I'm suddenly terrified. In fifteen years, I'll be older than the age Mart Thigpen was when he seduced my mother. "Dr. Chin," I say, "I have this one problem."

"I hope it's not seizures."

"No, no," I say. "I have an animal nature, deep down. See, my biological father, Mart Thigpen, a man I've never met, is the kind to cheat on his wife with other women and not really have regrets about it. I'm a little worried that I'll be like him fifteen years from now. Maybe it's irrational, but do you think people are kind of genetically programmed to become their parents, on some level?"

Chin sighs. "I believe in free will."

"Huh, I see. Is that a no? You don't think I'm going to turn into my biological father, right?"

"I think you're you, for better and for worse."

I nod but wonder if Chin put just a tiny bit more emphasis on *for worse*. Should I feel insulted?

"Can we proceed?"

"Sure," I say, "of course."

"Okay, then. After you take the pills, you'll get very sleepy. You won't actually fall asleep, but your emotions will no longer affect what your brain conjures. You will still react to the images, but those emotions won't block your brain's power. Images that appear in your mind will appear on the screen."

"Why no brand names?" I ask.

"Some people were using that information for financial gains that led to legal battles. It was ugly."

"Why don't the future lovers come in clearly?"

Chin shrugs and goes on, "Audio will pipe into the headgear. There will be a little intro." He puts a joystick into my hand. "Control the volume by pressing here." It has a thumb button and is wired to the wall. It would be easy to pretend I was on a quiz show.

"What if I don't believe in all of this?" I ask.

"I don't understand your question," Dr. Chin says in that way that Ivy League types can not know an answer and make you look like the stupid one.

"Is this one of those things where you have to believe in it to have any results?"

"Are you asking me if this is like pixie dust and that you have to repeat 'I can fly' so that you can fly?"

"I guess I am."

"You don't have to believe in anything," Dr. Chin says. "It'll work. Unless, of course, you have no future; then the screen will stay blank."

"What do you mean?" I ask.

"Well, if you're going to die young, the screen will stay blank."

"Jesus Christ!" I say loudly before I whisper it again and again.

"And sometimes you only die young in certain futures and in others you live a long life. But sometimes death is death."

"Holy shit!"

"That reminds me. You've signed off in triplicate, right?"

"Signed off?"

"The last page. Here it is." He boyishly shoves his blond hair off his forehead, and pushes the papers at me. "We really aren't responsible for any trauma caused by this process. But we will refer you to a professional, if you happen to, well, become troubled by anything you see here today." He hands me a black ballpoint. "Seeing futures, well, as you can imagine, it's tricky business."

"Tricky, sure. I can understand that." I pause, the pen frozen over three dotted lines.

"Are you okay?" Dr. Chin asks. He puts his hand on my shoulder.

"Do you look into your own future?" I ask him.

Dr. Chin claps me on the shoulder. "No. Of course not." He says this while smiling broadly. It's the kind of smile that makes me think of the expression *a winning smile* and then immediately I wonder if there's such a thing as *a losing smile,* and suddenly I'm sure there is. In fact, I'm sure that I'm smiling a losing smile right now—a smile that turns down at its edges and the eyes well up, nervously—but I can't help it. I'm still smiling while I sign my name—once, twice, three times.

I DOWN THE PILL and, in a few minutes the screen goes blue and the words *Madge Hedgeworth and Godfrey Burkes / A Chin Production* pop up like the low-budget video production of a shitty wedding—the union of two people with criminally awful taste. A rose lying on its side underlines the title and then a dubious copyright symbol, the year, and *A Chin Production* appear in cursive letters.

My thumb is poised on the joystick. This has been a waste of my copay money, my insurance company's money, and my time off from Unclaimed Goods. But I can imagine how I'll tell it, that I was in it for laughs all along, the blond Dr. Chin, the signing in triplicate, the idiotic leather straps on the metal helmet. My parents will say, *Oh, Godfrey, you're such a wonderful storyteller!* And Bart and Amy will have to concede that their envisionist was pretty hokey, too, worthless in fact. Bart might say, *I'll probably be completely bald in five years!* And *We don't even like tennis and boating!* Maybe even Madge would laugh along and then cup my face in her hands and say, *Poor Godfrey, I can't believe I put you through all of that.*

I start to feel a little loose and dreamy just as the first image appears on the screen—a small green car pulls into a driveway. A teenage girl gets out and starts across a front yard to a house. She's pretty with pale eyes and dark hair. She looks barely sixteen. She's wearing a skirt and a jean jacket—it surprises me how jean jackets refuse to become obsolete.

And that's when a man appears. He's holding a watering can. It's me, of course. I recognize myself. I'm forty, wearing what my father would call *trousers*—those almost high-waisted pants with pleats down the front. I wonder if I have a better job now; the pants seem to indicate a higher function in life. At forty I appear relatively fit, but the problem is that I have gelled hair, which is obviously lame. The first thing I realize is that in this alternate future I have very little, if any, personal dignity. My future self says to the girl, "Hey there."

"My mom wanted me to tell you that she dropped off some seed packets. They're in the backyard, under a pot."

"Great!" future-me says.

"I'm sorry about your mom," the girl says.

I look down at the watering can. "Thanks, but it's okay. I don't like to talk about it." I shake my head and stare at the ground. I recognize this as my sympathy pose; it's the one I strike when I'd really like someone to feel sorry for me. I hadn't realized until this moment that I have such a pose, but I can tell that this is a fake little moment.

The two undeniable facts of the situation are these: One. Something awful has happened to my mother. Two. In this alternate future, I've taken to hitting on teenage girls.

"Where's Madge?" the girl asks.

Future-me raises my eyebrows. "Just calling her Madge now?"

The girl nods.

"She's taken her latest dog to a restaurant. She's, you know, *socializing*." What in the hell does this mean? Is Madge openly cheating on me? Do people in the future openly cheat and call each other's latest lovers *dogs*? The girl doesn't seem surprised by anything future-me is saying.

"Well," the girl says. "See you later!" She walks to her tiny car, hops in the driver's seat, and waves through the open window.

"See you later, Lib!" *Lib?* This name means nothing to me. Future-me watches the girl, this Lib, ride off, and then I plod on. Future-me walks like now-me walks, with a small bounce forward with each step. I can't deny that this is, in fact, me. A forty-year-old man about to water his wife's flowers while she's out possibly cheating on him in broad daylight with his full knowledge. And is my mother really dead? What's happened to my mother?

Future-me stops suddenly. He looks down the street, watching the car drive out of sight. But then something else catches his eye. Someone's legs are pumping a bike. A woman's legs. Her skirt is flipping up on her thigh, six houses away or so but heading toward future-me—it's a close-up on the legs and the skirt and a big blue bike—its brand blurred out. The legs are beautiful but not really young. They strike me as the legs of a woman my age now. Where did the bike come from? The legs? I want to will myself to look at this woman's face, but I don't. She glides on by. Future-me turns around and walks back to the front of the house. He plops the watering can, a prop after all, down on the stoop. Evidently I had no intentions of watering Madge's flowers or finding some seed pack.

Do Madge and I get married and stay in the Baltimore area? Could be. The houses are boxy, older. A few are strung with Christmas lights, although by the looks of the small green yards and the sunlight, it's late spring. I watch myself walk into the house. It's design is all Madge, retro and antiqued.

As future-me walks through the kitchen, which is unremarkable, the screen fades and then there's a picture of a tall blonde woman standing at the foot of a hotel staircase. I don't recognize her. She's gorgeous though, looking busty in an angora sweater. She introduces herself as Svetlana and explains that she's a "vivacious Russian woman, looking for a strong American partner." I feel immediately deflated. Svetlana isn't part of my future. This is a fucking commercial. Dr. Chin's voice pipes up in the background while the screen cuts to footage of Svetlana walking through a meadow. Chin says, "The future can take many forms. Please talk to Dr. Chin, offering the future for curious people, to see your future with Svetlana or one of her many friends." Svetlana is now sitting alone at a lovely picnic, beckoning to the camera. I am disgusted; this whole interruption seems intentionally cruel.

The screen fades and my own future starts again. Future-me opens a door that leads to basement stairs. He claps and the lights flip on. He claps twice and then there's music—it's the first few chords from the Cure's "Love Song," one of my favorite songs from high school. The basement is awful. Lined with boxes and paint cans and an extra roll of brown shag, there sits my old furniture—an old sofa, coffee table, lamp, and surfboard—in the same pitiful configuration that I had as a bachelor, the same configuration that is now likewise arranged in our cramped spare bedroom. Has Madge forced me to re-create my old life in the basement of this new life because she just won't give me one square inch? All this while she's out with some *dog, socializing* in restaurant bars? I watch myself sit down heavily on the sofa, open the drawer in the coffee table, and pull out a pump bottle of lotion.

"No," I say aloud in the small waiting room. "Don't. Jesus. C'mon." There's no way I'm not pressing the button on the joystick if I start to masturbate. But if I press the button on the joystick, will the screen freeze-frame? Would some nurse waltz in and see me on the screen—a close-up on the action? That would be worse.

I close my eyes. But then there's a knock on the audio, some scrambling noises. I open my eyes. Madge is at the top of the stairs. I can only see her ankles—which reminds me of seeing them in the pool, underwater, last summer. But this time she's wearing her ultrasuede comfortable shoes—the ones she's just started buying. They're expensive and bulky and unattractive.

"I'm home," Madge says.

"How did it go?" future-me asks.

"She's doing well," Madge says. "I figure she'll be ready for the intensive training in two weeks or so." Madge doesn't walk down the steps. She's frozen up there. I lean forward on the examination table, as if I can see more with an upward angle. Madge says in a hushed voice, "Good girl. Stay."

And now I can hear the nails clicking on the kitchen linoleum. Madge is training an actual dog. She'd mentioned this once a while back—something about seeing-eye dogs. We'd seen a woman with one at the movies. Madge isn't cheating on me. She's turned into a good person. And I'm a masturbator, possibly a chronic one. Lovely. The worst part is that Madge refuses to walk down the stairs to actually look at me.

"Godfrey," she says. "Are you okay? Do you want to talk about it?"

Future-me shakes his head; his eyes go wet. This isn't a fake moment. He presses the tears out of his eyes with the heels of his hands. He clears his throat. "What?" he says. "I'm fine. We didn't even really get along. You know that." I know that this is about my mother again. She's dead. I can feel it.

There's a long pause and then Madge quietly says, "Okay, then. Okay." Her ultrasuedes turn on the stairs and disappear.

THE SCREEN REVERTS TO snow. I am sitting there in my paper gown, all of the gear still firmly in place on my head, holding the joystick midair. My future with Madge is worse than metal detectors on the beach—at least in that scenario there's a beach. What am I going to say to Madge at lunch? What is she seeing at Plotniks? Does she know that I'm a chronic masturbator who hits on teenage girls and has gelled hair? I wonder if Madge will cry. I hate it when she cries. Is this the end of our relationship? Are we calling off the engagement? Were we even engaged to begin with? She has the ring, but she's not wearing it. Is it possible to be halfway engaged? Would we be calling off our almost engagement? I feel relief over not telling my parents about the proposal. I'd hate to have to explain this. *This.* My mother is going to die fairly young. She only has fifteen years. No one needs to know that.

But now that I know that my mother is going to die, there's a tender swelling in my chest—an undying love for her. *All mothers die,* I tell myself, trying to stop the ache, but it doesn't do any good.

In spite of the bad news of Madge in her hardy shoes and me in the basement with lotion and my mother's death, or because of it, I feel alive—awful but fully alive. My skin is warm, fresh. The hairs on my neck are standing up. My heartbeat has made it all the way up in my ears.

I push the button on the joystick to call in a nurse. Moments later, the examination room door flies open. But it's not Dr. Chin or a nurse. It's the woman from the waiting room who lost her license. She snagged an appointment after all. She's barefoot, wearing her own paper gown—one hand on the knob, one hand holding together the gown in the back. "What in the hell are you doing in my room?" she asks.

I look around. "This is my room," I say.

She glances over her shoulder to the number on the exam room door: 3. "Oh," she says, "I have a lousy sense of direction." And then she glances at my spread legs and short paper gown. "You might want to . . ." And she makes a little gesture like she's closing a book.

I bring my knees together, trying not to blush. "Well, if you weren't in here . . ." I say.

She looks like she's about to burst with laughter. She's wearing the paper gown but also a dainty silver choker with a little doodad that's bobbing with choked laughter. "So sorry," she says, showing the thin gap in her two front teeth. Then, recovering, she points to the television. "Addictive, isn't it?"

I think it might be, I want to tell her—my knees pressed so tightly together I can feel my blood clipping quickly through my body. But the woman has already shut the door. I miss her immediately, and then I think of Mart Thigpen. My love of women is an animal love.

I push the button on the joystick again and wait.

Evelyn
MAYBE TRY A LITTLE BUDDHA

As the drugs settle into my bloodstream, it feels like my body is a raft on the Mississippi under an incubator-bright, incubator-warm sun. I say, "Godfrey Burkes, Godfrey Burkes, Godfrey Burkes. What's a Godfrey Burkes?" I think of him pulling my license from my lips and then in the examination room staring at me like that—like what? I don't know, maybe in a way that's quite typical of a Godfrey Burkes.

But I'm not here to see my future with Godfrey Burkes.

I have run through a list of people I loved or almost loved or should have loved or failed to love enough. I wanted to make sure that I hadn't broken up with or allowed myself to be broken up with by someone who would have been perfect for me under different circumstances, which might include now and/or ten years from now. None of those futures panned out. Some were flaming disasters; others featured plenty of embittered wreckage that I recognized from my parents' broken marriage; and some were what I would simply call a stalemate—no one throwing down, just lots of stubborn resignation.

And so, with my past clearly behind me, I'm moving on to present possibilities—no matter how farfetched, including one session with my landlord's younger brother, Teddy, who came by to unclog a drain once.

I hear the ambient noise of a crowd. The monitor reveals that Jason Binter and I are at a mall, but I hate malls, or at least the now-me hates malls: the recycled circulated air, the two lanes to walk back and forth but nobody can figure out which way is back and which is forth what with all the old people doing laps.

I could have a not-weird future, right? I'm capable of that. Maybe it's even something to aspire to. And, so far, so good. Binter and I are here, together, at a mall—being not weird at all.

And I quickly remind myself that it's too easy for things to start so well. That could be the first line to the memoir I'll never write: *It's too easy for things to start so well.*

At the top of the staircase, Jason turns around. Even through the fuzz, he looks like he did the last time I saw him, about a week ago, pawing through African American sheet music. Maybe his frat-boy vibe transcends aging.

"Do you want a pretzel?" I ask him. I point to what I assume is an Auntie Anne's pretzel kiosk, if those are still around fifteen years from now; the sign above the pretzel kiosk looks like it's covered in a mirage. "Something cinnamon maybe?"

Jason opens his mouth, but nothing comes out.

It was a simple question. I ask again, "Do you want a pretzel?"

But his mouth—just nothing. Is he thinking over the existential crisis of salt or no salt, to splurge on a side of icing? Adrian couldn't shut the fuck up; Jason can't seem to get himself started.

"Carbs," he finally says, shaking his head.

Jason doesn't eat carbs. This is bad. I love bread. My favorite food groups go cheese, bread, cheese bread, and soup served in a hollowed-out loaf of bread.

Half of the mall is blurred because of brand merchandising. Half of the nonblurred parts of the mall are foggy anyway, because this is the future and the future seems insecure in completely showing itself. I sympathize.

I wonder which mall this is. It's so blurred I could have been here a thousand times and wouldn't know it. I try to find a specific landmark: a fountain, maybe that hallway I dipped into to kiss Josh Teerman through most of middle school, but nothing.

The session is briefly interrupted—I've gotten used to these advertisements. This one is to adopt a baby from a third-world country by way of Chin's adoption program.

And then I'm back at the mall. Jason and I have wandered to a kiosk selling nail buffers. We're discussing the pros and cons of buffed nails. We also discuss, in no particular order and with no depth and/or irony, painting a living room beige or off-beige, which is different from ecru; a couple who wants to join our bunco group, but the wife lacks a filter and sometimes states things she shouldn't—for example, that her male collie often gets humped at the dog park by girl dogs, which strikes us as completely inappropriate conversation for our bunco crowd; a brief comparison of kitchen appliance brands; the benefits of galoshes; and why we love Crate and Barrel.

I realize quickly that this conversation represents a long, slow death in suburbia, the quiet suffering of the imaginationless masses, the soul dulled by commercialism. We might as well be screaming *We're dead! We're dead! We're dead!* Or, better yet, stuffed and arranged in a display case of a mall—beside a tiny nail-buffer kiosk—by Fadra the taxidermist!

I look down at my ring finger. The diamond is the size of my knuckle. I would never wear anything this gaudy. I bet this future-me doesn't ride a bike; instead, she opts for an elliptical in an air-conditioned gym while reading *Us Weekly*. I realize I'm being judgmental, which feels bitchy even though it's self-directed.

Then I look through the glass storefront of a clothing store and see a fogged and pale version of a self I do not ever want to know. I'm in better shape than I am now; I'm tan in an orangey way; my face is slightly injected. Binter has rubbed off so hard on me that I look like an aged sorority girl.

And beside me, there's someone else. Not Jason Binter at all. There's a man wearing . . . a white knee-length sundress? I can't really make out his face, but I see that he's handsome, maybe even honest-looking. Could it be a paper gown? Is this some escaped mental patient? My future self turns, away from the reflection, to the man himself, but he's gone.

My future self rubs her eyes. This is a strange mall. She runs to catch up with Jason. Who is she? Do people make us who we are or is every future possibility just different pieces of the same self?

The screen goes to snow, and I actually whisper a thank-you.

But this blank screen is my least favorite part of the day. Some would say the future never ends because it hasn't happened yet, but that's bullshit. They've obviously never sat in this chair.

Dr. Chin pops in after a few seconds. "How'd it go?"

"I can cross him off the list." I swipe an imaginary pen through the air. "Jason Binter, gone. See, so easy." There's a feeling of relief that I've narrowed down the possible futures that endlessly splinter out in front of myself. I'm pruning, and eventually there will be one future in front of me—obvious and clear and knowable.

"This is your fourth time in two weeks, and you're not following the healthiest pattern."

It's actually my fifth time, but I don't correct him. "What pattern?"

"Usually clients get exasperated, completely fed up. Heartbroken. They're ready to storm out of here if they haven't already. You, on the other hand, seem *excited.* Almost renewed by each failure."

"Well, there *are* three billion men out there, I think—ballpark figure."

He squints. "It might be better if this is your last appointment."

"That seems like a bad business model," I joke, but inside I feel a rise of panic.

"There've been cases of this," he says. "Studies done."

"Of *this*? What's *this*?"

"We call them—we call you—the Obsessives."

I want to laugh, tell him it sounds kind of badass, something out of a S. E. Hinton novel. Or maybe from a Broadway musical: *The Obsessives*—we'll sing before we cut you, but we'll cut you bad, bad I tell you. "Do we get name tags, a tattoo for every failed envisioning?" I try to smile, but he's not buying. "Look, I'm curious, sure, but hardly obsessive."

Dr. Chin rubs his neck—the front first, working his way to the back, under the collar of his dress shirt. I feel like I'm doing something wrong. "We could argue semantics all day, but your insurance only covers so much. Plus, you shouldn't get in any deeper."

"You make it sound like a cult."

"It might be worse," he says. His hand is still rubbing the back of his neck. "There's no Kool-Aid at the end."

"What is at the end?"

"Trust me, it's not pretty. The future, the desire to know it and feel it—that desire can swallow you whole."

"Look, I'm a nice, well-adjusted girl," I say, and everything's relative. "Worst-case scenario, I just run out of men."

"Do you have a career goal? I mean, is there something else you'd like to do with yourself?"

"Are you insinuating that I'm just boy crazy?"

"We do get a lot of that here."

"I'm a feminist."

"I'm not sure what that means anymore."

"I love my job and . . ." And what? And I was born in a generation where girls should be ambitious and men shouldn't matter. I'm of a generation of girls pushed into science and math, encouraged to play violent video games to subvert stereotypes, a generation fast outpacing boys in college entrance and graduation stats. A generation of women for whom men are optional, unnecessary, purely decorative. Still, I want a real love. I believe love matters. I want it to matter and to be true and to build a family with that love—the kind of family I was cheated out of as a kid. "I'm human. I still believe in love. Aren't we wired for it? Aren't you?"

Chin draws in a deep breath and then lets it out. "You know, people were happy before all of this." He points to the cheap screen, the shoddy B-movie alien helmet. "There was me and my wife. And for you there *will be* whoever it is you're supposed to end up with."

"'For time and the world do not stand still,'" I say. "'Change is the law of life. And those who look only to the past or the present are certain to miss the future.'"

Chin looks up for a moment and then says, "JFK, right?"

I nod.

"Maybe you should try a little Buddha. 'Do not dwell in the past, do not dream of the future—'"

"I know," I say. "Buddha's a real stickler about the present, a real *obsessive* about it, some might say."

"And JFK didn't get much future, did he?"

I sigh. "No, he didn't."

"Look, I just want you to be sure about your next session. Don't come back until you need to come back. You hear me? You don't want to be put on probation."

"Probation? But I could always go to another envisionist."

"Nope, we've got a system. When you're blacklisted, we all know it."

"You can't do that to people, can you?"

"We can," Chin says, "so just take it easy."

"I'm not obsessive. I just happen to live in a time in history when one can see the romantic future. I refuse to apologize for taking advantage of my time and place in history!"

He picks my chart off the table. "Look, it could be worse," he says, but I don't know how it could be worse because he's already left the room.

I put my clothes back on slowly, as if I'm relearning how to be real-life again, how to not watch myself do something I haven't done yet. I walk out of the room feeling sick and dizzy. What would happen if I got blacklisted? The idea of not coming back makes my head feel lighter than a balloon, taut like it's ready to pop.

Godfrey
PLOTNIK'S DISCIPLE

"I think envisioning must make you hungry," Madge says, cutting into a rib eye. "Dr. Plotnik explained how the whole thing works, the physics behind it all, how we're the source of manufacturing the images, as if our very own cells know all of this information. It's fascinating, right?"

I nod my head. The waitresses at this place all wear nylons and orthopedic-looking lace-up shoes; the shoes remind me of Madge's future ultrasuedes, which are exactly like her current ultrasuedes. And maybe that's the worst part about envisioning, I think. How things don't change as much as you think they should. I feel sorry for the waitresses each time they go shooshing by.

"Plotnik really took his time," she says. "He's a genius." I'm relieved to be here with the real Madge. I tell myself, *Here she is.* In the flesh. At this moment, she's explaining all the things that Plotnik told her but with her beautiful hands moving through air and her face lit up. This is the Madge who stopped me earlier this winter to catch snowflakes on our tongues, who tracked down a slightly used and now vintage action figure I was obsessed with as a child. This is the Madge I love and this is the Madge who's actually important.

"What did your place smell like?" I say.

Madge looks up, flabbergasted. She often gets flabbergasted in her conversations with me but not usually so quickly.

"What?" I say.

"You're not going to fixate, are you? I hate it when you do that."

"Mine smelled like egg rolls. That's all. I mean, yours could have smelled like borscht. I'm not fixating."

She shakes her head and picks up her knife and fork reluctantly, like she's rethinking the rib eye. "You've just been through a life-altering experience. Could you please act like it?"

"I'm not sure what that's supposed to look like." I pick at my mashed potatoes. I'm not hungry.

Madge rolls her eyes. There's some chewing.

"So," I say, "what did you think of it?"

"What? The smell?"

"No," I say. "What you saw."

"I don't know if it matters."

"What do you mean?"

"I mean . . ." She wipes her mouth, smearing her lipstick just enough to make her look like she's been freshly kissed. When was the last time I smeared her lipstick with a good old-fashioned kiss? I love kissing Madge. "I mean that it's the whole experience that counts. We can *know* things. It's a new way of life!"

"I know and love you now."

She blushes. I can still sometimes make Madge blush like when we were first dating. "I love you now, too," she says. "That's un-questionable."

"What if it's all just a racket?" I say. "They have whole packages, five-for-threes, that kind of thing. It's not very medical."

"Don't be jaded."

I think that's a yes. "I'm not jaded," I tell her.

"Yes, you are."

"C'mon," I say. "What did you see?"

"I ran into Elizabeth, for one. She was beautiful!"

"Elizabeth?"

"My sister's daughter. She'd dropped something off at the house and she waved me down as I was coming home."

"Lib," I whisper, too low for Madge to hear. "Short for Libby. Short for Elizabeth." The girl on the bike was the fat toddler whom we visited just a month ago—a two-year-old. She spent most of the visit throwing things off her high-chair tray. "But she's practically an infant," I say, letting my fork sink into the mashed potatoes and stop eating altogether.

"Well, she is going to grow up!"

"I know, I know."

Madge salts her potatoes. "What did you see?"

"I only saw your ankles. They looked good, but . . ." I keep going because I don't want to know if Madge's envisioning led her to believe I was about to jerk off. "Somewhere along the line, I start gelling my hair. Can we nip that in the bud?"

"That's the thing," Madge says. "We can. Of course we can. We can affect the future. We have two more tries left."

I'm not sure what to think. Maybe her view of things is a little brighter. Maybe I caught myself a little too vulnerable. My mother had recently died. I wasn't myself. "Do I have to set up my old bachelor pad in our basement?"

"Do you *really* believe that Bart and Amy are going to be yachting and playing tennis?" She leans forward. "I think they were lying."

"I think I might have a better job in the future," I say hopefully. "I had on very mature, upper-management pants."

Madge reaches over and touches my sleeve. "I'm sorry about your mother."

I think I nod.

"Elizabeth told me you looked really upset about it."

"Maybe I can talk to her about her health," I say. "Screenings and vitamins."

"Well," Madge says, lifting her wineglass. "Two more tries! Plotnik says that some couples have had a good bit of success in two more tries!"

I lift my mug of beer, wishing it were a keg. "Two more tries! We aren't sunk yet!"

We clink our glasses, sip and set them down.

"How do we affect the future?" I ask. "I mean, how do we make it less, less, you know . . ."

Madge is cutting her meat into little pieces as if she's preparing the plate for a child. She shakes her head. "I'll ask Plotnik," she says, fitting the last three pieces of beef onto her fork. "I trust him." She puts the fork in her mouth and glances at me. She's chewing but smiling and chewing. Her cheeks, like little shiny bulbs, bob. Her eyes are moist. With fear? With hope?

The waitress shooshes by. I lift a hand to get her attention, which she ignores, and I reach for my wallet with the other. It's not there.

I toss my napkin on my plate. "Shit. Did I lose my wallet again?"

"What?"

"I must have left it at Chin's."

"Do you just hate to pay for things? Are you *that* cheap?"

"I'm not cheap on purpose!"

"Are you *subconsciously* cheap? Jesus, I think you're subconsciously cheap! This is becoming a real problem." Madge sits back, full of herself. "Oh, I know what it is."

"What?"

"It's an identity issue," Madge says.

"What does that mean?" I don't like her tone.

"You keep losing your identification. You keep losing yourself. Purposefully."

"Not *purposefully*," I tell her.

"Well, it seems like it's on purpose to me. There are no accidents."

"There are accidents all the time!" I look down at my plate. My fork has been completely submerged in mashed potatoes. "*No accidents.* I hate that saying." Am I having an identity issue?

"It isn't a saying," Madge says, putting her credit card down on the table and hailing the waitresses. "It's psychology, Godfrey. It's part of our brains. It's science." And she smiles at me with her head tilted. I'm not going to lie, Madge is pretty, even when she's being condescending.

"Since when is psychology a science?" I say under my breath.

"What was that?" Madge asks.

But I'm just nodding my head.

Evelyn
BORROWERS AND THIEVES

Dot and I walk into the library's open airy entranceway, the expanse of skylights overhead, the massive portraits of austere human beings gazing down on us in our puffy coats.

"It feels like a museum," Dot says. She has a broad face, almost moonish, with great short choppy bangs and big eyes that make her look almost Manga.

"It's more like a zoo that lends out animals. The books are living, breathing, heart-beating creatures."

"So a lot of lives are at stake?"

"Actually, yes. We are the protectors of dangerous materials." I want to tell her that if not for me, a lot of the children of Baltimore would be doing meth in dark basements, but that's not completely verified.

"I see."

She doesn't see. I can tell.

As we peel off all our winter wear, we run into Chuck, our overly large-headed deputy. I introduce him to Dot who seems a little wary. She has anxiety around cops. Chuck says, "New pics!" and he waves his smartphone. "Chuck E. Cheese!"

Chuck has the cutest offspring in the world—fat and sassy. His wife dresses them in matching handmade costumes to coincide with current events and pop stars—the royal wedding, Lady Gaga, and an occasional uninspired bear suit. These kids, though, the dimples and snotty noses, the milk mustaches.

Chuck guides us through the latest series, and honestly, by the end, I'm a little choked up. That is how relentless the cuteness is. He's invited me over a few times and I bring the kids Slinkys and Silly Putty, and I feel like, if I play it right, they might soon be calling me Auntie Evelyn, which I would love more than a normal person would. Families, I can't stop myself from building them out of thin air.

"How are you doing these days?" he asks me.

"Still no cat!" I've promised him to one day adopt a stray cat and compete in the themed-costume department.

"When you do, it's game on," Chuck says.

"Game on!"

As I lead Dot behind the check-out desk, she says, "Is he always here? And armed?"

"Pretty much. Sometimes there's stand-in Chuck, but he's a little bland. Like real Chuck but just lesser, you know?"

Dot nods. "It's a library. People take the books. It's okay to take the books." She's really just talking to herself. She's jangled and I am, too—Chin's warning echoes in my head. Am I even still a feminist? Shit. I don't think *anyone* knows what that means anymore.

Ruby is checking out books.

"I'm going to see Mr. Gupta."

Ruby says, "All right."

"Ruby, Dot. Dot, Ruby. You two converse. I'll be back in a minute."

I'm actually here so I can beg Mr. Gupta to give Dot a job checking out books at the circulation desk. She was fired from a Barnes and Noble a couple months ago for not-so-accidentally taking things that weren't hers. But as I explain the situation to Gupta in his cramped office, I don't mention the stealing and instead use the term *let go.*

But Gupta, who's eating a grilled cheese sandwich over a brown paper bag on his desk, doesn't let that glide by. "And what was she *let go* for?"

"She tended to borrow things," I told him. "Books, mostly. And of course, only the really good ones."

"So, stealing. This is what you mean?"

I switch gears. "But here's the thing. This is a library." I press my fingertips together and bounce my hands a little. "And the beauty of libraries is that you're *supposed* to borrow from them. She always gives things back. She's a natural borrower. It's like hardwired."

Mr. Gupta considers this. "I remember the old days, Evelyn, when libraries were holy. When I first got my graduate degree and before the Internet, we were the gatekeepers of knowledge. We stood up against censorship, and now we pack the shelves with *Fifty Shades of Grey* because the people want their light porn. We were anticommercialism once—as un-American as any institution was allowed to be—and now we call the patrons 'customers' and we walk around asking if we can help them *find* something." He's got a good head of steam going. "We used to be democratic, buying all those lonesome titles, and now we're up to our necks in best sellers. So why not hire bookstore staff? Now that the brick-and-mortar bookstores are crumbling, we *are* bookstores, Evelyn Shriner! We *are* bookstores!"

I've heard this speech in snippets, but Gupta has really stitched it all together in dramatic fashion. I pause to let the speech air out a little, have its moment, and then I say, "Is that a yes?"

"She's a thief. Chuck will not like that."

"Really, Mr. Gupta, she's a borrower and you could go so far as to say that this building wouldn't exist without the Dots of the world."

Gupta perks up. "Her name is Dot?"

"Yes."

"Like the astronaut ice cream?"

I nod. I hadn't thought of that before. "Yes, just like the ice cream the astronauts ate."

"I used to enjoy getting a cup of it at the mall." He pats his midsection nostalgically.

"Who didn't!"

"I'll have to see her résumé and interview her and all of that. Can she work mornings?"

"Absolutely."

"We need someone for mornings. I've had to rearrange the whole schedule since Rita followed that boy to Africa."

"I think they joined the Peace Corps."

Gupta isn't paying attention. He glazes over, like Rita's leaving has caused an atmospheric shift and now a meteor the size of Texas is headed straight for us. "Mornings!"

"Dot loves mornings. She wakes up for mornings."

"And you can promise me she will always only *legally* borrow from us?"

"It's a given," I say, knowing that this might not be entirely true. "She's here. You could interview her now. She brought her résumé!"

He takes another bite and waves his hand, meaning *Sure, sure, bring her in.*

I send in Dot and tell her I'm going to wait outside by the bike racks around the corner on Mulberry. I usually love the library because of its echoing hushes, its gluey, dusty smell, its preservationist quality—everything loved, everything in its place—but today I feel like being in the open air, as if open air will clear my mind. And what is my mind cluttered with? Well, Chin's warning. How long should I wait before I go back? And when I do get unflagged, who will I next envision my life with?

I think about Jason Binter and I'm mad I wasted a precious session on him—not knowing how precious the sessions are.

I think of Godfrey Burkes, too, sitting there in his paper gown, pressing his knees together. I wonder who he was there to envision a future with. And I think of Adrian, because it's impossible not to. Adrian. Where is he now? Is he even thinking about me? When's he coming to pick up his little box of left-behind shite?

Eventually Dot appears, her coat stuffed, and I hope to God she hasn't already stolen stuff. She looks fifteen pounds heavier, but maybe she's just three thousand pages richer?

Before I can ask, she says, "This legally stealing shit could become a drag. I have to wait in line with all the regular people."

"Oh, to be the Normals," I say.

"I got the job—on a trial basis. Thank you," she says. "And you know how hard it is for me to say that."

"It didn't even sound sarcastic!" I want to reach out and hug her, but I know better. Dot isn't huggy.

"I'm trying to work on my sarcastic problem," she says. "You should be able to compliment someone on their outfit without them calling you a prick."

"Who was it?"

"My sister-in-law. I was being serious. It was a *nice* outfit," Dot says, and then she adds, "Did that sound sarcastic?" She sets the books down, shoves them in her backpack.

"It sounds like your sister-in-law was wearing a rainbow unitard or something."

"Shit. Well, I mean it—thank you."

"You're welcome," I say.

We unlock our bikes. Dot gets on the bike slowly, wobbly under the weighty books, and we begin to pedal the few blocks to our favorite diner, Café Honeybun, where the waitresses call the patrons "hon," Baltimore's most beloved pet name. They know Dot there, which means they're not upset when she steals stuff. They know she's going to bring it back. It's hard to find places that are cool with thievery as a nervous tic.

At a red light, Dot says, "When are we going to get a car? It's winter for shit's sake." Dot would like to see us driving an eco car one day, like a Leaf or something. "Electricity is easier to steal than gasoline. Plus, you know, the world and everything."

"Dotty Dotty Dot Dot," I say. "I don't *want* a car!"

A car would be nice, but even in the cold with these gusts, stuck in the sincerity of this silly Baltimore weather, I am happy on my bike. I wasn't allowed to ride them as a kid because my older sister died on one. Of course no one can blame my parents for not liking bikes, especially children's bikes. I have a picture of my sister, Meg, on her twelfth birthday when she got her vintage banana seat. She died not three blocks from the house. A drunk driver midafternoon.

I'm not trying to upset my parents by riding a bike instead of driving, though, to be sure, bike lanes are rare, and riding can get scary sometimes; I'm just trying to make up for a lost childhood. If they want to take that personally, there's little I can do about it. Dot thinks I'm an only child. Not a lie. I was born an only child.

We stop at another red light. I touch the curb with one boot. This is the spot where Adrian and I broke up. I pretend I'm a tour guide of my own life. "And here, when Evelyn was approximately twenty-five years of age, she broke up with her boyfriend, Adrian Kleivling, lead guitarist and sometimes background singer for the not-ever-famous band, the Babymakers."

"Right here?" Dot says. "This just feels really public." Dot's a private person.

"It was a now-or-never moment." A fork within a fork. "It felt right, right then. Or as right as any of those moments can ever feel."

"Adrian was sweet but kind of dense," Dot says as if he's dead.

"He's still sweet and dense, Dot. He didn't blow up when I broke up with him."

"I'm just saying."

We ride the final block to Café Honeybun, lock up our bikes, head inside, and take a table in the back. Dot's cheeks are bright red as if she's been slapped. Mine are, too, I guess.

Our favorite waitress, Delores, hands us some menus. She's very maternal and calls us both hon without any irony at all. She has these doelike eyes, now sagging a bit with age and little pouches on either side of her cheeks that remind me of Frances McDormand who I hope never gets that surgically fixed. Delores loves to give unbidden romantic advice.

Today she tells us that we need to use the Internet to meet nice guys. "It's how I met up with Joey," she advises us without our asking for advice. "The nice ones are all on the websites these days. They're shy, you know?"

I imagine a site just of the door openers, the check reachers. "I'll look into it," I tell Delores, though I'm kind of working on my own plan here.

Dot says, "You can also cherry-pick." She's a thief at heart.

"Steal someone else's husband and someone will give you a world of hurt. An entire *world* of hurt! Especially *me*," Delores warns, as if Dot were imagining her Joey, at this very moment, walking out of rough surf in slow motion. "I love that man. You know"—Delores leans down now—"you once told me a quote from the unibrow artist."

"Frida Kahlo?" Dot says.

"That one," Delores says. "How'd it go?"

"'There have been two great accidents in my life," I say. "One was the trolley, and the other was Diego. Diego was by far the worst.'"

"Joey's my Diego," Delores says. "We all have to have one, right?"

Adrian is not my Diego. I haven't had a Diego and neither has Dot, to my knowledge, but I say, "That's right." And Dot holds up her hands in surrender.

We order a mix of sides as if we really want the diner to be a tapas place. And I do.

I ask Dot, "Are you a feminist?"

"Of course. Fipps and I are both feminists." Fipps is Dot's bichon frise. "I wanted a girl dog because we'd be united." She raises her fist.

"What does it mean to be a feminist?"

"Equal pay for equal work, bitch."

"Does it mean we aren't supposed to put love first? I mean, aren't we supposed to know better or something?"

"Wasn't there a memo about how we're supposed to have it all? But women who are like now in their fifties must have rolled that back, right? I mean, we can't have it all, not easily at least. That's what I've heard. Word on the street."

"Can we still want to fall in love and have a family and have that be a priority? I just feel like men were workaholics, right? And women taught them that, look, there's something to be gotten out of being nurturing, of showing up for your kids—emotionally—something in it for you personally."

"There was that old saying like 'No one on his deathbed says "I should've spent more time at the office."'"

"Actually, that's pretty much what Da Vinci said on his deathbed. 'I have offended God and mankind because my work did not reach the quality it should have.'"

"Wow," Dot says, "because I really thought he gave it his all."

"Me, too!"

"If I got to pick what the next wave of feminists might do, it would be this." Dot puts both elbows on the table and leans in. "Let's not be all women cutting down other women. Let's let each other breathe a little, you know? If we stop judging each other and instead set our sights on some real shit, we could get stuff done. You know?"

"So I can make love a priority—one of those big sweeping wholehearted lifelong loves—and you'd support me? The Aristotle kind of love, 'a single soul inhabiting two bodies.'"

"Don't make me quote Pat Benatar. It's all I've got."

"I know, I know. Love is a battlefield."

"Okay, you can be a feminist with love and family as a priority," Dot says. "There, I said it. If you need to take it to the pope of feminism, she'll say the same thing."

"Steinem?"

"No, Pat Benatar. Seriously, sometimes I wonder if you're listening at all."

Delores brings us our food and we dig in, eating heartily. Dot and I are eaters. We take that shit seriously.

But in the middle of it all, Dot takes a moment to touch the ketchup bottle like she's thinking of slipping it into her oversized pocketbook.

Dot launches into the details of her mother's upcoming visit. "I'm trying to gear up. You know, she doesn't steal *literal* stuff. She steals other things—like love and honesty and hope. I wish she'd just show up and take my toaster and shit, but no, no, no. That would be way too literal! And I'm the one with the problem?"

"You actually do have a problem," I say. She really needs to work on the stealing thing.

"She was normal when I was little. And I don't think that's just because I was too young to know any better. I swear, she was like a regular human being who bought me what I wanted for my birthday, not like subscriptions to Weight Watchers, you know? But now she's mean—even when playing charades. Who can be so mean while just acting out books and movies?"

"I know." Once, she told me to get a haircut because I looked like a gypsy. Still, I've been weaseling my way into Mrs. Fuoco's slightly wizened heart, and even went so far as to tell her that "Dot is like a sister to me"—twice, hoping she'd catch a hint. I don't say this in front of Dot because she has a kind of allergy to sentimentality. Mrs. Fuoco isn't the type to let you just chum up and pretend to be part of the family.

"I'd love to have parents who I could play charades with, even mean charades. My parents don't know what to do with me, and I've never known what to do with them not knowing what to do with me." It's like they decided to love me just a little less, in case I died, too. But I can't even take it all that personally. They decided to love each other a little less, too. Maybe they decided to love everything a little less—matinees, rich appetizers, big sky country. They kept me as an idea, a centerpiece. I just remembered our yearly family Christmas cards. They were always a picture of just me, front and center, my hair perfectly curled around my ears. Above my head: HAPPY HOLIDAYS FROM THE SHRINERS!

"My mom didn't believe in Christmas cards. She said they were for people with too much time on their hands."

And that's when I segue to Dr. Chin's. "You should go," I tell her. "Just try it. Once. One time."

"I don't get the fascination," she says. "I mean, it's like alien technology without the aliens. And what's the point of a brain-melting machine without the flying saucer and beaming lights?" She's finished eating and wipes her mouth with a paper napkin.

"It's based on neuroscience," I tell her. "Don't you want to just pin the future down a little?"

"No," Dot says. "I don't think I do want to pin down the future. Do you really want to watch a movie of yourself pulling weeds with a man past his prime in a future where you're past your prime?"

"Is this my prime?" I say, staring around the restaurant, a little terrified.

"Me? I'd rather go to the dentist."

"Really?"

"Really."

"It's not the same for you as it is for me. You like the past. Your mother was once normal. You had a happy childhood!" I'm afraid I sound accusatory. There's something a little vicious in my voice.

"Yes, I did. And the future is the unknown. I like it like that." She stands up. "Let's go."

"We haven't paid yet."

"I'm nervous. I'll wait outside." She punches her arms into the armholes of her coat, shrugs on her oversized bag, and walks out.

I look down at the table. Aside from our dirty dishes, it's empty—no ketchup, no salt or pepper shakers, no Splenda or sugar holder, no forks or spoons. Mine are even gone and I'd barely finished. How does she do it?

Delores swings by and slaps the check on the table. Since I pissed Dot off, it looks like I'm paying.

"What's the extra damage?" she asks.

"She got everything this time, I think."

"Long as she doesn't upgrade to stealing other women's men, she's a good egg," Delores says with admiration.

"She's a really good egg. She has a great heart." She stole stuff, but I'm the one who feels bad. I hurt her feelings.

And as I bundle up, I wonder what I really know of judging hearts. I feel like I can't find my own. Mostly, I feel alone. Even with Dot, sometimes I feel alone. Reading into a little recording device for the blind revising literature, I feel alone. Maybe the only time I don't feel alone is when I see myself on that screen, existing in the future—maybe only where there are two of me. Really, though, maybe even then.

Alone is alone. Sometimes I think I've got a permanent condition.

Godfrey
FROG CALLS

When I arrive at my desk at the Department of Unclaimed Goods, there's a note on my chair from my boss, Chapman: *We need you in Lost Cell Phones—all afternoon. —C.*

Chapman is an idiotic prick—the kind of idiotic prick who knows he's an idiotic prick and uses this knowledge against himself before you can. It's kind of brilliant. When I went in for my annual review last year and asked for a raise—because Madge badgered me with little speeches that ended *You've got to ask to receive*—Chapman rubbed his chest and said, "You can die from a duodenal ulcer, can't you?" I said, "I think you can. Um, did you hear my question?" And Chapman said, "About the raise? Didn't I say no? I thought I said no in the middle of the question. I must have just said no in my head and thought I'd said it aloud."

Because Chapman is an idiot *and* a prick, it's hard to tell whether this temporary demotion to Lost Cell Phones is a mix-up—maybe

Chapman has confused me with someone of a lower rank—or a reprimand for a fake doctor's appointment. Either way, I'm pissed. Lost Cell Phones is the lowest rung on the ladder and it's the only office lodged in the basement, which is cold and damp and feels like a basement. It's where most everyone starts out. I moved up from there two years ago and I never planned on going back.

I punch in before walking down the rows of cubicles, angrily wrestling my jacket. Standing in front of Bart, I say, "Where's Garrett?"

"How's your gallbladder?"

"Fine. Where's Garrett?"

Bart shrugs.

"Chapman's put me in Lost Cell Phones."

"Shit."

"I take a few hours of personal time and I end up in Lost Cell Phones? Is that fair?"

"Personal time? I thought it was medical."

"That's what I mean." I lean against Bart's desk so that I can look down on the bald spot of Art Gunston in the next cubicle. "Where's Garrett?" I ask Gunston.

Gunston looks up, startled, as if God is speaking to him, but then he sees it's just me. "Oh, you." I once stamped UNCLAIMED on Gunston's cheek while he was sleeping on the job, and he didn't take it with the good humor in which I obviously intended it. There's been tension ever since.

"Where's Garrett? He's supposed to be in Lost Cell Phones."

"He's driving the truck."

"The truck?" I say, astonished. "The fucking truck?"

Bart doesn't like this at all either. "I've never driven the truck," he says sullenly.

"He has some kind of license," Gunston says. "Chapman just found out. So he's doing pickups."

"And so I'm the one Chapman tells to take over in Lost Cell Phones?" I've got a year's seniority on Gunston, easy.

"Ha!" Gunston says smugly.

"Shut up," Bart says.

"What?" Gunston asks innocently.

"You know what," I say.

THE BASEMENT SMELLS OF mildew. The lights are dim. They're fluorescent, which is how Bart avoided starting out here. He claimed he was an epileptic and that the fluorescent lights could cause a fit. Chapman demanded a physician's note, which Bart got from his brother-in-law's cousin, a podiatrist in Boca. That's the kind of typical shit Bart does that I find both despicable and admirable.

I didn't want this job. I have a college degree in business. Madge wasn't the first to talk me out of early education, to be fair. My freshman-year roommate said, "Seriously? That's a sorority-girl major. Why not just buy a MINI Cooper convertible, get a mani-pedi, and be done with it?" That was all it took. And could I get a real job in the business world? No. I relied on vague Bart nepotism and ended up in a basement surrounded by cell phones.

In Lost Cell Phones, your first job is charging the dead ones and finding out which ones are real goners, the permanent dead, the ones not lost so much as abandoned and mistaken for lost. There are tables filled with bins of phones and extension cords connected to outlet strips. I inspect the plugged-in phones. All of them are fully charged except for a half dozen or so that are still dark. I unplug all the phones and sort them into two boxes—one for the living, one for the dead. There are rows and rows of living bins, rows and rows of dead bins and rows and rows of unsorted bins. Every phone has been initially handled, stickered with a number and listed on a chart and—this is most crucial—set to vibrate. This department is always sorely understaffed, but whoever is in charge learns quickly to set them to vibrate, or else you've got bins of phones all going off in various ring tones. This will eventually make you insane. The vibrations are bad enough, all of the phones thrumming against each other. The vibrations are constant, though sometimes they seem to move in waves from one area to another. At certain times of the day—a mad rush at around 10 a.m., then again just after 3 p.m. until closing at 5 p.m.—the volume of calls shoots up and the basement office buzzes like a living thing.

I plug in a new batch of phones and sit down on a stool. I should be sorting through the living bins, listening to people's voice mail messages. The smart cell phone owners call in and leave messages with new numbers where they can be reached. It's depressing to listen to frantic message after frantic message, not to mention the calls left by friends, lovers, bosses—some of them angry, some desperately concerned. I've heard people getting dumped, being fired, being pleaded with, being cursed out, being coddled—it's too much humanity boxed up into these voices that always seem tinny and distant.

The big influx of calls hasn't started yet so I put my forehead down on the table and close my eyes. Am I doomed to become a lonesome perv? I'm already showing signs of a lack of dignity that will eventually manifest themselves as clumps of gel in my hair. Can *that* be fixed? I hear a cell phone jingle, the same exact ring tone as my own. Garrett missed one, what a jackass—and Chapman trusts him with the truck? I don't move, although I know I'll have to at some point. If I fall asleep like this, I'll have a red circle on my forehead, and if anyone pops in—like Chapman, checking up—it'll be undeniable. I wonder how many phones Garrett has missed. How many times this afternoon will I have to listen to little bits of "Hollaback Girl"?

On the third ring, however, I realize it's my own phone ringing in my own pocket, a private embarrassment that seems worse because there's no one I can kind of look at, shrug, and say, with a laugh, *I'm such a dipshit*. I shake my head by rolling it back and forth on the table while reaching into my pocket and answering.

"Dr. Chin's office." It's the receptionist, Lisa. "Is this Godfrey Burkes?"

"Unfortunately."

There's a moment's hesitation. "We have your wallet," she finally says.

"Oh, thanks." I lift my head. "Can I pick it up tonight? At around quarter to six?"

"That's after hours. But someone will be here. You'll have to knock."

"Okay," I say, "thank you."

I hang up. Dr. Chin's office has my wallet! I consider calling Madge and telling her my problem is solved—I'm not subconsciously cheap and I've found myself. All's well, right? Happyish now, I listen to the vibrating phones. They remind me of something I can't place. I close my eyes again and just listen. I remember the lake house my parents used to rent up north each summer; there was this same sound when I was falling asleep at night—this deep humming and chirruping. The curtains over my bed billowed out and then were drawn into the screens when my mother opened the door to say good night. It was like the house was breathing. *Good night, Godfrey-boy. Little Godfrey, my sweet.*

"Bullfrogs," I say aloud. "They sound like bullfrogs at night."

But this is all unsettling, how seemingly easy it is to shift to such a different time and place. I actually feel smaller, boyish. If I try hard enough, I can smell my mother's perfume and the cabin's damp fireplace. Do I really have an identity problem? Do I really know who I am or who I was?

I need to talk to my mother. It's necessary. She's going to die on me. I only have a short time left, really, to understand her. Who was that woman in the doorway of the lake house? Who is Gloria Burkes—once so young and naive she was seduced by a Thigpen?

The upside to working in Lost Cell Phones is that, in a sea of cell phones, you shouldn't have to waste your own minutes. It's against policy to use a lost cell phone, but who's going to figure that shit out? I pick up a phone from one of the living bins and dial my parents' number and wait. After two rings, my father answers.

"Hey, it's me," I say.

My father pulls the phone from his ear—I can tell because he sounds trapped in a tunnel—and announces, "Godfrey's on the line! It's Godfrey!" like he's sounding an alarm. I know that my mother is stopping whatever she's doing. I'm not quite sure what she does exactly, besides bunny rescue, but she's always busy at it. Within seconds, she's on the line.

"Godfrey?" she asks, breathless, a note of disbelief in her voice.

"Yes, it's me."

"How are you?" she asks.

And, not to be outdone, my father chimes in, "Yes, how are things?"

"Good," I tell them.

"Is there something you need?" my father asks.

"Can't I just call to say hello?"

"Of course you can," my mother says, letting the rest of the sentence go unsaid: *but you never do.*

"Are you okay?" my father asks.

"I'm fine," I say. "I just think we should know each other better. As adults. To have a real relationship."

"A real relationship? Do you hear that, Gloria? Another person in the family wanting a real relationship! I'll never understand what you all mean by that."

"Hush, Frank," my mother says. "Let the boy talk to us."

"He *is* talking to us!"

"What do you want to say?" she asks.

"I don't know," I admit.

"Well, how do you feel?" my mother asks.

"In general?"

"How does he feel! Men don't have to feel things all the time, Gloria." His voice becomes softer. "You don't have to feel things all the time, Godfrey."

"I may be having an identity problem," I say.

"An identity problem," my mother repeats. "You mean you don't feel like yourself?"

"You're you, Godfrey. Trust me. I'm me. Your mother's your mother. There's no way around any of that."

"I keep losing my wallet." I wave my hand through the air, like that's supposed to show them how it just wanders off.

"Well, that's not an identity problem. You're just being sloppy, forgetful . . . um, what's that word?" I'm not sure if my father's asking me or my mother. "When you're thinking about something else all the time?"

"Preoccupied?" I say.

"That's it!" he says.

"Are identity problems the mother's fault?" my mother asks meekly.

"It's *always* the mother's fault," my father says. "Like Freud says." Does my father know Freud?

"I don't think it's anyone's fault," I tell them.

"Godfrey, you don't have an identity problem," my mother says with finality.

"I said that it wasn't your fault," I tell her.

"Did I tell you that I ran into Mrs. Ellis? Who had those two twin girls that you dated?"

"You just say 'twins,' Gloria. 'Two twins' is redundant."

"No," I say. "You didn't tell me."

"The girls are doing great. Klarissa is still single. I told her mother not to worry. Your generation will all pair up eventually." Sandra and Klarissa are identical twins, but Sandra was the pretty one, if I remember correctly. They had all of the same features, but one of them came out just slightly downturned and the other just slightly upturned—as if being smushed in the womb at different angles.

"That would help with your identity problem, Godfrey," my mother says.

"What would?"

"Pairing up."

"It's easier to define yourself when you're standing next to the same person all the time. You just let the other person define you. It's simple," my father explains.

"It happens naturally," my mother says wearily, then adds in a chipper tone, "How's Madge?"

"I have a question," I say.

"Shoot," my father says.

"If you could have looked into the future, you know, way back when you were young, would you have?"

"Goodness, no," my mother says.

"Why would anyone want to do that?" my father says.

"Why not? I mean, you can nowadays. It's possible."

"If you started down that road, how could you stop?" my father says.

"If you can know one thing, wouldn't you want to know everything?" my mother asks.

"I guess so." There's a momentary pause. I realize I haven't asked how they're doing so I do.

My father says, "Fine, just fine," as if proving that men don't have to talk about how they feel all the time.

My mother says, "I've just rescued five new bunnies. You should come visit them," which is a thin metaphor for Gloria Burkes saving five new vulnerable Gloria Burkeses and that I should come visit *her*. But my mother's going to die. She can't save herself. None of us can. "We'll get together soon. I promise," I say. I can get to my childhood home in Owings Mills in less than thirty minutes. "I have to go. I'm at work."

"How about I get in touch with Madge and we schedule a double date. Lunch!"

"That's great," I say. "I'd like that."

"We're glad you called," my mother says.

"Very glad," my father says.

"I love you," I say.

There's a pause. I've caught them off guard.

"You haven't said that since you were at that awful overnight camp," my mother says, sounding concerned.

"Don't embarrass him," my father says.

"I love you, too," my mother says.

"Of course," my father is saying, "okay? Okay, Gloria, hang up now." I imagine my father has walked into the same room as my mother. He isn't talking into the phone anymore. He's talking to her directly. And then my father has taken the phone from her. "Talk to you later, Godfrey. We really are glad you called," he says, and then the lines go dead, first one, then the other.

Evelyn
LOUD QUIET

It's the scheduled time for my biweekly phoner with my parents. I like to pace the apartment when I talk to them. They're slow talkers. They measure their words—small syllables, small words, small voices. Talking to my parents always makes me hungry. I paste a bagel together with cream cheese, and I'm on the move. I circle the coffee table. I pet the cover on the toaster like it's a legless cat. I punch the pillows on my bed. We discuss salting snowy sidewalks, purchasing paper goods in bulk, a sickly neighbor I don't remember that well even though I'm told I should. Keep moving. That's the trick, moving so much that sometimes I get winded. Once my mother asked me if I was on drugs. "Me, drugs?" I said. "No, no. I just have a quick little hamster heart." But maybe it wasn't so much the speed of my heart but the shrunken size; when I'm talking to my parents, I feel small of heart.

I imagine the calls are a chore for them, falling somewhere on their to-do list: *clean golf clubs, arrive at church fifteen minutes early, remind Evelyn she has parents, feed dogs.*

Still, I feel like I have to alert them to any changes big enough to alter my profile on Facebook.

"Adrian and I broke up."

"Let's reverse gears a moment," my father says. Both of my parents are good-looking, the kind of young-looking old people they put on brochures for old people things, like retirement villages with multiple tennis courts, Depends, Flomax. "He broke up with you?"

"No."

"You broke up with him?" my mother says, plainly surprised.

"Is that so hard to believe?" I walk to the doorjamb where I measure everyone who comes into my apartment, a tradition that my parents didn't approve of. Writing on walls? Once, though, I saw a faint outline of my sister's height on a doorjamb in the mudroom, lightly painted over.

My parents aren't responding. A quiet moment arrives, as if pulled up by a team of silent horses. My mother eventually says, "Of course it's not hard to believe. We believe you. You're our daughter," as if the only reason they believe me is because they're parentally duty bound.

"I think you're supposed to say, 'Are you okay?' or 'I'm so sorry, honey.'" It's not unusual for me to feed my parents their lines, like someone just offstage trying to help them as they blink into the stage lights.

And then the quiet. You almost have to respect the stuffy determination. I'd like to make a band of my parents' silence. It would be called Big Loud Nothing. Their first single would be a guitar being plugged into an amp, then nothing. Are they exchanging glances from their two cordless phones? "We are both so sorry," my mother says.

"Of course," my father says. "We understand breaking up. It was hard for your mother and me when our time came."

My parents are a divorced couple who still live together. I forget this sometimes. They divorced each other when I was twelve. They told me while driving back from a church-sponsored Easter egg hunt. I have a deep abiding distrust of fake grass. It's bullshit. By Easter, there's always plenty of real grass if grass is what you want to use to pad your basket, except maybe in the Dakotas and shit, where it's still cold. No one should ever trust fake grass. Its insincerity is hateful.

At first, my father got an apartment—a dismal bachelor pad— but after I'd gone off to college, he moved back in with my mother, as if he were really just trying to get out of half of my childhood. They live separate lives but under the same roof, the most solid container for all of their mutual—what? Sadness? Emptiness?

I decide to pretend that my parents understand me. If I bully on, will they? "Adrian and I loved each other, I think, but it wasn't enough."

They have nothing to say because I've uttered the word *love.* It hangs in the air, bobbing like that apple before Eve plucked it from the limb. I want to say, *I'm the result of dead love. Do you hear me? Say something something something.*

But there is nothing to say.

Again, there's my sister. My mother always curled my hair before school. Meg's hair was curly. I never got to pick out barrettes or scrunchies—my mother always had a box of them. I wouldn't realize until years later that they were Meg's. There are little things like that—the details of being raised in the shadow of a dead sister.

Still nothing from my parents.

I imagine the sound of our blinking eyelids. Ticking. A form of Morse code we can't understand.

Finally, I whisper, "I have to go."

There's a burst of adrenaline with their good-byes. *Take care! Be safe! Have fun! Talk soon!* I feel it, too, a diluvia of relief.

And I press end, grip the phone and pat my fridge, like it's the flank of a horse. "Steady now. Easy, big fella."

Godfrey
LET'S MAKE A DEAL

I knock on the door to Chin's office after hours. I can hear people inside, a lot of competing voices, playful yelling, and a stutter of laughter. Maybe Chin's having some sort of party. Two young manicurists from the Nail-A-Rama are out front smoking cigarettes in their matching green aprons, and shivering. They wave to me and I wave back. They laugh nervously as if I've waved incorrectly. Can you wave wrong?

I knock again, but I'm pretty sure no one can hear me, and so I give the door a push. It swings open easily.

The waiting room is smoky and full of people sitting in all of the spare chairs, pulled up around the coffee table, playing cards. They're using cone-shaped paper cups that you find in dispensers near water coolers to do shots of Jack Daniel's.

Chin's there. He's kicked off his slippers. They sit, pigeon-toed and empty under his chair. Chin's bare feet are tough and honestly corned. His legs stretched out, he's leaning back in his chair, squinting at his hand. He looks almost nothing like the doctor I saw earlier in the day. His chin tucked to his chest, his face looks bloated. His eyes, though squinting, are bleary and restless.

Lisa, the receptionist, and the nurse who told me to undress, are here, too, plus an elegant man with a gray pomp of hair, wearing some kind of pretentious scarf, an Asian man, and two guys who look like poker-playing clichés.

"Jump in next round," one of the strangers says.

The receptionist eyes me like I just dropped off a bunch of pizzas, collected my tip, but refused to leave.

"We need new blood," the stranger says.

Chin doesn't look up. He's intent on the game, although he doesn't look very good at it. I can tell from his furrowed brow that he's bluffing. Truth is, I would love to be dealt in. I'm not bad at poker. I'm a natural at bluffing, which, I figure, is probably a bad thing in the long haul—proof of my insincerity, maybe proof of my Thigpen nature.

I can't jump in; I haven't told Madge where I am. She'll assume I stopped off at a bar with Bart if I'm a little late, but if I start in at poker, she might get worried. And I don't have my phone with me to call her, because, in a sad, ironic twist, I left it in Lost Cell Phones. I worked hard for the last hour, to make up for lost time, and sorted it into a bin. Is a cell phone also a source of someone's identity? Does this back up Madge's theory about my identity problem? I'm pretty sure it will.

Without my cell phone, I feel weird like I'm in an antigravity machine. It's strangely liberating. No one knows where I am . . . not even my cell phone.

"I'm here for my wallet," I say. "I left it here today."

Chin looks up. He's clearly drunk. The squinting is necessary just to pin me down and focus. "Oh, the guy with all the questions. You sure you don't want in?"

Feeling warmly welcomed, I smile and joke, "Why don't you just put on the helmet and find out how the game ends?"

No one thinks this is funny. "Old joke," the man in the pretentious scarf tells me. He offers me a paper cone cup of Jack, which I decline and then briefly regret declining.

"Hey, wise guy," Chin says. "This is my brother, Earl. You didn't believe in him, did you?" Earl looks up and smiles. He's Chinese, his hair has a surfer feel to it, shaggy but lightly groomed. "Earl," Chin says. "Are you my brother?"

Earl nods and says, "Sure am!"

I smile and say hello. "So, is my wallet here?" I ask.

Lisa says, "I call." There's a small uproar. Folks put down their weak hands. She wins with three of a kind and rakes in the money. "Your wallet's on the filing cabinet."

"I'll take him back," Chin says, shoving his pale, corned feet into his slippers. He gets up unsteadily and leads me back through the door marked OFFICE.

"Seriously," I say, "you never glimpse into your future for yourself, not even a little bit?"

"You can't keep your eye on the distant horizon. It's disorienting." He picks up my wallet and throws it to me.

"Technically, the horizon's very orienting, if you're lost. Isn't it?" I say, thumbing through my wallet to make sure it's all there.

"How about this? If you keep your eye on the horizon, you're going to trip on the path."

"But you'd know what was coming, if you'd seen the rock or whatever up ahead a few years earlier."

"Okay. If you keep your eye on the horizon, you may miss the flowers on the side of the path."

I hesitate. "Okay."

"Why don't you try the Five-Pack? You look like someone who might have stumbled upon some worthy girlfriends at some point who might deserve a second glance."

"Thanks."

"I'll give you a discount. Five for the price of three. Can you come up with that many?"

"Yes," I say defensively. I'm already thinking about the Ellis twins. There's two right off the top of my head.

"Okay, then, you can tell me after it's all done if you're better for having known. Okay?"

"Deal."

As Chin heads for the door, I ask, "Why do you work in a business that you don't believe in?"

"Do *you* believe in *your* work?"

Chin won this hand. "Fair enough," I tell him.

"Most people don't believe in their work, especially the ones who start out believing wholeheartedly in it."

"Did you believe in all of this once?" I ask.

Chin's closes his eyes, as if he's been caught in a lie, and shrugs. "I might have."

"What happened?" I put my wallet in my back pocket.

"Life is disenchanting. The future is bleak and flimsy. Why rush into it?" He claps me on the shoulder. "But don't take my word for it. Find out for yourself."

WHEN I FINALLY GET home, it's late. I stayed on at Chin's playing poker, even smoking a few cigarettes, which I haven't done in years, and had a few shots, which I've never done out of paper cone cups. I made some money, though—some pocket change, the amount of which I can exaggerate for effect if Madge starts in on me too hard. I had to leave my car at Chin's. Earl drove me home. The trade-off of my wallet for my car feels like a net loss.

As I unlock the door, I brace myself. I know Madge might be sitting on the edge of the sofa, holding the remote, but the television will be off. Her face might be oily from her night lotion, and I'll have to start apologizing quickly. I'll have to explain about losing my cell phone—which is an excuse that may work against me—and how Dr. Chin *insisted* I play a few hands. I'll understand how worried she is, of course. I'll understand why she's angry, of course. And I'll tell her that's why I love her so much.

If I play it right, there may be conciliatory sex. (Why do I think this thought? I'm a Thigpen!)

The lights are off. I flip a switch. The living room is empty. No Madge.

I take off my shoes and walk into the living room and stare a minute.

Let me take a minute with the decor of our apartment. Aside from the re-creation of my bachelor pad in the small, almost closet-sized spare room, it's been taken over by Madge's retro style: a wall-mounted, spring-cord telephone, an ancient toaster oven. She once wrote a paper for a feminist studies course in which she made the case that the 1970s marked a decade of the height of American worship of masculinity, which was so strong that people actually made design decisions inspired by the chest pelts of some machismo actors—hence the abundance of brown shag rugs. (The paper includes old photographs of Burt Reynolds, shirtless.) In celebration of the A on her paper, Madge bought a brown shag throw rug for the living room. I don't have much use for the past. As much as I want to believe it was perfect, old things make me feel sad and fleeting, like a mere blurry image of myself, fading fast.

I rub my feet on the rug for a moment and then whisper her name.

No answer.

I rush through the kitchen, peek into the spare room—which may one day end up in a basement somewhere—then open the bedroom door.

There's Madge, her face oily with her night lotion, true, but she's fast asleep.

I put my hands on my hips and look around the room. Then I walk up close to see if she's breathing. Maybe she's dead and that's why she's not up on the couch holding the remote, with the TV off, worried. But her ribs rise and fall. Is she sleeping in anger? Is this part of my punishment? I look around the room some more. I don't get it.

I cough.

She doesn't wake up.

I walk to the squeaky board near the bathroom and bounce on it. Nothing. I bounce on it again and again. Still nothing.

I go to the bathroom, flush the toilet, run water in the sink, and bounce on the squeaky board; then I stand over the bed and cough loudly.

Madge rolls to her back. She opens her eyes. "I fell asleep," she says, a little surprised.

"I see that," I say.

And then without another word she rolls to her other side, away from the bathroom light, and falls back to sleep.

By the time I climb into bed, I'm thinking about my five-for-the-price-of-three deal. I lost my virginity with Liz Chase who was good and wholesome—I dumped her for no apparent reason, except that maybe I decided it was hard to be around someone who was so much better than I was—the constant reminder of how very much I fall short. And there were the Ellis twins. We'd grown up in the same circles, though they were both a little wilder than my crowd, as if they goaded each other. I dated the less attractive one during summer break from college and then stair-stepped my way to the prettier one. It's probably not surprising how much in the end they really hated me.

In any of those futures, would I be quarantined in the basement to jerk off? In any of those futures, would my mother still be alive? Couldn't Liz Chase's impeccable karma keep my mother—her mother-in-law—alive?

I plump the pillows behind my head and I sniff the air. There's a strange odor I can't quite put my finger on—deathy? Does our bedroom smell like it's suffered a small death? Can this be anything but a bad sign?

That night I dream that my mother and I are at an indoor hotel swimming pool. She's saying, "There's an endless supply of towels here, Godfrey. Simply endless!" She seems younger and more radiant— moist with steam.

I smile at her. "That's good to hear," I say. "It's a great place."

She hands me towels, one after the other, until I'm weighted down with them. I walk to the pool's edge. The pool is filled with people fully dressed in suits and dresses, an occasional ball gown.

Then I see a woman who's hard to place exactly. She's wearing a bathing cap and a nose pinch. She's pushing a kickboard through the crowded pool, her arms straight, her legs fluttering behind like a little motor. When she sees me, she stands in the shallow end, tucking her board under her arm. Then she makes a small gesture, like closing a book, and I know exactly who she is—the woman from Dr. Chin's office.

I instinctively tighten my knees against each other. "What are you doing here?" I ask, but the room is so echoey, she can't hear me. She cups her ear and mouths, "What?"

I repeat the question, but the words bounce and warble, like they're stuck in the dead end of a maze. She shrugs and waves.

I wave back.

My mother shows up again, grabbing my shoulder. She points into the pool and says, "Look, look! How pretty!"

And then I notice mice in the blue water, swishing beneath the surface in darting schools.

I wake up in the middle of the night, sweaty and breathless. I sniff the air again and now I can place the deathy smell; it's a mouse, dead in the walls somewhere.

Evelyn
DIRTY HARRY

I spend much of the workday at the computer in Youth Services, looking up quotes from famous people about the future. But all I come across are quotes that I want to argue with.

Steve Jobs saying, "Again, you can't connect the dots looking forward; you can only connect them looking backwards. So you have to trust that the dots will somehow connect in your future. You have to trust in something—your gut, destiny, life, karma, whatever. This approach has never let me down, and it has made all the difference in my life." I don't trust dots to connect themselves, Steve; this is one of our many differences.

And there's B. F. Skinner who said, "I did not direct my life. I didn't design it. I never made decisions. Things always came up and made them for me. That's what life is." Yeah, well maybe for an asshole who raised his daughter in a box.

Lincoln said, "The best thing about the future is that it comes one day at a time." This is precisely one of the things I hate about the future. It plods toward us, loping along. I want to rush toward it, my arms flung wide, and I can.

Once I'm worn out from arguing with dead people, I decide to hang with Dot at the circulation desk. We're talking and zipping through the checkout line when I glimpse Adam Greenberg out of the corner of my eye. Dot catches my gaze. He's walking toward us. His steps are careful, almost planned. Dot's body tightens. I worry she's forgotten how to breathe.

"I love him," Dot says. The words hang in front of her like a thought bubble in a comic strip.

Adam Greenberg is Dot's new crush. I've known him forever. He checks out Oprah's Book Club selections for his mother, who is wheelchair bound. He's new to Dot, though, brand new. Adam Greenberg, the sensitive boy with a sweater vest always glued to his thin but competent frame. Our Café Honeybun waitress, Delores, would approve. *Nice nice nice.*

Dot makes a habit of disappearing in front of crushes. "Doesn't he know that Oprah shut the book club down? That he's going to run out of titles?" She's sincerely concerned. "I'm going," she tells me. "Tell me what he smells like today." She starts pushing a cart of returned books away from the checkout desk, where she'll spend twice as long as she should shelving them.

I whisper, "I don't want to sniff Adam Greenberg for you. Sniff him yourself! Stay!"

Adam Greenberg is moving toward us in his checkered vest, his ironed button-down mostly hidden beneath it, the colors

mismatched just enough that they *actually* match (something neither Dot nor I can ever figure out), his green-framed glasses that
look too much like they belong there, like he was born with them.

And when Adam Greenberg is standing in front of me, I find
Dot's nerves running through me.

"Evelyn," Adam says, but he's not looking at me. His gaze is following Dot until she turns down an aisle, disappearing from view.
Adam turns back to me, gripping the Oprah-sealed book against
his chest.

"Hi, Adam!" I say.

He slides the book across the counter and hands me his library
card.

I swipe the bar code. "Two weeks and counting with *The Pilot's
Wife*," I say, suddenly aware that it sounds like I'm accusing him of
a two-week affair with the wife of a pilot.

"There are some new additions to the library," he says. He puts
his library card into his right front pocket and presses the book back
against his chest. "I like the . . . aesthetics."

We both glance at the aisle that Dot disappeared down.

I look at back at Adam and smile. "The aesthetics appreciate it,"
I tell him.

OUTSIDE, THE WEATHER IS gusty in clumps of gust, and
when I run down the front steps of the library, I feel a little giddy.
I told Dot what Adam said about her, and she was uncharacteristi-
cally giddy, which I absorbed.

And then I see a figure leaning over my bike, chained to the bike
rack, messing with my basket. It's a little foggy and so the person is
ghostlike. Once I'm close enough to hear him cursing, I see that it's

Adrian. Two steps closer and I see he's trying to tie a piece of paper to my basket with the wire of his ear buds.

"What are you doing here?" I ask in a quiet voice.

He pops up. "Shit! You scared me." He presses one hand to his narrow chest.

"I think you're the creeper in this situation."

"I was passing by and I wanted to leave you a note." The note dangles loosely, knotted by the black wires looped in bunny ears.

A car lays on its horn nearby. People yell at each other out their windows. I pinch the paper and say, "Do you mind?"

"It's for you!" he says.

The note is written on the back of a Babymakers advertisement. The first line is *We should hang out.* I'm not impressed. But then the next line is *Bruce and Caroline miss you.* And I know he's trying to lure me in with his parents. I briefly remember their porch swing. It's the kind of porch swing a kid could grow up reading books on. The third line is this: *And I miss you. Seriously. Fuck.* And that feels honest. I look up and Adrian looks a little teary. "It's hard," he says. "I love you and I want that to be enough. I really, really feel like that should be enough."

"But you know we aren't right for each other. We won't last."

"I know, I know. We're kind of doomed. I mean, I see how you're not really the one for me and I'm not really the one for you, but we do love each other, right? In some way? And so we're not wasting time. We're doing something good."

A few skateboarders clatter by on the sidewalk. In retrospect, Adrian's lack of composure when I broke up with him surprised and thrilled me at the same time. His fragility in public, a broad daylight of an emotion, like this little act of tenderness with the note and the ear buds, well, it's something Adrian always masks with overconfidence in his band, but it's important. It's one of the reasons I fell for him.

I say, "What if there is this time bomb to love. What if it's like you fall in love with so many people who just aren't right for you, and with each one, your heart toughens up, and you have to find the one who is right for you before your heart is completely calcified in your chest?"

"Like there's a closing window."

"Right."

Adrian shakes his head. "No. It's more like every person you fall in love with is right for you but just not at this moment. Like the now-you would be perfect for the me ten years from now, but because we can't sync it up, we'll never make it. Unless you're willing to wait for me to become that person."

"But my ten-years-from-now self can never be my now self, so I'd have to completely stop growing—deep down—so that we can sync up."

"It's not that I'm stunted, though. I could have just as easily said that your ten-years-from-now self would be perfect for my now self."

"Right, right," I say so quickly that he can't really believe that I mean it, and I don't really mean it.

We wait for a whining ambulance to pass.

"I've got to come by and pick up my stuff," he says.

"I've boxed it all up."

"None of this is going to go down well with me. I can tell that this conversation is going to piss me off in like T minus fifteen minutes."

I look around without moving my head because I wish someone

were here to witness Adrian figuring this out about himself, his delayed emotional reactions to charged situations. If I say anything like this, though, he will realize—much later—that it was condescending of me and be even more pissed off.

He opens his arms and we hug. It's a muffled and muted hug because of our puffy coats, a good thing.

He says, "Later."

I say, "Bye."

And then as I bend down to unlock my lock, I wonder this: In my newfound Time Bomb Theory of Heart Calcification, as I now name it, how much toughening of my heart did Adrian cause? How many small rejections, how many missed opportunities, how big of an accumulation of jadedness has taken its toll? I think of my heart. This isn't its first hardening of a loss. How much is left?

I RIDE THE FOURTEEN blocks from the library to Dr. Chin's office quickly. I make record time. I'm stuffy hot under my coat.

I walk into Dr. Chin's office, still thinking about Adrian, the way he looked at me, a little teary-eyed through the fog. I worry about my heart. I feel this new urgency, but I'm hoping for something really good this time, if for no other reason than to prove that my heart isn't so very calcified that I should start losing hope.

The office is crowded: an old man wearing a tuxedo, a couple holding hands, a young man complaining about a bank loan scam. Desperation Friday, I figure—everyone trying to build some hope before the weekend. "The mass of men lead lives of quiet desperation. What is called resignation is confirmed desperation." That's Thoreau, of course. Am I still desperate, or has my desperation moved to the confirmed column? Damn it, I think I'm resigned.

I don't have an appointment, but I've come prepared with a mani-pedi coupon with which to bribe Lisa. When she slides open the office window, I say not a word. I just slide it across the counter. It's a good one, 50 percent off. She looks at it, looks at me, and gives the nod.

I don't have to wait as long as I expect. Chin's reading materials include *Transworld Motocross* and a *Children's Illustrated Bible*. I'm about to choose one when my name is called.

I'm led into examination room 5, where I'm handed a paper gown and told to change.

Once I'm into the gown and am sitting in examination room 5, I realize I've blown through all of my envisioning appointments with nothing so much as a spark. I've thought about it—as Chin suggested—and decided on Godfrey. Godfrey Burkes. My first stranger. If I'm disappointed, at least it won't feel predictable.

Dr. Chin knocks twice before walking into the room. He sits next to me, rolls the tray holding the meds to the chair. We make small talk and then a pill, a sip of water. A second sip of water. Then one more sip of water until the paper cup is empty.

"Who's today's victim?" Dr. Chin says.

"Godfrey Burkes," I say, surprisingly out of breath. "G-o-d-f—"

"How do you know Godfrey?" he says, cutting me off.

I can't tell Dr. Chin I met him here in his office because I accidentally walked into the wrong examination room, and there he was in a paper gown. And there I was, staring at him in a paper gown. *It was a staring thing.*

"We go way back." He'll immediately blacklist me if he knows I've moved on to strangers. Is that a worldwide ban? "We went to high school together. He was too quiet to ask me out, but I always wanted him to. Every day through our junior year. We had PE and Spanish together, but nothing. Then I transferred schools my senior year because my father got a promotion—he works in plastics, and we had to move, which meant a different high school. I never saw Godfrey again." I'm a rambly liar.

Dr. Chin looks at me for a full minute until he just sighs before typing Godfrey's name into the computer. He hands me the panic button and gets out of the chair. "Fridays!" he says, exasperated. The door clicks behind him.

EXCEPT FOR WHAT WE'RE wearing, everything looks as if it's been shaded with pastels. It's like we are two charcoal sketches placed in the middle of a cotton-candy land, standing in front of a pool the color of a strawberry milkshake, surrounded by edible plants and trees. But this is real life, and I don't think real life will look like this in twelve years.

Why does everything feel so tilted?

On the screen, Godfrey is holding my hand. The thing most frustrating about envisionist sessions is that you can see the future in a decent amount of detail, but you can't *feel* it. I grip the joystick harder, as if I'm holding his hand right back. We're dressed in matching black—Godfrey in a well-fitted suit and skinny black tie, me in a black dress. Not a little black dress, something more somber. The matching heels are just tall enough to be considered heels. It's not a sexy outfit, but I look well intentioned.

Even with the sedative, I feel a surge of emotion something like nostalgia, but how can I feel nostalgic about a future? And Godfrey

Burkes is just more present than anyone else I've ever seen in these envisionings. I can't explain it except to say that he's simply more *there,* and this frightens me a little.

And then I see the bunnies! Too many to count. The meds make it impossible to try. They're fast, and every single one is the color of clouds. They blanket most of the grass. Godfrey and future-me watch them scuttle around our feet, up and down the edges of the yard and pool. Where the fuck did all of the bunnies come from?

The sky is the clearest ocean, like the future never met pollution and all the clouds became white bunnies.

It's deafening, the quiet. The camera zooms in. Godfrey and I are crying. I want Godfrey to say something. I want to hear his voice. I want him to tell me why we're crying. I want his mouth pressed against my lips, and I want to know everything he's ever thought. I want to learn it all slowly. I want the ridges of his teeth.

I notice the flush of my cheeks, the dimples in his. I'm smiling. Godfrey's smiling. Still, we're crying. Everything is so tilted. I feel completely alive and therefore vulnerable as if that's what feeling fully alive demands; this scares me, too.

I lift his hand and pull it to my heart and I *feel* his hand grip mine; I truly feel it! His fingers are colored, too, as if he's been finger painting.

He looks at me. I look at him.

A bunny hops by and dives into a bush.

But the tears. And the smiling. Is it the meds? A glitch in the system? Can too much of a good thing actually be too much of a good thing?

Godfrey. Godfrey. Godfrey. I can't take it. Are we so happy that we're crying? I grip the joystick tighter. My heart holds an incredible amount of everything. How can one future be so full of emotions, different ones at once? I feel . . . whelmed and quickly overwhelmed.

As if we're on a timer, Godfrey and I take off our shoes.

"On three?" Godfrey says. He looks at the pool.

I can feel my heart pulse through my fingertips. I wasn't supposed to have this session. Desperation Fridays. It's too much. I wasted a mani-pedi coupon on this? I had to pay for this incredible eruption of feelings?

"How about right now?" future-me says, and then we're off, running straight for the pool.

Right before Godfrey and I jump, I press my thumb on the panic button. I press it again and again and then I close my eyes and press down on the button as hard as I can.

WHEN I OPEN MY eyes, the screen is blank, but I still see fragments of things: clouds that have fallen to the ground and hopped away, Godfrey's tears, *my* tears, colors too aching to actually be colors, a constant tilt. I see streaks of light if I move my head too quickly, probably aftereffects of the medicine. I've never ended a session early—there wasn't even time for a commercial—so I don't know what I should be feeling. I'm groggy and yet there's buzzing in my chest. How can one future feel so intense and beautiful and sad all at once. I feel . . . *seized.* And everything around me is still a bit off, surreal. Maybe the screen is broken (this is Dr. Chin, after all) and that's why the colors were fucked up and once that was off, everything was derailed—a jagged spill into some emotionally complex world that can't possibly truly exist.

Plus, I can't swim. I never learned. There were lessons, sure, but I couldn't ever get over my fear. But that's not the reason I pushed the button. No. Why did I press the button? I was happy, but it was too much. We were wearing black—was someone dead? Who was dead? This future had too many questions. What I need are answers.

It feels like I've been sitting here for hours. Everything connected to me is numb except for my thumb, which has taken on a dull ache. My thumb is still pressed down on the panic button. It's lost all color. I let my thumb slide off the button.

I feel awful—am I pale and panting? I scan the room. I'm still alone. "Hello?" I say a little too quietly. I sound hollow. I don't know where that voice came from. I find myself embarrassed for it.

I look back at the blank screen. How did I feel Godfrey's hand like it was right here and not fifteen years away?

The stillness of everything makes me even more uncomfortable.

"Hello?" I say again, a little louder, less hollow.

Nothing.

I can't just sit still. The images won't leave—Godfrey's stiff frame, our tears, the clearest sky. I lean forward until I can reach the keyboard. *Any boy,* I tell myself. *I just need a name.* I want a safe future. And that's when I think of Adam Greenberg in his sweater vest. It's not because I really want anything romantic to happen between us. I don't. It's just that he feels like a future that could fit in a tidy box.

I can just test it and see if he still wears his green-framed glasses in his late thirties. Will they still make sweater vests fifteen years from now?

I type A-d-a-m G-r-e-e-n-b-e-r-g and press Enter. I look at the screen. Nothing happens. I wait. Still, nothing.

Did I spell his name wrong? The meds are still pulsing through

my system, so it's possible. I need someone else. I can't think of anyone. I've already used up most of my college prospects. Everything
is blank. Maybe high school?

It hits me: Mark Standing. He was a senior when I was just a
freshman. Girls would have sleepovers just to talk about him. Mothers thought about him when they slept with their husbands. College
girls dated him while he was still in high school. Mark Standing. Yes!
The wavy brown hair, the guitar he kept in his backseat even though
we never saw him play it.

What could be simpler and more reliable than choosing the
hunky guy from high school—the one every girl picks?

Before the fog completely rolls in, I type M-a-r-k S-t-a-n-d-i-n-g.
I hit Enter.

FIFTEEN YEARS FROM NOW, I look like a lion while I sleep,
a lion curled up to Mark Standing's fine form. My hair is curled
everywhere, some of it spilling across his chest. My hair is very
blonde. His hair is still wavy, though it's begun its recession. He
looks like he tastes like a sledgehammer, but in a good way. He's
stayed fit, Mr. Standing has. We both sleep naked. I think about
horseback riding.

There are clouds in the bedroom, a fog, dew on the sheets.
Future-me doesn't notice; she's still asleep. There are birds outside
and they want everyone to know they exist. I'm thinking it's spring.

Watching myself sleep curled next to Mark makes me feel warm.
I imagine myself sleeping in this bed forever. Nothing in this envisioning freaks me out. I've stopped sweating.

I am about to fall asleep with Mark and my future self when I hear a bang. Two bangs. Too many bangs. It sounds like a door, probably the front door, since the sound is too far away to be the bedroom door. But these aren't normal knocks—they're angry knocks.

Then a crack. I think of the show *Cops*—*that* kind of crack.

I lean forward watching my future self jolt up in bed. She holds the covers up to her neck. Thirty-eight-year-old me, lion-mane-haired, glowing an unnatural shade of sun and lit fog, eyes darting back and forth.

Mark barely stirs.

The bedroom door swings open. This wakes up Mark. He looks confused until he sees Adam Greenberg standing in the bedroom.

What the fuck is Adam Greenberg doing in my future bedroom?

Everyone looks scared now except for Adam Greenberg, who's angry. I've never seen him like this before, which is a shock in itself. He's also not wearing a sweater vest, instead opting for a V-neck undershirt—still something organic, I'm sure. No glasses either. I knew that shit wasn't prescription.

Adam is holding something in his right hand. It's fuzzy, so it takes a second for me to focus. Is that a gun? That's a gun! Silver, large, mean. He's pointing it at Mark and then at future-me before bringing it back to Mark.

Eventually, he lets the gun linger between the two.

"Dot's in jail!" The gun is shaking or maybe everything on the screen is shaking. Who can tell anymore?

"That wasn't our fault." Mark's trying to be calm, but he's up against the headboard, the covers draped around his waist.

"The bank was your idea!" Adam says. His pitch gets a little higher with every word. I've seen enough movies to know that's not a good thing.

Future-me is whimpering as quietly as possible.

What about Dot and jail? There is so much fog in this bedroom. Did someone leave one of the windows open and it just let itself roll in?

"You left her there," Adam says. "You just drove away."

"We had no choice," future-me says. "Someone tripped the alarm." I sound ragged, like I've been chain-smoking. Future-me isn't looking at Adam when she talks—her face is staring straight down at the bedsheets.

I've seen this gun before. It's the same one Clint Eastwood used in *Dirty Harry.*

"You didn't have a choice, and now I don't either," Adam says. He cocks the gun. Mark raises his hands. I hear someone calling my name. It's coming from outside. I run to the open window still naked, thrust my head out, and look down on a small yard.

There's Godfrey, wearing the same black suit from the last session. He shouts, "I know I shouldn't be here, but I need to see you, Evelyn!"

Mark Standing shouts, "It can't be that fucker! At my house? On my lawn?" He rushes at Greenberg, quickly twisting the gun from his grip, and still naked, too, he runs to the window, pushing me out of the way.

Mark takes aim. "Who the fuck do you think you are? She's my wife, goddammit!"

Before he can pull the trigger, I scream loudly. Love and fear swarming in my chest again, I hit the panic button with my thumb.

Fear and love. I keep screaming as I slam my thumb down over and over on the panic button.

Dr. Chin rushes into the room just as the screen goes blank.

I'm breathlessly pressing the panic button. "What the hell!" I shout. "What the hell!"

And then Chin puts his hands on his hips and frowns.

"Don't blacklist me," I say. "Please don't blacklist me!"

Godfrey
PLOTNIK & PLOTNIK

There are two Dr. Plotniks. Dr. Plotnik and his wife, Dr. Plotnik. She goes by Dr. A. Plotnik in an effort to reduce confusion. Dr. A. Plotnik specializes in reformatting romantic futures. Madge is explaining all of this in the bar called Fast Eddy's, which is near Fontana's. We're sharing a booth with Bart and Amy, who strike me as unbearably glib, and Gunston from work. Sometimes when I see Gunston out in the wild like this, set loose from his cubicle, I feel guilty for stamping him with an UNCLAIMED stamp while he was sleeping. Gunston is unclaimed with no prospects of getting claimed in the near future. But what's the difference between me and Gunston? Once upon a time, Madge found me and saved me. That's all. Here I am, sitting next to her, and with Gunston here, I feel lucky. *Claimed.* Though she's still not wearing the ring. And, believe me, I know that some other men would have asked her for the ring back. "Wear it or give it back!" they would demand, but if she gives it back then I feel like I'm one step further away from being engaged and I don't want the ground to just keep eroding under my feet. I'm trying to hold on to what I've got—a girlfriend who has the ring in her possession, if not on her finger, is better—to my mind—than one who's given it back. There's some logic to this.

Gunston is looking out the window.

It's a loud place. TVs stationed in the upper corners, guitar riffs screaming overhead, a noisy crowd. Rumor has it there'd been an area in the back room devoted to a mechanical bull, but the insurance had been too high and the era passed. I have my cell phone on me again without ever having to confess its temporary loss to Madge, which feels like I dodged detention. I had to claw through the bins in Lost Cell Phones for quite a while, and now that it's back I feel rooted again—not a bad thing, all in all.

"We didn't need any romantic reformatting," Amy says.

"Lucky, I guess," Bart adds.

"I don't think we should talk about our private life in public," I say, glancing at Gunston.

"Like he cares," Madge says.

Gunston taps on the glass-front window, trying to get the attention of a young woman at the bus stop.

"Don't tap the glass, Gunston," Madge says. "They don't like it."

"But she almost looked over," Gunston says. "I mean, she hears something. She's just not sure where it's coming from."

The woman at the bus stop is kind of beautiful. Her skirt is too short for the cold and I love the way she's hugging herself and stomping her feet to keep warm—innocent but sexy. I could probably watch her be cold forever, which sounds kind of mean and, yes, Thigpennish.

"I'm excited about it," Madge says, returning to the topic at hand. "I can't wait to meet Dr. A. Plotnik. It's all fascinating."

"It's a racket," I say flatly.

"Don't," Madge says.

Amy and Bart lean back in their seats, a unified gesture of shocked disapproval.

"You have to admit," I say, "it's a little convenient that Dr. Plotnik shows people bleak futures and then prescribes romantic reformatting, which his wife just happens to specialize in."

"I'd like to be romantically reformatted," Gunston says as the bus pulls away from the curb, taking the woman with it.

"You have to have a partner first," Amy explains.

"That seems backward," Gunston says.

"We're going to Dr. A. Plotnik," Madge says. "We're going and that's it."

"We don't have to," I say, but I don't think anyone can really hear me, just as my voice echoed in the dream I had last night, how it was swallowed by the glassed-in swimming pool. I remember the woman from Dr. Chin's in her rubber swimming cap and nose pinch.

Bart leans forward with his hand spread on the table. "Godfrey, listen to her."

Madge has gone flushed. "We're going," she says again. "Because it's a great way to better understand ourselves and because it's our only hope." She wipes her nose, pushes herself from the booth, and rushes to the ladies' room.

"Why did you do that?" Amy says.

Madge had been so full of bravado at the restaurant, talking about the new way of life and all of that, that I wasn't sure if she'd been disappointed at all. But she must have been actually feeling a little desperate. Knowing that Madge sees this as our last hope gives me some necessary hope.

"Go after her," Bart says.

"Don't go after her," Gunston says.

"You should," Amy says.

"She's in the ladies' room," I tell them.

"Knock on the door," Amy says. "Tell her you're sorry."

I stand up, walk slowly to the ladies' room, hoping Madge will pop out before I have to knock.

She doesn't.

Standing in front of the door, I look back at the table. Bart makes a knocking gesture. Gunston gives me the finger for no good reason.

I look at the door and knock. "Madge," I say. "I'm sorry. We'll go. Of course we'll go. C'mon. Are you okay?"

The door opens, and here stands Madge with fresh lipstick on. "It isn't a racket," she says.

I stare at her. This is an ultimatum. I have to choose correctly. This may cost me the engagement, actually. I can't help but be very disappointed in life at this moment: the embarrassing fact that big decisions can come just like so, standing outside of the ladies' room at Fast Eddy's.

"It isn't a racket," I say, a stab in my chest. It's the right thing to do, I'm fairly sure, but I can't help the feeling of immediate and deep regret. It's like giving to a charity only because people are looking on. But I'm pretty sure that Madge isn't the one who's the charity case. I am. In this relationship, I always have been and probably always will be.

THE PLOTNIKS' CLINIC—Meeting All of Your Future Needs—is sleek, streamlined, falsely pine-scented as if from an air freshener that dangles from a rearview mirror, but a nice air freshener, top of the line, in a very nice car, imported from somewhere where everyone is blond and happy.

The children in the waiting room choose from bookshelves filled with handheld computer games. The adults are well groomed. They read untattered copies of *Time* and *Vanity Fair* and the *New Yorker* and glance at their watches with immediacy. The fish tank is massive, clean, and built into the wall. There's a ceiling-hung flat screen television playing preprogrammed health news—a coifed woman behind a desk describes the pros of envisioning treatments for the elderly.

No one is holding a dog or digging for their license. The clinic doesn't smell like deep-fried takeout. I can fairly assume that Plotnik's machines are not coin-ops.

"This place is nice," I say, propping my elbows on the armrests.

Madge looks at me a little bewildered. "It's a doctor's waiting room."

"A nice one, though," I say.

Madge shrugs.

We're called to the reception desk to fill out forms. The receptionist is in her forties but is wearing braces—the kind that are almost invisible. She smiles so happily that I find myself thinking, *Good for you, opting for straighter teeth at your age.* It seems like an accomplishment of great self-esteem. Another receptionist is taking calls. There's no mention of notarizing or euthanizing or lancing.

I try not to act amazed by it all. I almost confide in Madge how bad it was at Dr. Chin's, but for some reason, I feel protective of Chin, and I don't want to badmouth him. Plus, my session worked. I saw my future with Madge—clear as anything—and Chin had offered me a deal. I haven't told Madge about *that*. She might take it the wrong way—me shuffling through futures with my ex-girlfriends. It's just an experiment, really, a bet I've got going with Chin, if nothing else. Why get into it?

Madge and I are escorted back and then we're standing in the middle of the room, which has a wooden desk with a chair on wheels, bookshelves filled with actual books filled with actual words, two tall plants and three armchairs.

"I never know where to sit in these kinds of situations," I say. "It's like the first test you get to fail." I move toward one of the chairs.

"Not there," Madge says. "That's her chair. It would be a power play if you sat in it."

"How can you tell it's her chair?"

Madge looks at the other two. "I don't know," she says.

"They're all so fucking equidistant," I say.

Madge shakes her head. "Don't swear. This is probably being recorded."

I walk over to one of the tall potted plants. "Fuck, fuck, fuck, fuck," I say into the closet branch. "Testing. Fuck."

"C'mon," Madge says. "Be serious."

I whisper to the plant, its leaves, its branches, "I am being fucking serious."

Just then, Dr. A. Plotnik swoops in. I jump away from the plant. Madge sticks out her hand.

"I'm Madge and this is Godfrey."

"Welcome," Dr. A. Plotnik says placidly. She's a dry woman,

somewhat brittle, wearing an oversized blazer with shoulder pads that accentuate her poor posture counterproductively. Her cheeks have pouches as if she's hiding something there, like acorns or sugar cubes or the secrets of the brokenhearted. But she's pretty in a papery way. She turns to her desk and says over one of her hunched shoulder, "Have a seat."

Madge and I look at each other and then at the armchairs. I start to sit in one, but Madge waves me off, then points. I move to the one Madge has indicated. We both finally sit down.

"I'm so glad you're here," Dr. A. Plotnik says. "Romantic reformatting is a real commitment." She sits in the third armchair and smiles at us. There's no seating reorganization necessary. We've passed the first test. I feel a surge of confidence. Madge and I are a good team.

"We're ready," Madge says.

Dr. A. Plotnik looks at me expectantly.

I nod. "We are," I say. "Absolutely."

Dr. A. Plotnik only partially smiles this time, as if reserving the right to be disappointed in me in the near future. "I use a method called positive memory concentration," she says. "Couples who foster positive recollections of their early relationship are actually creating a positive mythology, and these couples are seven times more likely to stay in their relationships and nearly three times more likely to describe the current state of their relationship as 'happy' then the group who reported 'rarely' or 'almost never happy.'"

"That's fascinating," Madge says.

"Positive memory concentration helps couples foster positive recollections of the early formative budding of their relationships."

I say, "What about the couples who meet in prison or during a war or working together at the DMV?"

"I don't understand," Dr. A. Plotniks says.

"It's a joke," Madge says, scowling at me. "He's trying to be funny."

I'm not joking. "I mean, what if a couple doesn't have any real positive recollections of the early part of their relationship?"

"Ah, I see. You're trying to break the ice with something humorous," Dr. A. Plotnik says condescendingly.

"Not really," I say.

"If you have to explain a joke, it isn't one," Madge says, under her breath. "I've told you that."

"Sorry," I say. "We can just move on."

"No," Dr. A. Plotnik says, with a knotted expression of deep concern and psychological know-how. "I think that your 'joke' is actually exposing an underlying fear. Are you worried that you won't be able to come up with positive recollections of your early relationship with Madge?"

"No," I say, shaking my head. "I can come up with plenty."

"Like what?" Madge asks.

"Like . . ." I'm thinking of the first time she let me have sex with her. It was supposed to be very romantic. I tipped over a candle and burned a hole in her sofa. I decide not to mention it. Sex would be too animalistic, and Madge was pissed about the burned hole. "Like when we ate tacos on our first date," I say. "And the waitress didn't speak English very well. She was great, wasn't she?"

Dr. A. Plotnik turns to Madge. "Was that a positive memory?"

"I think it's a positive memory of the waitress," Madge says.

Dr. A. Plotnik sighs. "I understand," she says to Madge. "I have plenty of positive recollections of my early relationship with Dr. Plotnik," she says. "Plenty. But he's always fuzzy on the details, and he has a little ADD and so his mind wanders in the middle of a session. And can I blame him for having a dysfunction? No, I cannot. I'm a woman of science." And this is the moment when something inside of Dr. A. Plotnik fissures. She slams a hand down on her thigh which, for such a contained woman, can only be described as a gesture of pure outrage. "But when he gave me a Moleskine journal three days ago—a late birthday present—which . . . don't even get me started on. I spend thirty birthdays with him and he still can't remember *not* to pick up a sixteen-dollar-and-ninety-five-cent journal from Target that I'm going to hate? I'm growing old with this man. I think that deserves a string of pearls." Dr. A. Plotnik gets up and shows us the evidence—one moleskine journal.

I look at the journal and then at Madge, whose heart is really going out to Dr. A. Plotnik, and then I look at the journal again. "Plus, how many moles died to make that journal?" I say, hoping to lighten the mood. The two women stare at me. I feel I have no choice but to soldier on with the joke now, hoping it gets funny somehow. "Um, probably about four and a half moles, tops. It's a small journal."

The extremely tense silence that descends can only be described as a pall. I've never experienced a real pall like this before.

Dr. A. Plotnik lowers the journal and puts it down on the ink blotter on her desk. She picks up a lime green folder and returns to her seat. I glance at Madge, but she won't make eye contact.

Dr. A. Plotnik says, "Humor. I get it." She smiles coldly. "Here is your workbook. It's a weeklong process of daily study. Each session should last one hour. And then each of you will return to your envisionists and reevaluate your future together. If this doesn't work, you return for another session with me, a more intensive session, and then try again. That will be your last try. Do you understand?"

"Of course," Madge says.

I nod, afraid to open my mouth.

"Okay, then," Dr. A. Plotnik says, standing up and reaching out to commence another round of handshaking, Madge first, then me. "Hopefully I won't need to see you again, and this will be our final visit. I wish you both the best of luck." She turns quickly back to her desk, flipping through her appointment calendar, signaling an abrupt end to our meeting.

I shuffle quickly to the door, but Madge stops and says, "Thank you so much. And thank Dr. Plotnik for us, too. I really appreciate all of his time and effort on this relationship."

Dr. A. Plotnik's head whips around. She eyes Madge suspiciously. "His time and effort?"

"Yes," Madge says, a little surprised by Dr. A. Plotnik's tone. "He's been really fantastic."

"Well, isn't that nice?" Dr. A. Plotnik says, and then she regards us very seriously. "Listen, I think you two have an excellent shot at true happiness. Work very, very hard on your sessions. Rarely do I see a couple with such potential." She squints at us.

This catches me completely off-guard. "Thank you," I say, giving a little nod. Me and Madge? We have rare potential? I'm embarrassed by my sudden hopefulness. I think back on the ultimate seating decision earlier. "We're a good team," I tell her.

But Madge is a little stiff. "Yes," she says. That's it, just *yes*.

We walk out of the office, and shut the door behind us. We look at each other, but I'm pretty sure I'm looking more at her than she is at me.

"Did you hear that?" I say. "Rarely has she seen a couple with our potential."

"Yes," Madge says, "I heard her. It's just that it sounded, well"—she lowers her voice—"hard to believe. Didn't you think? I mean, *us?*"

I think about it. I look up toward the ceiling, replaying the moment in my head—Dr. A. Plotnik's pinched eyes, the squirrel cheeks. I linger over the notion of Madge and me—rarely does Dr. A. Plotnik see a couple with this much potential? Do we really inspire that much hope? I've always thought of our relationship as one of those hidden gems. You know, the couple who might bicker some in public but that's just a sign of how damn healthy and confident they are in their deeper bond. Outward signs of potential for the long haul, well, that's not our thing. If I asked Amy and Bart and even Gunston if they thought we had real potential, would they say yes? Unlikely. Plus, Madge is good at reading people. She knows when they're being just a little bit offish. There was a moment when I believed Dr. A. Plotnik, that brief moment, now barely a memory, when I believed that Madge and I were full of potential, when we were rarities in love.

"Maybe it was a little hard to believe," I admit. "Maybe so."

We walk down the hall toward the waiting room, but then Madge stops abruptly and turns to me. " '*About four and a half moles, tops? It's a small journal?*' I mean, what were you thinking? Moleskine journals aren't made of actual moles."

"That's why it's funny." I shrug. "Or not."

THAT NIGHT, I EMERGE from the bathroom to find Madge standing on the mattress of our bed. She's clutching Dr. A. Plotnik's workbook (written by Dr. A. Plotnik), which she'd decided to read cover to cover before we did any of our sessions. This postponement was fine with me, as I've been dreading the sessions. I'm fairly sure we'll have to look deeply into each other's eyes, and I'm dead set against mandatory gazing.

"It's right here," Madge says. "It just hovers."

"What's right where?"

"That smell!"

"Oh, right. The death," I say.

"It is death, isn't it? This isn't good, Godfrey. Death is hovering above our bed. The place we're supposed to make love. Death!"

"I didn't say it was good!"

"It's worse than your identity crisis."

"I thought it was an identity issue. When was it upgraded to a crisis?" I ask sarcastically but also a little alarmed. "I found my wallet, you know. I told you that."

She flops onto the bed. "What are we going to do about it?"

"I think it might be a dead mouse."

"That died in the air above our bed?"

"Stinks move and linger and hang. It's probably just a dead mouse in the wall."

"We're fucked."

"Why would you say that?" I say, crawling across the bed to her.

Madge lies there, closing her eyes tight. "You should read the examples in the book. Some people have had such great romantic beginnings. People talk about buying peaches in a market together and getting lost on a bus together. One woman talks about this carriage ride. A *carriage* ride! I mean, how can we compete with that?"

"I don't think we're supposed to be competing."

"You know what I mean." She rolls away from me and pulls her knees to her chest. "We're doomed to that shitty little house and that fucking stupid seeing-eye dog and you creeping out my niece!"

"What?" I say. "I didn't creep out your niece!"

"She told me, Godfrey, that you *creep her out*. She's a sweet kid! Completely innocent!"

"You think I liked seeing an old pervie version of myself in the basement? With my gelled hair? You think I liked looking at your ugly shoes?"

"Hey, I wear those shoes now!"

"I don't like them. There, I said it."

There's a quiet moment. I flop back onto the bed. I think of origami and how I wish it were human. One minute I could be a puffed-up box and the next minute a crane. "We *are* fucked," I finally say, agreeing. "You really didn't like the house?"

"No. And the seeing-eye dog growled at me in the car," she says. "Those dogs are supposed to be completely gentle. And then I hit it. I don't think you're supposed to hit seeing-eye dogs in training."

I love Madge for confessing she hit the seeing-eye dog. I do. I roll toward her. "Look at me," I say.

She shakes her head.

"C'mon, Madgy."

She slowly turns.

I look deeply into her eyes. "I think you're beautiful. I thought you were beautiful the first moment I saw you. And I didn't love the waitress. I loved the way you talked to her in Spanish. All chopped up. The way your mouth worked out the words so beautifully. And you used your hands." I pick them up, place them in mine. "These beautiful hands."

Madge smiles. These are the moments I pride myself on—quiet

ones that the public never sees. We do have potential, even if it's not completely obvious to anyone else.

"That's pretty good," Madge says.

"Isn't it?" I say. "Screw that woman and her carriage ride! We've got a mythology. We can do this."

Madge kisses me passionately, and I'm pretty sure that I'm going to call Chin and cancel the five-for-three deal. I love Madge. *It's decided,* I think as I undo the row of three small buttons on her pajama top. We're going to do this.

We start to have sex and she closes her eyes and keeps them closed. I don't think it's that she doesn't want to look at me. It's something else; I feel it, too, the overwhelming fear that we're about to crash into something. The stench of a small death still lingers while we keep going. I imagine the disintegrating mouse and then remember the mice in the swimming pool, how they glinted and pivoted like fish and the woman, her rubber cap wet and shiny like a dome, waving to me.

Evelyn
BEES AND BEARS

I flop down on my couch with my coat still on, breathless from the bike ride, and I just stare. Chin didn't blacklist me. He ferreted his fluffy blond eyebrows, and said, "Sister, you need to Zen your shit out." He sold me a box of tea—handmade from some ancient mee-maw of his and it smells like a mee-maw a little, mints and mothballs—and he sent me home.

And now I sit here, like I've just come down from a bad trip—shrooms or frog licking or something—and I'm thinking, *In my future with Mark Standing, I have an affair with Godfrey Burkes? What the hell? Who is Godfrey Burkes? Why was he on our lawn? Why did Adam have a gun? And, Jesus, Dot went to jail!*

There's a line from Chin's forms that's always stuck with me: *In the case of true love, there can be system failures.* Is it wise to trust a doctor who believes in true love? Probably not. Still, I wonder—for one brief moment—if I've just experienced a true-love-induced system failure.

No, no, no. None of it was real. I just put in too many names and screwed it all up.

I tell myself to breathe. I quote some George Burns to soothe myself: *Look to the future, because that is where you'll spend the rest of your life. Look to the future, the future* . . . I lift the cardboard box of tea bags and sniff a mee-maw and wonder if I should drink mee-maw-flavored tea and, if I do, will it Zen my shit out?

I don't know how long I sit there like that, but eventually I snap to attention because there's a knock at the door.

"Coming!" I call out. I don't have a doorbell—I find their buzzes jarring, like little electric shocks. When I moved in, I disconnected it, ripped the wires right out of the box, meaning I will probably not be getting my deposit back.

I peer out the peephole. It's Adrian. He's stepped back from the door, his arms crossed on his chest. I can tell immediately that he has processed our conversation and is now more pissed off than he was while trying to attach a love note to my bike basket with ear bud wires. It's a small apartment, and he knows that I'm already at the door. He doesn't knock again.

Through the door he says, "I'm here to pick up my stuff. I texted earlier." A couple of days ago, he left an exhaustive list of things I struggle to find significant.

I open the door and we look at each other like strangers who've just happened to constantly fall into bed with each other over the last few years.

"Come in," I tell him, but he doesn't move. His arms are still crossed on his chest. I don't know what he's waiting for. "You can come in." I point behind me, toward everything I own. "It's just a couple of steps, I promise."

Finally, he walks into the living room. I point to a cardboard box. "It should all be in there."

Adrian isn't making eye contact with me, but he's burned holes through my carpet, the hem of my skirt, and for a second, my collarbone.

He gets on his knees and starts shuffling through the box. I stand behind him as he sorts through his stuff, including a broken drumstick and a map of Carrboro, North Carolina.

"You could've put my toothbrush in a Baggie or something," he says, holding the purple toothbrush in his hand, his thumb running over the worn bristles.

"You're supposed to switch your toothbrush out every three months," I say defensively.

"Has it been that long?"

I nod.

"Still, you have small sandwich bags."

"I'm sorry," I say, but really, I'm not sorry. The toothbrush is a cesspool of the worst parts that have crowded both of us. When did we invite such things in? I'm wondering how clean my mouth has been these last three months. "I'm sorry," I say again. "I found the map, though."

He drops the toothbrush and picks up the map, touches it gently. "Cat's Cradle is one of the greatest venues in the country," he tells me. "Too bad you won't be with us when we play there."

"I'll have to read about it on the music blogs."

"What about the Wii?" He pulls it out of the box. I left the cords attached—they dangle half inside the cardboard box and half out. "We went halfsies on it, so it really is both of ours."

"Our child."

Adrian doesn't say anything. Is he getting sentimental?

He stands up and immediately starts fishing through his pockets. He pulls out a few crumpled bills and hands them to me. "I owe you for the Wii. Here."

I don't bother counting the money even though I know it can't possibly cover half of the game system. *A gesture is a gesture,* I tell myself. Besides, I was the one who broke up with him. Let him keep the Wii.

"How are our Caroline and Bruce?" Adrian's parents.

"You shouldn't miss them."

"But I do."

He sighs. "You want too much, Evelyn."

"What's that mean?"

"I don't know. It's like there's some hole in you that no one can fill up."

"I think everyone has a hole inside of them that can't be filled. I mean, that's why religions exist and why some people excel despite all odds."

He shakes his head. "Yours is personal. I'm just telling you this for your own good."

I yearn. So what? "I want things that normal people want, Adrian." I want to pick the right person and build a family of my own. What's wrong with that?

"You want those things too much, and as long as we're being painfully honest—"

"You're being painfully honest. I'm not."

"You're also afraid of things that are out of your control," he says. "That's why you like to spend all day shelving books in alphabetical order."

"You have no idea what a librarian actually does," I tell him. We've been over this.

"And it's why you're obsessed with that Chin guy, who's a flim-flam man."

"He showed me our future, Adrian. We fought over cheese."

"That doesn't sound so bad to me, Evelyn. Does it? In the long run? Sometimes you just have to commit to something that's not perfect. And you have to commit to the whole future of it. And that can't be known and it can't be controlled. I think that's just life, you know? The sun wakes us up every morning and you don't know what the day will bring."

I don't want Adrian to be right, but what if he is? And then my mind pivots because something doesn't quite sound natural. I tilt my head. "Are you writing a song about this?"

"What?"

"That last part sounded like bad song lyrics. You're testing out song lyrics on me, in the form of an argument, aren't you?"

"My life and my art are very entwined," he says defensively.

Now his tangibles, what few there were, are in a cardboard box and that box is leaving. His stupid broken drumstick. His stupid map of Carrboro, North Carolina. His stupid fucking cesspool of a toothbrush. Damn it. I don't want him to stay, but I don't want him to go.

Adrian picks up the cardboard box. "I guess I should pretend to have somewhere important to go," he says.

I follow him to the front door and open it.

Then the lag. We both want this to end, but we don't know how. Or we both want to stay, but we don't know why.

I feel stuck to the doorframe. I think of spiderwebs stuck to trees, gnats stuck to the spiderwebs.

Adrian is at the other side of the doorframe. Is he also stuck? He's holding the cardboard box like an infant he took out of the hospital for the first time. The box isn't heavy, but it looks like it's weighing him down, causing his feet to sink beneath the hallway carpet. Soon his ankles will be gone.

"Is this the last words part?" he says.

Last words? Last words of famous dead people are some of my favorites. My head is flooded with them. Churchill's "I'm bored with it all." Joan Crawford telling her praying housekeeper, "Damn it . . . Don't you dare ask God to help me." Pancho Villa saying, "Don't let it end like this. Tell them I said something." Emily Dickinson's "I must go in, the fog is rising." Oh, or Oscar Wilde, "Either that wallpaper goes, or I do."

But I choose to say, "Beautiful."

"Beautiful?"

"Those were Elizabeth Barrett Browning's last words. Her husband had asked her how she felt."

He shakes his head. "The quote machine. I always thought you were kind of like a bottom feeder of other people's words," he says. "But shit. I miss the quotes."

"A bottom feeder?" This is the worst thing Adrian's ever said to me, but it's also one of the smartest things he's ever said. It doesn't hurt as much as it baffles me. Did I ever really know Adrian? "Have you changed on me already?"

"I've changed a lot."

"How?"

"For one, I'm going to a legit envisionist, not that Chin bullshit."

"But I thought you said it was all new-agey bourgeois bullshit."

"I'm part of the bourgeoisie, I guess." He shrugs and then nods toward the kitchen. "I want my height erased from the doorjamb."

"Seriously?"

"Seriously. I came to erase myself completely. I'm trying to move into the future now, Evelyn. You should be able to get that."

"You think I can erase your height and it'll be like you were never here?"

"I just want it erased. Okay?"

"Fine."

He stands there. "Do you have any last words for me that aren't ripped off from someone else?"

"Yeah, I do. Don't wear your own band's T-shirt on stage," I tell him.

He looks down and I know that under his sweater he's wearing one of his own band's T-shirts. "I wouldn't have had to if you were any better at selling our merch."

I want to tell him the music might be the problem, not the way I stood behind a card table, with an assortment of demos and T-shirts splashed out in front of me. I don't say it because I don't actually want to hurt him.

I'm already beginning to feel lonely—the hole in me that maybe no one can fill. Or maybe I'm lonely because Adrian is more outside my front door than inside my front door and that means something. Even inches mean something. First it's inches and then it's feet, yardsticks laid out into football fields, a printing press and then so many spines filled with ink that every county needs a library, sometimes dozens. At some point, continents shifted and this is all because some Neanderthal was once closer to being outside a cave than inside it. Small stays fragile and even big is still fragile. Possible futures are the most fragile but they always end before something can truly break. Were Adrian and I small, or were we big? I know which crashes harder, but which crashes longer?

And what if he's right and fighting over cheese isn't so bad in the long run? What if not committing to something that's imperfect is just a way of avoiding the future?

Adrian nods. His nod says, *I've got a cardboard box with a broken drumstick, a purple toothbrush, a Wii, and a map of Carrboro, North Carolina. I'll be fine.*

I lean forward, unsticking myself from the doorframe and kiss Adrian on the cheek so lightly I will probably forget I did it. Adrian shifts the cardboard box a little to the left and shrugs. I watch him walk away—seven steps to be exact—before turning down the stairwell.

I stand at the door, staring at the chipped paint, the dirty knob. If someone asked me what I was doing, I would say, *I don't know. Please tell me.* I am not waiting for Adrian to come back. I know that.

I don't move. I stand at my front door for minutes. This is not a habit, but maybe it will turn into one. Me, waiting at doors, for nothing in particular. On first dates, men will ask me about my hobbies and I will tell them, *Standing at front doors,* as I scrape the cheese off the top of my chicken parmesan. *It's a lifestyle choice.*

One half-filled cardboard box gone, and once inside the apartment, it feels completely empty, like movers just showed up and packed up everything—even stripped the paint from the walls. Sound was evicted. Here I am, alone. My choice but still alone. The quiet gets loud—this buzzing. Louder.

I think maybe there are bees in my apartment.

I am certain there are bees in my apartment.

A whole hive of bees. Two hives. A dozen hives. Soon the bears will come. I will die in a quiet apartment, alone and stung and mauled. My choice but still alone.

Godfrey
FIVE FOR THREE

So I decide to go through with the five-for-three deal with Chin. How do I rationalize this? It's an opportunity I'll never have again and completely harmless, as no one will know, and I can't contract any diseases in the process. I'm not going to a topless car wash or anything. I'm pretty sure that Madge would take this opportunity if it were offered to her. Then I wonder if Madge is taking an opportunity like this. And I say to myself, "Good for Madge." At our five-year anniversary, we'll confess to each other and it'll be this little silly moment. "Can you imagine doing that now? Insane! Ridiculous!"

And honestly, it's not like I'm going to look up some old girlfriend in real life because we have some exquisite life, in which we, what? Shop together at IKEA without bickering?

I look up benign yet stubborn gallbladder issues, which ends up to be unnecessary because I successfully peel out of work before I collide with Bart and his genetically compromised gallbladder and arrive for my appointment ready to take care of all five sessions at once.

While I strap on a helmet, Chin assures me he'll closely monitor my needs. There's the noise of coins clunking in the coin-op and a light fog rolls over my eyes. I hear the door open and close.

My first envisioning choice is obvious: Liz Chase.

Liz Chase and Godfrey Burkes A Chin Production

Future-me looks like he should be worried about his cholesterol. If he isn't worried about his triglycerides, I'm worried for him. Maybe this is what happens when you marry your high-school sweetheart, the one who took your virginity and didn't complain when the condom didn't stay dry long enough to get through a commercial break for *Friends*. Now when I think of Liz Chase, I think of her sweetness, how she pretended it was always supposed to be like this—so succinct, so quiet.

I loved her in a way any sixteen-year-old boy could love a girl named Liz Chase and her practicing for future sexy bras (not yet lace but teasing in that direction with the little bow where the clasp goes in the front) and her smiling as she slid shut the bottom drawer she designated the "elephant graveyard" for the sports bras of her youth—that being from when she was fifteen, of course. By all of this, I mean I loved her hopelessly, and even now, she is still the first woman I think of when Madge is at Fontana's picking up something to make for dinner, and I am alone with a box of tissues, a bottle of lotion, and a complete lack of self-worth.

After I broke up with her for no good reason, she got into the back of Rob Linger's father's Chevy pickup, and I regretted letting her go—especially to Rob Linger.

But this time, fuck you, Rob Linger.

In fifteen years, future-me is shaving. He nicks the bottom side of his left cheek, and he's stuck a piece of toilet paper over the cut. Then he straightens his tie, but it doesn't work. No matter how long he tries to fix the tie, it just can't get itself down to his belt. That stomach—who let *that* happen?

Future-me leaves the bathroom and heads downstairs. The house is middle income. In this future, I wear a tie to work, but I'm not raking it in.

Downstairs looks like a Reagan wet dream: a long, wooden kitchen table with place settings, pancakes in the middle, syrup, butter, toast, and kids—all 2.5 of them. The kids are a complete blur, but the high chair is pink, so I assume the little one is a girl.

Liz always wanted a girl. She wanted to name her Annabelle. *There were so many different ways you can go with it,* she used to say. *Anna, Belle, Bells. Or, you know, Annabelle.* I would just nod, barely listening, wondering when I'd be allowed to unzip my pants again.

I want to fast-forward this session to the part where I redeem myself, but I think if it were possible to do that during an envisioning session, I might be fast-forwarding forever.

Past the kitchen table, Liz closes the fridge and turns around. She looks weirdly the same, just slightly stretched out like the dummy my mother had for sewing—the one with the expandable body. Holding a carton of orange juice, Liz is in a bathrobe she's probably owned since the birth of our first child. I can't tell what's a stain or fabric pattern.

There's no good morning from Liz. Future-me doesn't say anything either—he just sits down at the head of the table, between two of his kids. The only thing not fuzzy is the food, and really, it's the only thing worth looking at. It's lush and glossy and brimming.

Liz walks around the table, pouring juice into the kids' cups first, before filling mine and then hers. Still, she says nothing. She sits at the other end of the kitchen table, next to .5 in the pink high chair.

"My neck," future-me says. "It hurts when I turn to the left."

"Then just don't turn that way," Liz says. Her voice is colder than I remember, like it got stuck in an ice storm. Even after fifteen years of marriage, what if I still can't give her an orgasm? I remind myself to send Rob Linger a thank-you card.

Why does my neck hurt? Is it from constantly shifting the belly weight? I imagine even my arms must feel heavy, my feet the equivalent of anvils.

Future-me answers my question when he says, "How many more nights on the couch?"

Liz shifts without looking over, like I'm the reason malaria still kills millions every year or why so many in this world go without potable water.

What did I do to deserve the couch? Not take the trash out? Forget an anniversary, miss one of the kid's clarinet recitals? I don't even know how old my children are. When does one start playing the clarinet?

But I know the truth immediately. I'm a Thigpen. I've been caught seducing other women. Even in this bulbous state, I've become the animal I always knew I would be. (Does my mother know?)

If winning is 2.5 kids and a wife who makes you sleep on the couch, you can keep it all, Rob Linger. (Madge wants one supersmart kid, so we can "maintain some semblance of our selfhoods." Me? I'd like a brood, but I don't ever say that because it makes me sound like a Neanderthal.)

"It's your turn to carpool," Liz says.

Here I am, a bloated Thigpen who has to drive half the neighborhood kids to school.

"Okay, kids," Liz says, standing up from the kitchen table, "time for school."

The kids moan and slide out of their seats. Liz takes .5 out of her high chair and follows the kids into the other room.

Future-me barely touched his breakfast. Maybe this rough patch in my future marriage will save me from an early heart attack. He heads outside and gets in the driver's seat as the older kids pile into the minivan. They're faceless, my kids, and it creeps me out something awful. I'm surprised I've stuck with this session for so long. I'm depressed now, and it looks like I'll be just as depressed in fifteen years. Do good envisioning sessions even exist, or are they all secretly backed by big pharmaceuticals with the intention of peddling more antidepressants?

Future-me starts the minivan. Barry Manilow's "Mandy" comes on the radio. I don't know what's more surprising: the fact that they still play Barry Manilow on the radio in fifteen years or that I'll be okay with listening to Barry Manilow on the radio in fifteen years.

Future-me hums along—I like humming—and checks the rearview mirror before putting the minivan in reverse. He tenses. I worry he's about to grab his left arm, grunt, and die right there, in front of his children who will grow up to resent him, not fifty feet from a wife who will quickly remarry (probably Rob Linger). I wait for his head to fall against the steering wheel, causing the horn to blare, right before a slow fade to black.

But then I notice why future-me tenses. In the rearview mirror: legs.

What feels like miles of them.

Miles of legs the color of butter on a bike that might be the sky if the sky were coasting along pavement in rain boots with flowers sprouting on them. It's a brief moment that stretches in super slow-mo for hours, years. Still, it doesn't last long enough. A kick in my gut that just makes me hungrier. It's one of those moments—a butterfly you touch—that will last.

A pair of legs and a realization that right here, paper-gowned, doped up in a renovated Chinese restaurant turned new-age tarot card reader, I'm staring at a future that—in this moment—makes my heart pitch forward in my chest in a way I haven't felt until right now watching those legs go through a rearview mirror of a minivan I haven't purchased yet.

YEAH, LIZ CHASE WAS a mistake. All I want to know about are the legs. I start to unhook the helmet, but Chin walks in and says, "Whoa, whoa!"

"What if I'm not cut out for futures? I might be peaking."

Chin looks at me doubtfully. "Well, you can quit if you want, but you still signed up to pay for three—just instead of five, you'll get one."

"Seriously?"

"Seriously."

I look around the room and then, for the first time, taped to the wall next to the examination room door is a sign: PLEASE, NO MASTURBATING. THANK YOU, THE MANAGEMENT. But someone had some fun with a black marker and now it reads PLEASE, NO MASTURBATING THE MANAGEMENT.

"Look," Chin says, "what if high-school Godfrey Burkes really underestimated himself? Maybe you should set your sights a little higher. Not too high, but, you know, higher."

Chin's right. What if high-school Godfrey Burkes could've been head of the football team, what if he could've thrown a football through a tire swinging from the branch of a linden tree? I decide to go for it.

Tina Whooten and Godfrey Burkes
A Chin Production

Future-me stands in a large kitchen, hands in his pockets, between the sink and the island. He looks uncomfortable, as if he's never been here before. I notice a bowl of fruit that might be plastic, and then Tina Whooten walks in wearing a pencil skirt. I wonder if I'm the kind of husband who picked out this skirt for her before going to the movie that we left early so we could have sex in the back of our sedan before getting back to the kids and babysitter who charges twice as much as she should because she can, because even after fifteen years I can never get enough time alone with Tina Whooten.

Everything is so clear I wonder if this is a reality television show or an actual envisionist session. Maybe this is just someone who resembles me, standing around and being awkward and getting paid for it because he's on TV.

But then Tina looks over at future-me, surprised but only for an instant.

"Oh fuck, again?" It comes out as a sigh, like it's the third time she's said it today. She walks past me and pours a cup of coffee, not offering me any.

Maybe it goes without saying, but "Oh fuck, again?" is not what I hope to hear my hot future wife say when she sees me.

"Godfrey Burkes, right?" she says as she starts to peel kiwis at the sink, not looking back at me.

I'm kind of jacked that she remembers me, but then shouldn't she know me because we're married?

Future-me shifts helplessly while I do the same thing on the examination table, the helmet making me feel like an astronaut with nowhere to go.

Then I remember the rules. Or part of them—God knows what little attention I was paying to them. There was a line that if you don't believe in your own future with a certain person, it cannot really be envisioned.

Seriously, can I not even dream of being married to Tina Whooten?

And suddenly I feel like I'm in tenth-grade biology, sitting behind Tina Whooten, *the* Tina Whooten who filled the stands for every home volleyball game, even though the school team hadn't had a winning record since the late 1970s. Tina Whooten, two years older—why was she even in tenth-grade biology as a senior?

"Tenth grade was it? You couldn't keep your eyes off my tits," she says.

Real-me nods. I couldn't keep my eyes off her tits, but neither could half the class. That included more than a few girls and every teacher with a moderate amount of testosterone.

If it were a yearbook category, Tina Whooten would've been voted Most Likely to Be Envisioned Fifteen Years from Now.

"Don't you have something better to do?" she says.

Future-me, he or I or we, still hasn't said anything. Sometimes it's distracting to breathe in two different places at the same time. Future-me shrugs. He seems just as confused as I am.

Everything is so goddamn clear, especially Tina's shiny skin. I wonder if she applies lotion on it or if the lotion does it itself. Like the lotion says, *No, no, I've got this. You just keep lying there.*

There's a pause. My mouth is dry.

Tina calls out, "Sarge!" and I expect a retriever, but a man's voice calls out from another room and then he appears. He's holding a trash bag. Tina holds her coffee and smiles at him. He's just as clear as Tina and so good-looking I want to cover myself, call my mother and Thigpen and say, "Can you try again?"

Tina looks at the man like she always wants him to be pinning her against a wall. He smiles at her before looking at future-me, who is now even more confused.

"Oh, hey man," he says to future-me. "Sarge." There's a pause. "I'm Tina's husband." He shakes my hand with his free hand. He only looks at me for a second, and then it's back to his wife. His hand stays gripped around mine. "From high school?"

"Yeah," Tina says.

Sarge finally lets go of my hand. Future-me tries to rub his hand as subtly as possible.

"Makes sense." He looks back at future-me. "She looks even better now," he says. "Yearbooks. She dusted them off when all of this started happening, you know?"

"What started happening?" future-me manages to ask.

"You know, all these guys who were once in love with her started showing up to see what their futures would be like if they'd gotten her." He laughs. "As if."

"As if," future-me says meekly. I want him to say, *But wait, this is all a product of my mind. You don't really exist, do you?* But future-me is either too dumbfounded or embarrassed to question their reality. In point of fact, it would be stupid to doubt Sarge's existence. He could easily prove it by beating future-me's ass.

"Third one this week," Sarge says.

"Fourth, actually," Tina says. "You're forgetting the one who showed up during the movie." She turns toward future-me. "Scared me so bad I spilled the popcorn all over that couple in front of us."

"That's right!" Sarge says. "Pretty much ruined the movie."

"I'm worth it." She winks, and Sarge's eyes cover her entire body in one swoop.

Sarge hands the bag of trash to future-me. "Could you drop this at the end of the driveway on your way out?"

Future-me takes the bag of trash from Sarge, who may or may not have been on the cover of an *Esquire* stacked on the back of my toilet. I feel pathetic, bottomed out. I hope future-me feels just as pathetic. I hope future-me hates himself right now. I don't want to be the only one, even if it's another version of me feeling this way, just older with a semireceding hairline.

"Sorry," future-me says. With his free hand, future-me waves good-bye and lets himself out.

It's dusk. The neighborhood is quiet; the houses are spread apart. The community is probably gated. Will I even be able to get out of here? At the end of Tina and Sarge's driveway, I put the bag of trash in the green trash can.

Across the street on the sidewalk, in front of a house that looks exactly the same as Tina's, I see the bike. I see the boots. *That* bike and *those* boots. I want the camera to zoom in closer, but it won't. I lean forward on the examination table, but it doesn't help.

Kneeling in front of the bike is the woman in the boots. I can't make her out. She has her back to future-me as she pumps air into the back tire. She's wearing a dress. It silks off of her like it's telling a story: all of the girls who wore dresses before her were just practicing for *this* moment.

I am thinking, *She is here,* and then I'm thinking, *She should always be here.* But then, why is she here? It seems like a glitch in the system. A fantastic glitch. My favorite glitch in the history of glitches. Her image freezes. The screen starts to skip before it goes black.

A NURSE COMES IN this time. She's got this permanently bored expression. I was hoping for Chin. I have a few questions—thank you very much—about someone (in rain boots) photobombing session after session. What's it mean? How can I actually see more of her?

The nurse looks at my chart. "Who's next, lover boy?"

"I once dated these twins . . ."

"One at a time! We don't do any of that kinky stuff."

"I wasn't—"

"Save it. Pick one."

Sandra Ellis is twelve minutes older than Klarissa Ellis, but Klarissa Ellis looked older back then, even though they looked almost exactly the same. I end up saying, "Klarissa Ellis," because she swirled her tongue like a whirlpool. That was long ago, but I figure, once a whirlpool . . .

Klarissa Ellis and Godfrey Burkes
A Chin Production

The session opens in a windy car, driving fast. Night. My view is shaky, like the opening scene of *Saving Private Ryan,* but there's no gunfire or Tom Hanks before he put on his sincerity weight.

Klarissa Ellis is driving the car, I'm in the passenger's seat, and the radio is loud. It's the Smiths' "Heaven Knows I'm Miserable Now." Along the road, there are a few unlit strip malls. It must be very late.

Klarissa isn't saying anything, but she's only in a bra and a pair of torn jeans, faded, a wedding band attached to a necklace around her neck.

Future-me is gripping his seat belt frantically. He's wearing glasses, a fitted suit, a shadow of an incoming beard. This is the best I've looked in the future so far, but I've never seen myself so frightened.

There's rattling so loud I can barely hear the music over it. Empty pill bottles are scattered on the floor of the car. Future-me looks back at Klarissa, who is staring at the road. He then looks at the speedometer; it's nearing 100 miles per hour.

"Klarissa," future-me says. I can just hear him over the music, and I know Klarissa didn't hear him.

Future-me looks back at the road. He freezes.

Klarissa laughs. "We'll try not to wake up this time," she says, and then the car runs straight into the side of a Walmart.

I'm back at Chin's with the helmet strapped on.

The nurse is standing there, looking concerned, which concerns me because she seemed so good at looking bored. "You okay?"

"Next twin!" I shout. I'm still bracing for impact.

"One twin killed you, and you want to try again?" she says.

"I'm a slow learner. Besides," I tell her, "that was the best movie I've seen in months."

Back to bored, she shrugs. "All righty."

Sandra Ellis and Godfrey Burkes
A Chin Production

Bunk beds. I'm on the top bunk. The bunk below me is empty. I try to think of the last time I was in a bunk bed. Third grade, maybe, a sleepover. I remember being too scared to fall asleep. But I was maybe eight—why would I be in a bunk bed when I'm thirty-nine?

The shot widens and now I know. Future-me is in jail. I jump down and start getting dressed in my orange suit. I am fucking ripped. There are muscles on top of my muscles, like I have built mountaintops and they didn't know how to end so they just kept growing more mountaintops. Ripples. When future-me moves, the muscles crash into themselves. I imagine this is how the ocean must feel. I wonder if it'd be worth it to go to prison just to get this physique. Hard call. I look that good. There's a loud buzz. Someone announcing visitation hours. The clanking noise of un-locking doors.

A guard walks up and down the cell block. All of the inmates, including future-me, line up single file and follow one of the guards down the stairs, through thick doors and into a large room.

Future-me sits down at a small metal table, across from whom I assume to be Sandra Ellis. There's no touching, but she stretches her arms out as far as she can and balls her hands into fists. Future-me does the same. Maybe this is how people hold hands in the future. I doubt it.

Truth is, Sandra doesn't look good. She's tan but kind of homeless tan, not to sound like a judgmental prick, but she looks like she's been out in the sun, wandering. She's lived hard and maybe done a little too much meth; her teeth are in bad shape.

And for the first time I am wondering why I'm in jail. Who the fuck did I kill to end up here? (I kind of hope it was Tina Whooten's husband. I mean, if that effer could see me now.)

The visitation room is large, sunken—everything seems to cave toward the middle. Everything is gray, and I don't think that's entirely because of the blur.

Maybe if I close my eyes and open them again, this won't be happening. I do. But I'm still in an orange jumpsuit, sitting across from a woman I sloppily made out with once because there was more vodka than punch in the hunch punch.

Future-me is looking at Sandra, but I'm not. I'm scanning the visitation room of the prison, looking looking looking. I don't know what future-me is looking for—someone with a shiv? But I know what I want to see—those boots, those legs.

I'm hearing bits of conversation to the left, then the right, then Sandra, but I do my best to tune her out. She's saying something about our kids needing new jeans for school. One of their backpacks ripped and he loved that backpack because Spider-Man was on it and he just fucking loves Spider-Man. How is she going to buy a new backpack when they're cutting down her hours at the diner?

Why do I always have kids and why am I always a terrible father to these kids? I should probably start seeing a therapist now so I can figure this shit out. Must be my Thigpen?

All of a sudden a woman's voice comes through like radio static: "Dot's trial starts in two weeks, but the lawyer doesn't seem optimistic."

That voice! I know that voice. Do I know that voice?

"What do lawyers know?" It's a man now. I can't make out any distinct features, but his jumpsuit matches mine. They're sitting at the metal table directly to the right of me and Sandra.

Everything looks like space gas, but there they are—the boots with the flowers. I try to make out what kind of flowers they are. Daisies? Lilies? Chrysanthemums? I don't know anything about flowers so I don't know why I'm even trying to guess.

The guard makes an announcement over the intercom that it's time to go and then adds, "Evelyn Shriner, your driver's license has been found. Please report to the front desk. Evelyn Shriner?"

It's her. The girl from that first envisioning session, the girl from the dream of the pool. She's the girl on the bike, the beautiful pumping legs.

She's blonder and older this time—she's aged the same amount of years as future-me, but it's obviously her. There's no mistake. But what rain boots last fifteen years? The boots still look brand new. This is the closest I've been to her—five, six, seven feet at the most. Future-me could almost reach out and touch her. Future-me is looking at Sandra Ellis as Evelyn calls to a guard, "Oh, that's me! I lose my stuff all the time! I think I have identity issues!"

· · ·

THE MEDS ARE ALMOST completely out of my system now, but I still feel foggy. Chin's there and could be saying anything to me right now, but I'm not paying attention. Evelyn Shriner from the waiting room on the first day, with the driver's license in her mouth! How long ago was it?

"You have one more session. You want to do it today still? You look a little wobbly."

It has to be Evelyn. Surely I could think of someone else I could waste it on, but it's always been Evelyn. Those boots! Everything above those boots! Hell, everything inside those boots! I mean, she has to take them off in bed, right?

I say to Chin, "I read in the materials, at the beginning . . ."

"The release of liability forms."

"Yeah, those. I think it said that people could recur in your envisioning and maybe in your dreams. And . . ."

"Are you having a situation like that?" He sounds suspicious.

"Maybe."

"It's rare, but it's some serious shit when that happens."

"Serious how?"

"Serious as a heart attack."

"What?"

"That's just an expression."

"Not when it's coming from a doctor!"

"Listen, it means that you've met someone who's important to you—even though you're not consciously aware of it—and they're so important that your mind is causing them to barge into your dreams and envisionings. Those times when your rational mind and your fears and desires aren't playing interference. You know, when you're actually pure, running on your own fuel."

"And there's that one line in the rules about true love."

"I don't like to talk about true love."

"But you wrote it."

Chin nods. "Well, yes, I did with the help of my brother, Earl, who practices law on the side."

"It said something about system failures . . ."

"I've only seen it a few times myself."

"What happens?"

"Anything and everything. It just means our systems no longer work. Weird shit occurs. That weird shit varies. And that's about all I can say."

"Weird shit occurs? That's all you've got?"

"Look, science and the mysteries of true love can only coexist for so long before weird shit occurs."

And then I realize that using my last envisioning session on Evelyn is nothing but a lose-lose situation. If it goes badly, then it goes badly, and all of these feelings are more cloudy weather in an already shitty Baltimore winter. And if the session with Evelyn is a knockout? I'd feel like a complete asshole. I would've cheated on Madge—not physically, but isn't emotionally cheating in some future scenario the same thing? Maybe it's even worse.

Madge might not be the best girlfriend—how can I say fiancée when she refuses to wear the ring?—but no one deserves to be cheated on. Even if it's fake or at best, *alternatively* real. The emotions are there; those can't be faked. We always shed our skin but our hearts stay the same.

I can be loyal and true.

I am no Thigpen. I am no Thigpen.

"I wish I had rain boots," I mutter.

"Would be good. The weather warmed up some. Expecting a light rain, they say. So," Chin says, "number five? Yes or no?"

And, regardless of everything I've just worked out in my head, I say, "Evelyn Shriner."

"Huh," Chin says.

"Why huh?"

"Did I say huh?" Chin asks.

"Yes. Why?"

"No reason."

Evelyn Shriner and Godfrey Burkes
A Chin Production

This Godfrey is on his hands and knees crawling in what seems to be a large hard-plastic tube, like the Habitrail I once had for my hamster, Elminster. Future-me stops and looks down through the orange-tinted plastic and sees that the floor is far away. My God, this contraption is suspended from the ceiling. There are children far below, running everywhere. This future-me spots a woman below. She's scanning the tubing frantically, and then she gives up on scanning; she's taking matters into her own hands and is heading into the tube, too. Future-me doesn't like this at all. I start pounding on the plastic. I shout, "Evelyn! No!" but my voice is trapped in the tube. She can't hear me at all. And in she goes.

The ruckus of children screaming is mostly muted by the plastic, though it's clear that some are squealing joyfully and others are crying their heads off. Inside the tubing, there are shouts and cries, too—sharper and more piercing.

I start crawling again, faster now. I shout, "Dotty! Dotty!" And then under my breath, I mutter, "Jesus H. Christ, Dotty." And it's clear that Dotty is the product of me and Evelyn Shriner, and she's the kind of jackass kid to get lost up in hamster Habitrails connected to a ceiling (as if this is a good idea for any child whatsoever at all). What kind of psycho Skinner protégé thought this shit up?

I'm obviously not enjoying myself. In fact, I look a little pale. Is it possible that instead of getting a good clear look at Evelyn Shriner—who's now up here crawling around somewhere, too—I'm going to have the opportunity of watching myself spray-barf? I have a very sensitive stomach. I sometimes get nauseated in elevators, to be honest. I haven't done any kind of amusement park ride more robust than a merry-go-round since I was seven.

I start to alternate now between shouting, "Dotty!" and shouting "Evelyn!" while padding along as quickly as I can.

And then I get shoved in the butt. I spin around. "Hey, watch it!"

There's some chubby, sweaty, cheeky kid face saying, "Mister, you're not supposed to be up here! There's a weight limit!"

"I lost my kid!" I shout back. "One day, when you're a father, you'll understand that you don't abandon your own child just because of a weight limit!"

But there's a sharp nervous twitchy glance that I give the tube all around me like—shit, I'm going to die in this tube and I'm going to take my whole family and all these kids with me.

I'm perspiring all down my shirt; even my pants are soaked.

But I persist and, God bless it, I kind of love me for pressing on. I mean, I have no real choice, but still I keep shouting, "Dotty! Evelyn! Dotty!"

And then just when I think things can't get much worse, the lights go out. Kids scream. Music blares. And there's some kind of laser light show—the kind they do at bowling alleys nowadays for no rational reason. What does bowling have to do with laser light shows? What does *anything* have go do with laser light shows, really?

And then there's a fucking fog machine that sprays—inside the tubes!—as if kids today aren't already, by and large, asthmatic!

I'm pissed about this. I know my pissed face and, holy shit, this is it, dear God.

And that's when I lose it.

I stop moving altogether; I lock it up like an angry camel. And I start screaming. Just a high-pitched hysterical scream.

And the screen goes blank because Dr. Chin Productions is, one assumes, trying to show this from inside of my very own point of view; and, with my eyes closed, I can see nothing.

But then there's this slap. It's a loud ringing snap, and it cuts through all the noise. My own cheek goes warm in an instant as if my cheek knows it's been slapped before the screen even pops back into focus.

Of course *focus* isn't the right word because there's pretty much only fog lit up by laser lights playing in rhythm to some screaming guitar rock-opera bullshit.

But I hear a voice and the voice is Evelyn.

"Quiet!" Evelyn says. "Godfrey, I've got Dotty. She's right here. We're fine."

"I'm so sorry," future-me says back to her. "I looked away for one second and she just shot right up. I'm a terrible father. Jesus, I'm the worst father."

"I love you, Godfrey Burkes. You're a fucking superhero. You've got a good soul, and this isn't your shining moment, but I will always love you. No matter what. In fact," she goes on because her heart must be pumping pretty hard with adrenaline right now, too, "I will always remember you in this stupid tube. I will always remember how you went after her. It's proof. You hear me? It's proof that no matter what we will endure."

It's a beautiful speech, especially from a woman holding on to a little kid—our Dotty—cursing pretty hard amid flashing lights in a foggy tube during a rock-opera crescendo.

And even though I can't see her face clearly and can only make out the squirming shape of our daughter, I see a glint on Evelyn's shirt. It's a brooch. Is it a pear brooch? Jesus, it's exactly like the one found in Wickham Purdy's safe deposit box.

"Now don't barf," she says. "And let's go home."

Evelyn Shriner. My wife. The mother of at least one of my off-spring. God, I love her.

I stare at the blank screen. My heart seems like it might burst from my chest, and I realize—with a feeling of elation—that I have access to Wickham Purdy's brooch, which Evelyn Shriner will wear in some future. It's like a small baton that could pass from my hands and somehow to hers, a baton that could be passed through time, through futures. It's a kind of lure. If I somehow put it out in the world and she takes it, what would that mean? Nothing or everything? This is about fate. I'm not baiting fate, but I am, yes, testing it a little, maybe shoving it in the chest, like I'm saying, *So, fate, you know futures? Prove it.* If there's something here, between Evelyn and me, and it's true love, and it's as serious as a heart attack, I can't give up on it.

I know I shouldn't do a damn thing with Wickham Purdy's brooch and I know that I will.

Evelyn
A COLLABORATION

Shaken by my last disastrous envisioning at Chin's and the encounter with Adrian, I've got new resolve. I go back through my old recordings, put in new endings, and upload them to the database. It takes a while, but I save them—one by one. I reunite lovers and families and push many great and tragic literary figures to better fates, and damn it, it feels good. I'm just now getting back to *The Great Gatsby*. Mr. Wilson comes over to Gatsby's with a gun but not to kill him. He invites Gatsby and Nick hunting in some East Egg woodlands. "The boar was almost too heavy for the three of us to lift," I fake-read. "Gatsby thought it better to just leave it." I flip a page, for effect mostly.

I'm getting into the rhythm of it when there's a knock at the door. I wonder if it's Binter coming to apologize for . . . what? Wanting me to be not-weird when that's just not realistic at all? Or it might be someone interested in postcards about Salisbury Cathedral or cable cars (both found in box 2).

Mr. Gupta says, "Evelyn, can I talk to you?"

I wonder if he's mad at me. I'm not volunteering on library time. I can prove this with time cards. "Sure," I say. A key in the lock again and there's Mr. Gupta, "Jesus, Evelyn," he whispers. "Why do you do this in here?"

I open my mouth to explain, but Gupta raises his hand then squeezes his forehead as if his head is about to explode and he's trying to mitigate the spray of his brains on the holdings within Special Collections. "Look," he says. "We got a call."

"From who?"

"A blind person."

"Oh."

"I know what you're doing." He lowers his voice. "And *Charlotte's Web*! That's for children, Evelyn Shriner! You can't revive Charlotte and think that sight-impaired children won't know the difference!"

"I assume they know," I tell him frankly. "In fact, sometimes I talk directly to the listener. I talk about sorrow in literature. Sometimes I talk about sorrow in life. Sometimes I whisper to them that it's just me in a room and that there's been enough sorrow. Every book has a past, a present, a future, and the future, by definition, is splintered, Mr. Gupta, so I'm being true to a larger order here, if you get what I'm saying."

"I do not get what you're saying. Not at all. What would Salinger think? My God."

"I never touched *Catcher in the Rye*. I feel like you should know that."

"This is literature, Evelyn. Literature is a language handed down from one generation to the next. Without that consistency, the world order breaks apart completely! You're fired."

"From my job?"

"You're fired from this volunteer effort."

"But can you fire a volunteer?"

"Would you prefer to resign?"

"I would."

"Then . . ."

"I resign, but I would like you to tell the board—"

"I'm not going to relay this to the board."

"Tell them that I believe in—"

"What *do* you believe in?"

I grip my copy of *The Great Gatsby* and my digital recording device. "I believe that nothing is set in stone. That each reader is an interpreter. Reading is collaborative. I was just . . . collaborating."

Gupta sighs.

"And I hope we're still on good terms otherwise," I say. He's my boss after all. I don't want to call him a father figure, but there's something there.

"You're on secret probation. I'm worried about you," he says, as if reading my mind.

"Don't worry about me!" I say, but I'm worried about me, to be honest. I feel shaky and loose in the knee joints. Why did I think I could change endings to great works of literature?

Gupta opens the door for me. There's Binter, sitting there at his desk, looking completely unwittingly good-looking. I want to say the right thing. I'm trying to be not-weird. "I'm sorry about the complaint you got," I tell Gupta in a formal tone. "I'm sure it was embarrassing. And I didn't mean to . . ."

"Well," Mr. Gupta says quietly. "It wasn't exactly a complaint."

"What was it then?"

"Technically, it was a fan."

"A fan?" I glance at Binter to see if he's overhearing this. He's staring at his computer, oblivious. "I have a fan?"

"Actually, a couple. One of them wanted to convey his gratitude. This person said, 'Tell her I like what she did with *Anna Karenina*.' Evidently, he'd listened to it many times and, well, found your version refreshing."

"I see," I say, trying to take the high road. "Well, I hope you told them that we aim to please."

"We don't aim to please," Gupta says. "We're a library of books. They are fixed in time and space by language." He opens the glass door to Special Collections.

I give a wave to Binter, saying, "Bye-bye, Binter!"

And as the glass door swings closed between us, I'm sure I hear him say, "Bye-bye, weirdo." Just like that, but that's fine by me. My weirdness got me more than one fan; I have *plural* fans.

Gupta peels off, duck-footing toward the front desk.

I get my coat from the mail room and then make my way out the main doors, down the large marble steps. I wish I could walk straight into Mr. Chin's waiting room. I close my eyes and try to imagine it. But all I see is Gatsby floating in a pool. Sometimes I wonder if the future is the future, and no matter what you do, you're bound to meet it. A fast car, a gunshot, a crumpled bike.

Inevitability. What if every fork in the road is leading to the same conclusion? This scares me most of all.

It hits me that Chin was right and wrong about me. I'm an obsessive, but I'm not obsessed with the promise of a man in my life or even love and family, which aren't antifeminist but noble, damn it! I'm obsessed with the future and the future only. I'm terrified of not knowing what will happen to me—and my heart, yes, my ever-calcifying, one-love-at-a-time heart. Is this a young-life crisis? Is there such a thing? I once knew step-by-step what would happen next and next and next. I went to high school. I graduated wearing a black gown. I went to college and then got my master's in library science. I graduated in another black gown. And now the rest of my life lies before me, stretching on and on.

I do not know how to get from here to there—I do not know where there is. If I knew that, I'd have a better chance of getting there. I am not a grown-up. I ride a bicycle and glue flowers on my rain boots. Last year, I hosted a cocktail party but realized I didn't know how to make any cocktails. We drank out of mugs and jelly jars. I have a job and a best friend who steals things like a juvenile delinquent. We talk about our crushes. What if life goes on this way—on and on. It can't. Once, I was an eleven-year-old who was terrified that I would never be able to give up playing with Barbies. I'd be a closet Barbie player my entire life—a dark hidden shame. Were there more like me? Was there a support group? And then one day I realized I hadn't played with them in ages. It was over. How will this part of my life be over?

And worse, why would I want it to ever end? So that I can become my parents and stop yearning?

I know that life makes demands on a person. It wants things that you don't want to give. Sometimes it asks for your firstborn. Sometimes it wants you to love a child you can't love. Sometimes it says just try to divide up your grief between two people. You still won't be able to bear it.

I need to know *something*. And Chin can provide a piece of the future. I will keep going back until I have that one fucking thing. Is that thing love? Love is how you build family, how you combat loneliness; maybe it's how you fill a deep unfillable hole. I can't stand the futures—millions of them—chaotically rolling out before me in all directions.

And this is how I know I'm not an obsessive anymore. I'm a junkie.

Godfrey
LEARNING TO ABSTRACT

Every day is fix-our-relationship day at the Madge and Godfrey estate, and I'm running late. I'm in Fontana's Super Mart and Pawn Shop. Mr. Fontana is turning the pear brooch around in his hands, holding it up to the fluorescent lights, as if that'll do anything. I shouldn't be here. I can't stop thinking of Evelyn. I want to hear that speech one day in a foggy tube of flashing lights. This is what I can't explain to anyone. Who would understand? "I'll give you five bucks if I sell it, and frankly, I doubt I'll sell it. It's pretty much crap."

"You can keep all the money, Mr. Fontana. All I want is for you to give this note to the person who buys it and not to share this information with Madge."

Fontana reads the note aloud. "We should have lunch. I think we've got a bright future together. Sincerely, Godfrey Burkes." And then he reads my phone number. He looks at me and smirks, his chins squeezing together tautly. "Is that supposed to be romantic or some kind of job application?"

Because I don't trust Fontana, I say, "A kind of job application. And can you display it prominently?"

Fontana scratches his chin. "That'll cost you."

"But I'm already giving you the entire proceeds!"

"This isn't about proceeds, is it?"

He's got me there. I give Fontana ten bucks and he promises to keep it out from under the glass, right near the cash register.

WE'RE ON DAY 4 in Dr. A. Plotnik's workbook, and Madge is so happy she doesn't even care that I'm late. As soon as I see her beaming face, I remember how happy Madge and I can be together. I decide, right then, that I will call off my brooch deal with Fontana as soon as humanly possible. No excuses. No rationalizing. I love Madge, and I love how she's throwing her energy into fixing us. I don't need to test fate. This is fate—me and Madge. Right, *right*? Dotty doesn't even really exist. She's a figment. What kind of a name for a little girl is Dotty anyway? I wouldn't ever name a child Dotty. And no one would actually let loose a fog machine in an elaborate Habitrail for human children.

I'm with Madge. I can do this.

Honestly, the envisioning experience can really warp your mind. I mean, I fell in love with a girl in rain boots while watching my future self locked up in prison and then fell more deeply in love with her because of just one beautiful heart-pumping speech? After a good night's sleep and with a happy Madge, things are a lot clearer.

The expression "serious as a heart attack" does come back to me from time to time—it does—like an unpredictable missile attack. But I keep going.

Madge marked this day on the calendar that hangs in the kitchen with a big heart. Inside the heart, Madge scribbled, *Abstract painting—4:30 p.m.* Every month on the calendar is a different kitten. February is a Maine coon wearing a scarf dotted with hearts and a matching beanie. I'm not going to lie, it's cute as fuck.

Today, our living room is half–art supply store. I feel like I'm at summer camp. I used to be a counselor at summer camps. That's where I first figured out I'd like to teach kids, before I tamped that down deep. Today Madge is head counselor. She's going to teach us how the abstractness of abstract art is going to save our relationship. Out of sheer confidence and optimism, Madge invited Bart and Amy over after for cheese and finger foods, things that you would find on the decks of yachts, things that don't actually equate to meals.

"So it's not a dinner party?" I ask Madge. It's hard to hear her. She has her computer plugged into the stereo speakers, almost full blast. I'm not familiar with the band; I've never heard these songs before. See, this is how a relationship can be made new—little things.

"No, just hors d'oeuvres." She looks me up and down, lingering on the down, and frowns. "No jeans," she tells me.

For just a split second, I want to say, *So we're having a dinner party but with no dinner. And I have to dress up for this dinnerless dinner party where our only guests are just Bart and Amy?* But I don't. I just go and change because saying those things would be petty. Pettiness is one of the traits to avoid, as listed in Dr. A. Plotnik's "Guide to Romantic Success."

I put on khakis and walk back to the living room.

Madge says, "Sit down on the rug." It's the old Burt Reynolds–inspired shag, which sometimes makes me feel slightly less masculine because I'm just not that furred.

Somehow the music gets louder when I'm on the floor. And I really don't like the music. I guess hot air rises, but shitty beats lower themselves, probably heading for the graves they know they're destined for. The devil is still probably listening to Creed.

Do I say any of this? No, I do not. Self-restraint is listed as a positive quality to have in Dr. A. Plotnik's "Guide to Romantic Success."

Madge sits across from me, Dr. A. Plotnik's workbook in her lap. Between us, there are two canvases, paintbrushes, paint. While Madge flips through the workbook, I wonder how we'll afford to eat next week.

I say, "Who is this?" I point to the air, then my ears.

"Oh," she says, smiling. "They're called the Babymakers. They're a local band."

"Oh, local." Baltimore's local scene has its highlights. This isn't one of them.

"They've got a gig at Club Q coming up," she says. "I think we should go."

We both sit on the floor and listen for a minute. Most likely this is a self-produced EP. The Babymakers haven't recorded more than four songs, but Madge has them on a continuous loop. But why?

"Do you like it?" Madge wants to know.

"'You are only aware of love when your lips are drenched in sun,'" I say, quoting the song that's playing right now. "It's just that same line for like four minutes straight."

"Well, what do you think he's saying?"

"That she really gets off on being outside?"

"Oh, Godfrey." Madge actually puts her hand against her chest. "They say so much in such a simple way. It's heartbreaking."

"It sounds like it was made in a bedroom."

"It was," she says. "Adrian said it was all made on his MacBook. An entire song done on one computer, all made next to a bed and dresser. Can you believe it? Those aren't even real drums. The drummer got mono or something."

Listening to the songs, I want to say, *Yes, yes, I can absolutely believe it*. Then I think a little longer. Adrian, I don't know an Adrian.

"Who's Adrian?" I say.

"The lead guitarist and backup singer." Madge's face says, *Obviously. Keep up, dumbass. You shouldn't fail a take-home test.*

"You know his name?"

"Yeah," she says a little quieter. If I weren't sitting so close to her, I wouldn't have heard her. Then Madge straightens up like something climbed up her spine. I think of a wooden roller coaster. "He's the one who gave me the demo, along with this." She reaches across the living room floor for her purse and pulls out a flyer. She hands it to me.

It's a cheap cutout, something mass-produced in a hurry, with THE BABYMAKERS written in a bold, all-capped font on the top. Underneath the band name: GET YOUR ASS OFF THE SOFA AND LIVE A LITTLE. Am I jealous? It's not like me. Maybe it's because I just envisioned my future with four women from my past and a stranger I'm afraid I fell in love with. *See how these little secrets erode trust*, I tell myself. *See?*

"I don't really know him," she says, and then she holds up a book. *Abstraction: The Past, Present, and Future of Abstract Art.*

"Hey, hey!" I say. "That's cheating."

The catch about this Dr. A. Plotnik assignment is that we're supposed to make an abstract painting "of our own relationship." I don't even know what abstract painting is, but Madge urges me to relax. "It can be whatever we want it to be."

I bet the book told her that.

"It's just research," she tells me. "To save . . . whatever this is."

"You mean, to save our engagement?"

Madge begins to read from the workbook. "'Be in the same room but barely.'" She looks at me. "She must mean that we're together but aware of our selfhoods most of all." I've never been clear on Madge's use of the term *selfhood,* so I just nod.

"'Take exactly one hour.'" Next to her is an egg timer. "Okay," she says, "it's all ready to go. Any questions before we start?"

"Which color is that?" I say, pointing to one of the darker colors in the middle of the paint pile between us.

Madge barely has to look at it. "After Midnight Blue."

"So, a light black?"

"It's a blue." A sigh that sounds like frost. "If you were listening. After Midnight Blue."

I nod. "So the lighter blue is *Before* Midnight Blue?"

"No," Madge says, "it's just blue." She grabs my hand. "So, we're going to do this?" Madge's eyes look like Christmas morning.

"Yes."

Madge sets the egg timer. "The timer's on. Pick your corner."

WHEN THE EGG TIMER goes off, I'm grateful—an hour is a long time to try to be abstract. I set down my paintbrush and look up from my canvas.

"Don't show me! Don't show me!" Madge cries.

She's already out of her corner, walking back toward the center of the living room. If the room were larger, she'd be skipping. She loves this. And I love that she loves this. And I wish that I loved this.

I follow her lead, getting out of my corner and walking back to the center of the living room. I sit back down across from her. Our canvases are facing away from each other.

"Okay," Madge says. "Who first?"

I can tell Madge wants to go first. She's lightly drumming her fingers against the back of her canvas. "Why don't you?" I say. I'd do anything to score some points right now.

Madge's painting is intricate. There are so many lines and small dots of color that I wonder if I should be picking out Waldo. Is this one of those paintings that only make sense when you stand very far away or if you relax your eyes so you can see the lady or the witch?

I back up a little. That's when I see the penis. My penis, I'm guessing. And my penis doesn't look very happy—or robust. I want to tell Madge how buff I look in prison—*that* Godfrey Burkes would have been drawn with a robust penis, believe you me. But I can't tell her this because I'd have to explain why I saw myself in prison.

"Well?" Madge says.

I don't know how long I've been staring at the painting.

"This is where you say something," she says. "The workbook says that first impressions are the most important. Godfrey, what's the first thing you see, feel?"

I clear my throat. "You didn't make my penis very life-sized." I pause. "Or maybe I've been looking in the wrong mirrors."

"What are you talking about?" Madge is doing her best to keep a

neutral facial expression, but her lips are trying not to do something—
I'm just not sure what the *not* is.

"Underneath the After Midnight Blue," I say, pointing to the center of the painting, at a long strip so blue it's black. Madge follows my finger as it goes underneath the dark strip, hovering right over a flesh-toned cock.

Madge's brow furrows, her lips purse. I keep my finger there. She knows I'm right, but I won't win this. I'm surprised I'm even willing to try.

"You have to see it," I say. "You painted it."

"Oh, Godfrey," Madge says. She's still looking at her painting. She finally lifts her head up. "I really hoped for more from you today."

"What?" I'm trying not to laugh, but my self-control is shaky. "It's a cock. I mean, not an impressive cock, but it's a cock!"

"Language," Madge says in a tight whisper.

"I'm sorry," I say, lowering my voice, too, even though nobody else is in the apartment, even though that music is still playing on a continuous fucking loop, and even though both of us curse freely in front of each other.

Madge sets her painting down. "It's hopeless," she says.

"What is?"

"Us."

"But I haven't shown you mine yet," I say, trying to backtrack. Something can be saved. Something can always be saved.

"You were barely doing anything over there. I saw you." Madge sighs. "I bet it's two stick figures holding hands, maybe a quarter of a sun in the upper-right-hand corner of the canvas."

My face goes red. How the fuck did she know that? Still, I say, "That's not even close to being true."

The room is stale. Madge is about to lose her shit. "This is fuck-ing typical," she says.

"I don't know what you're talking about," I say.

"You're so . . ."

"Say it." Now I'm getting worried. I don't ever remember seeing Madge like this.

"You're so like you!" She's breathing through her mouth because she can't fit enough air through her nose right now. "You're always so . . ." And then she just stops. Her arms don't move. She looks like a marionette, hanging from invisible strings. "You just have no idea how to be in a relationship!"

"That seems really unfair."

"Do I have to rehash old Godfrey relationships to make it clear? Wasn't your last relationship a short-lived romance with a woman who lived in a 'very confusing' part of town? And on your third date, you got lost while on your way to pick her up, and because you were too embarrassed to admit it, you never showed up."

"In my defense—"

"She never called, and neither did you. Was that going to be your defense?"

It kind of was. This is not a story I told Madge, by the way. It's a story I told Bart, in confidence. But I don't mention this because Madge's face has gone all stony, and she's stopped talking.

"Madge," I say. That fucking music. That same line—"You are only aware of love when your lips are drenched in sun"—over and over again for four minutes. "Madge, say something."

"What if I'm only drawn to you genetically," Madge says.

Is she breaking up with me? "Only genetically?" I say. "What else is there?"

"Everything."

"I don't like the sound of that."

"You know what you are?" Madge says, her voice low and rough with anger. "You're an overrepresented demographic. The neurotic, needy white male demographic."

"And yet I still don't think anyone's quite represented *me*—you know, accurately and precisely—in art or literature or film."

"That's because of the blur of so many representations of your demographic."

"The blur might be the best I can hope for," I say. And suddenly I can feel it—like a downy coat on my skin—the fuzzy outline of my soul.

"You," she says, still not moving. "You're always so like you."

"And this is bad?" I want to say, *And this is why you're not wearing the ring?* I want to tell her that doesn't make any sense. I am obviously always like me, but her face is so red and we've dated for so long that I've learned when it's best to just shut up. "I'm getting a drink," I say to Madge's vicinity. I can't look directly at her or I might break something and then break something else. This might then go on forever.

I leave Madge in the living room and walk into the kitchen. I take a Heineken out of the fridge before three heavy consecutive knocks on the door.

I open the beer bottle with a bottle opener attached to my keys as I head over to open the door, but Madge stops me.

"I ironed you a white oxford button-down. It's hanging in the closet." She's dressing me in parts. And I can tell she has more to say, but then there are more knocks on the door. "Hurry."

WHEN I RETURN FROM the bedroom, wearing the starchy white oxford, I find Bart and Amy settled onto our couch. I head for the kitchen and find Madge struggling with a bottle of champagne. I lean over and whisper into Madge's ear, "Boat shoes. In the winter. In Baltimore." I take a sip of my beer. I can't *believe* my best friend is wearing boat shoes! "He'd probably wear them to visit me in prison. Does he know how stupid he looks?"

"What are you talking about?"

I finish my beer. I set the beer down on the kitchen counter and run my hands down the front of my white oxford. "It's very crisp," I say, hoping to change the subject. "You did a great job with the iron, thank you." *Complimentary* is one of the positive traits in Dr. A. Plotnik's book on romantic success. I'm still trying, if for no other reason than I don't want to fail in front of the futuristically successful Bart and Amy.

"The boat shoes are simply preparation," Madge says, louder than necessary. "Some people like to plan ahead." Does she mean that the shoes are part of a larger plan for Bart to buy a boat? She picks up the cheese tray we can't afford and crackers we probably can't afford either. "You know, when there's something worth planning ahead for." And with that, she walks out of the kitchen.

I open the fridge and take out another beer. Bart and Amy brought the champagne, but the champagne can suck it. I open my beer in the kitchen. I'm buying as much time alone as I can. It's going to be a long night. Who the fuck would name their band the Babymakers? Who the fuck would name their kid Adrian? Why am I still thinking about him? Luckily, Madge turned the music off when Bart and Amy got here. The flyer for the Babymakers is rolled up next to my empty Heineken bottle. I pick it back up and stare at it.

I take another sip of beer and count to one hundred. I've heard this helps—the counting, not the drinking, though I've heard that helps, too, just for different reasons. I'd check my pulse, but I can never find that shit. I'd be a terrible doctor. *This one's dead, too,* I'd tell the nurse. *I just don't feel anything happening. Must be an epidemic or the zombie apocalypse.* Would the nurse call the CDC or would I?

I'd stay in the kitchen the entire night if I could, but I know with every minute, Madge is getting angrier: I'm being a bad host.

I chug my beer, get another, and walk into the living room.

Bart and Amy are still sitting on the couch; Madge is across from them in a chair.

Bart stands up when I walk into the room. He puts a hand on my shoulder like we just finished a business transaction. "It's good to see you, friend," he says.

Bart looks even more ridiculous up close. He's wearing a navy blue blazer, something rumpled around his neck. And the boat shoes. In the winter. In Baltimore.

"Is that an ascot?" I ask.

Bart lightly massages his neck. "Amy picked it out." He looks over at Amy and smiles. Amy smiles back. "She says it makes me look older."

"Soon, you're going to want to look younger," I say.

Amy ignores my comment. "It's silk, like a cloud."

I nod, take another swig. Bart sits back down on the couch.

Madge looks at me, appalled. "You didn't offer our guests a beer?"

"It's all right," Bart says. "We brought champagne."

Amy nods.

Four champagne flutes are lined up next to the bottle of champagne in an iced bucket on the coffee table. I wonder when we got champagne flutes. Did Madge buy them for tonight?

"We should get this thing open," Bart says. He leans forward and pulls the champagne bottle out of the bucket of ice.

"Be careful with the cork," Amy says. "We all need our eyes."

Everyone but me laughs.

My mind wanders to Evelyn Shriner. I wonder if she's the champagne type, if her rain boots are the champagne type, if she would look that lovely visiting me in jail.

Madge is staring at me. Amy is staring at me, too. Why? Because I'm just quiet? It always seems to be the quiet things that make people stare. I didn't hear the bottle pop, or Bart fill up all four flutes with champagne, but they're raising glasses.

"A toast to the bright days ahead!" Bart says, like he's practicing driving his new off-white Mercedes, pretending to take a call at a red light just as the war vet is hobbling toward his window, shaking a change jar made out of a used Wendy's cup, a sign hanging around his neck that says HUNGRY—just HUNGRY, because he was too hungry to write more than that. Is there some doomed future where I'm that guy with the sign?

"Yes!" Amy says, holding her champagne flute up. "Bright days!"

I wonder how many times they practiced this before they came over.

"Lovely," Madge says. She looks at me. "Are you going to put down that beer, Godfrey?"

"No," I tell her. "So, what else are we going to toast to?"

"I don't know," Madge says. "Why don't you give a toast, Godfrey?"

I smile at everyone. "Would love to."

The four of us form a circle. I grab one of the glasses. We raise our champagne flutes.

"To Bart and Amy," I say, "our best friends and future Republicans."

They glance around nervously, but we all clink our glasses. Everyone is about to take a sip when I stop them.

"Wait!" I say. "I have more."

"Godfrey, please," Madge says.

I ignore her. "To possibilities," I say. "To the lack of understanding through understanding too much."

"Let's drink," Bart says, his glass of champagne still hanging in the air.

"Yes," Amy says. "We wouldn't want the champagne to get warm." She laughs nervously.

Madge doesn't say anything. She's still staring at me.

But I don't drink. Not yet. I'm not done. This is that fuck-it moment and I've already lost. Why not go out big?

"What about in fifty-one years?" I tell them. "What if there's a hurricane, and it sinks your fucking yacht?" I point at Bart. "What if you can't get your cock to go up anymore at year twenty, but you didn't know that because all you got was one glimpse, just an ounce of a forever? An ounce can seem so big when you're looking at a screen in an ex–Chinese restaurant, but in reality, it's still just a fucking ounce." I take a breath. Bart is staring at me, sharing the same look as Madge. Amy is drinking her champagne very quickly. "What if Amy catches you with a nineteen-year-old hostess at the country club you're members at? What if she forgives you and stays with you because of the money, because of the grandchildren and only slightly fucked-up children who didn't know what to do with all that money, so it was just line after line after line of coke off their framed Harvard diplomas with their American Express Black cards?" I turn to Amy. I only need a second to catch my breath. I haven't felt this good all day. "What if your ass won't stop growing? What if the envisioning missed Bart's heart attack by one day?" I turn to Madge. "What if your ass won't stop growing? Or my ass or Bart's ass? I look really good in a prison jumpsuit. Did you know that? Do you see me bragging on and on about that? No you don't!" I point at Bart. "What if at year fifty-one, the skies open up and Jesus is like, 'It's time. You're so boring I'm tired of yawning,' and you're like, 'Holy shit, I only stayed with her because my insurance has a good copay, so on a whim I saw this weird doctor.' What if that's your last thought? What if the money and the yacht that may or may not sink are the only things that keep your marriage wet?"

Everyone is staring at me. Madge's face is red. Bart and Amy's mouths are open so wide, birds could nest in them. I down the champagne in one gulp. I set my beer down on the table.

I look at Madge. Her face is screwed up and she's about to say something—but she's got so much to say she doesn't know where to start.

Amy and Bart are staring at the floor, or maybe Bart is staring at his boat shoes. I bet the floor is wondering why it's getting so much attention. I imagine the floor doesn't want the attention—it just wants to be a fucking floor.

"You shouldn't have told Madge about that girlfriend I broke up with because I got lost, Bart! You shouldn't have done that!" I grab my coat. "I need to get some more beer," I say as I open the door and walk out of the apartment, run down the stairs and out the door.

I'm in trouble. I'm in deep. Things are really bad and yet I feel good. I feel really good. It's cold and I don't have a hat or mittens. I'm just loose in the world.

I head over to Fontana's. I check my watch—I have about twenty minutes till they close, which is probably just enough time for Amy to console Madge in the bedroom while Bart finishes the cheese in his goddamn boat shoes. I'll grab a six-pack and some gum; it's impossible to have too much gum. Maybe for once I'll be a winner. I'll rush back to Madge waving my receipt and say, "Look at what your fiancé got you, 20 percent off your next purchase of Gouda fucking cheese."

Does Fontana's even carry Gouda cheese? It wouldn't matter, I'd say it anyway. I'll be a winner, so I can say whatever the fuck I want.

And then I realize I left my wallet in the apartment. I can see it on the edge of the kitchen counter—next to my cell phone and keys, also left behind—but I go through all my pockets anyway. I've got a ten-dollar bill and three singles that have been balled up like an empty gum wrapper.

How could I forget my goddamn wallet and phone—*again*? There is something seriously wrong with me and the loss of personal items is an iceberg tip. I imagine myself drunk and lost and finally packed under twenty feet of snow; one by one my fingers turning blue, unable to call anyone. And when they finally find me, no one will know who I am.

Fuck it. I breathe in the cold. Everyone I talk to is in the apartment anyway, and they all suck right now.

I look back at the apartment and then up and down the street. I am trying to figure out what exactly went wrong. Then I realize: maybe Madge has never been good at being a person. Maybe she's someone else's version of a great person. Maybe it's not so much that the person she believed I could become was deep inside of me and only needed to be drawn out. Maybe she never wanted a better me, but a different me—for me to be someone I'm not.

The sidewalks are sludgy. Tonight is a good night for rain boots. I look down the street and zip up my jacket. I could go back, beg forgiveness, but I don't. Keep going, I tell myself.

IT'S LATE ENOUGH THAT I know I'll be the only patron in Fontana's before I even walk through the front doors. And I am. And I'm drunk. And I'm going to get drunker. There is champagne and beer in me. If the two fought, which one would win? I would say champagne because it costs more, but the rich don't work harder. That's bullshit.

It's twelve minutes to nine. Fontana's closes at nine. My life at twelve minutes to nine: thirteen crumpled dollars in my pocket, an angry not-really-fiancée at home, pissed-off friends, and I'm freezing as fuck. I make a beeline for the beer.

Behind the cooler doors there aren't many choices—the normal domestics, the normal imports, the forties I haven't touched since sophomore year of college when I went to a party and a Colt 45 was duct-taped to each hand, and I wasn't allowed use the bathroom until I finished both—I want them all.

Thirteen dollars cannot buy them all.

I do some slow math in my head before walking away from the rows of beer. I need to be smart with my money. I need liquor.

I scan the shelf of spirits. Vodka, no. Rum, God no—never again after that night. Whiskey. Yes. It's cold out, and whiskey is just really fucking good anyway. I'll count that as a double win. My eyes keep going until they fall on a bottle of Jack Daniel's. Too rich for my blood. Then I see it: On the bottom shelf, a fifth of Evan Williams. And the price below it: a smooth $11.99. There's only one left. I grab it, cradle it like a firstborn, and walk to the checkout. As I set the whiskey on the counter, my brain says, *Where's the pear-shaped brooch?* It's not on the counter. I look up expecting Mr. Fontana, but it's Mrs. Fontana.

"This is it?" Mrs. Fontana says.

"No," I say. "I paid Fontana ten bucks to keep the pear brooch out where everyone could see it. So where is it?"

She glares at me, but this time I hold her gaze. Finally she pulls a cell phone out of her pants pocket and hits a speed-dial number.

I wait.

She says, "That little shit who wears the mittens is here." The little shit who wears mittens? I don't care for that at all. She pauses, listening. "Yeah, he says he paid to have some brooch on display. That right?"

Mrs. Fontana raises her eyebrows. "What? When?" She's pissed. She looks up at the surveillance camera. "How much are we out?" She waves her hands in the air. "I'll tell him. He's here right now, drunk off his ass, staring at me." She hangs up.

"What happened?" I ask.

"Stolen."

"What?"

"Somebody stole it."

Now I look up at the cameras. "Did you get 'em on tape? I have to see who did it."

"Like I'm going to stare at all that footage to see if something that we didn't lose any money on got stolen." Mrs. Fontana scares me. I once heard her tell a vendor that she'd gouge his eyes out, and I kind of believed her.

I feel sick about the brooch. Gone. Some fucker stole it. Evelyn Shriner will never get my message. "This all you getting or what?" Mrs. Fontana says.

I nod hesitantly.

Mrs. Fontana rings me up. She hands me the change, then, glancing at the receipt, she says, "You're a winner?" She's surprised. I don't blame her. I'm surprised, too. In fact, I don't believe her until the receipt is between my fingers, the black ink already too dry to smear. I stare at the words: *You're a winner.* I run my thumb over them.

"I'm a winner," I say.

"Twenty percent off your next food purchase," she says flatly.

I'm a winner. This means something. This strip of cheap paper—a transaction for a fifth of whiskey—is giving me more hope than Madge has in the last month. That's some kind of fucked up.

I look past Mrs. Fontana. What would a winner do in this situation? I could go back to the party and apologize for the toast, for the abstract art. *I'm not an artist,* I could tell Madge. *I am just a collector of lost goods.* And I could apologize to Bart and Amy. I'm an ass; they should expect this by now. Besides, they're just boat shoes. Thousands of people wear them, and now someone I know wears them, too. It happens.

Mrs. Fontana puts the Evan Williams in a small brown paper bag and hands it to me.

I don't want to go back. I want to go forward.

Someone stole the fucking pear-shaped brooch and now no one will deliver my message. I'll have to deliver it myself.

I turn to walk out of the place but then I see a pay phone. Those still exist? It's been here all along? This might be the last living pay phone in Baltimore. And under the pay phone, a phone book. How many times have I been in Fontana's and I have never seen the pay phone? They say you won't notice a piece of art on the wall until you're ready to, and maybe it's the same for pay phones.

I walk up to the pay phone and for a minute I forget how to use a pay phone. How long has it been, years? The phone book's locked to the pay phone, like phone books are in demand. I imagine Mr. Fontana waking up in the middle of the night in cold sweats, throwing on his shoes and driving to the store to check on the phone book.

I flip through the book. The thin pages stick together, and I have to lick my finger to find S. I get to P and then somehow I'm at U. This goes on for about two minutes. I check the time. Fontana's closes in three minutes. Finally, I find the S's. I scan through the pages with my finger. My finger stops.

And she's listed.

I didn't expect to find her, but of course I should have. I'm a fucking winner, and this is what happens to winners. I have a receipt in my pocket to prove it. I look at her phone number and then remember the change Mrs. Fontana gave me. Eighteen cents won't pay for a call.

I look back toward the cash register. Mrs. Fontana is reading an issue of *Soap Opera Digest*. Her head is down. It's now or never.

I check the time: two minutes until close.

I can't decide if I should fake a cough or sneeze, so what ends up coming out is a hybrid. But there's enough noise that I'm pretty certain Mrs. Fontana doesn't hear me rip out the phone book page with Evelyn's address printed on it. In moments, the page is folded and in my pocket, nestled with the eighteen cents.

I'm out the door.

Evelyn
THE SMELL OF HAPPY

Dot and I are getting drunk on my California king. We were waiting for the glue gun to get hot so we could glue plastic flowers to the new rain boots, which Dot says she paid for with her own money; I'm proud of her. But, fact is, we're too drunk for glue-gunning and so we decide to concentrate on the matter at hand. We've got a mission. This is a purposeful drunk we've got in progress.

Dot's finished her second glass of wine and is pouring her third, topping mine off, too. "Look, we're going to set this shit straight," she says.

"Right. And how do we do that?"

"You think of everything that's wrong, one by one, and as you think of it, you sprinkle-tap your forehead and say, 'It's all bullshit. It's all bullshit. It's all bullshit.'"

"Hmmm." I feel like my bed is a giant ship deck and we're at sea.

My bed is so big it takes up 90 percent of the room. My dresser lives in the closet. My record player lives on the bed. It's playing some Pixies; we've picked through my Modest Mouse, Silver Jews, the National, and Elliott Smith. I look at the poster of Bruce Springsteen's ass—the album cover for *Born in the U.S.A.;* it was something my sister had in her bedroom when she died. I found it in a box marked MEG in my parents' attic. "And sprinkle-tapping your forehead works?" I ask.

"It's how I got over my mother voting for George W. Bush twice. Twice! And middle-school gym class. It's how I combat my loathing of Christmas-themed sweaters and dogs in cute outfits and guys who drive Hummers. It's how I put one foot in front of the other, Ev. For real."

"My life is in your hands."

"What's first?"

"I got fired from a volunteer job," I say.

"You did?"

"Reading to the blind."

"How?"

"I made up alternate endings."

"You can't do that. It's literature."

"Are you here to judge me or to help me move on?"

"Okay. Say it out loud and tap your forehead."

I tap my forehead. "It's all bullshit. It's all bullshit. It's all bullshit."

"See?" Dot says.

Weirdly, I feel a little better. It could be that I'm getting drunker. But I want to go again. "I broke up with Adrian and am now afraid that I will die in this apartment alone, mauled by bears."

"I don't think there's a real bear threat in the city."

"Is this practice reserved for rational problems only?"

"Sorry."

"And I'm concerned about the calcification of my heart. I mean, what if my past loves, including Adrian, have each effectively toughened a part of my heart, and what if I've got three more bad relationships to go before it's completely hardened? What if it's worse than that and there's only one more relationship until it's just a chunk of char or ice?"

"I have more confidence in your heart than you do," Dot says, taking a swig. "Tap it out."

I tap my forehead and say, "It's all bullshit. It's all bullshit. It's all bullshit."

"What else?"

"I had an insane envisioning session that scared the hell out of me. And Adam Greenberg was in it. He was wielding a gun."

She looks at me askew. "Why was Adam Greenberg in it?"

"I might have punched his name in—it was a moment of panic."

"Should I be jealous?"

"I'm not going to steal Adam Greenberg from you. Don't worry. But I want to tell you this: that man is crazy about you. I know you don't believe in this stuff, but he's kind of a badass when he's not wearing a sweater vest."

"Okay," Dot says. "I trust you. Tap it out."

"Oh, and Chin almost blacklisted me." I tap my forehead. "It's all bullshit. It's all bullshit. It's all bullshit."

"What about you?" I ask Dot.

"What about me?"

"Don't you have something to tap out?"

"I'm fine."

"Really?"

"My mother is staying with me for twelve days. So I'm like prepping for a PTSD situation."

"Tap it out."

"I have. I do. It's a regimen."

It's quiet a moment. "What if it's not all bullshit?" I say.

"Some stuff is bullshit and some stuff isn't."

"How can you tell the difference?" I ask.

"One wrecks your heart and doesn't go away, even if you do a hundred 'It's all bullshits.'"

I think of Godfrey Burkes, declaring his love for me by the pool.

"Do you think Greenberg really gets all those books for his mother? Sometimes I think she's just a cover, and he reads them himself," I say, changing the subject.

"I like him either way."

"Eventually Adam will have to pick something to read all by himself," I say. "You don't just stop reading because Oprah did."

"Tell me what happened in the session," she says.

And so I do, as best I can.

"I was really in jail?" she asks somberly.

I open the next bottle of merlot, a five-dollar one we found on sale. We go cheaper and cheaper as the night progresses—finally ending on the worst tasting since we've basically lost taste by that point. I refill our glasses. "Adam Greenberg was not happy about it."

"I bet he was cute in his rage."

"So dreamy in that V-neck undershirt," I say, "waving that gun."

"He was fighting for my honor." She brings a hand to her chest. "Unlike someone I know."

"Sorry, I was busy sleeping next to Mark Standing. I'm just a simple girl with priorities." I lower my voice and make it sound smoky. "'I require three things in a man: he must be handsome, ruthless, and stupid.'"

"It's weird that I know your Dorothy Parker voice," Dot says, and then she sits upright. "I almost forgot!"

"What?"

"I got you a gift!" She crawls off the bed awkwardly, then down onto the floor where her coat is. She digs through a pocket. She climbs back up on the bed and holds out two fists. "Eenie meenie."

I close my eyes. "Eenie, meenie, minie, moe. Catch a tiger by the toe. If he hollers, let him go. Eenie, meenie, minie, moe. And my mother said—"

"Here!" Dot says, opening one of her fists.

And there sits a little pin with a pear on it. I screw up my face and give her a look. "Did you pay for this?"

"Yes, kind of."

"Yes and kind of are different answers."

"I was caught in a smarmy overly earnest look-at-me I-might-be-important-one-day part of town at this supermarket/pawn shop, and I overpaid for about seven items, which added up approximately to the price of said brooch."

"Give it back." I push the brooch at her.

"I can't," she says.

"Why not?"

"Because it's yours. I mean, I rescued it from that completely bullshitty part of town, and I mean, who else would wear this pear brooch? Plus, it was on display like *Please for the love of God take me!*"

"I love the pear brooch, okay? I love it in all of its pearness and broochiness. But you have to give it back."

Dot shrugs. "I'm just going to reverse steal it." This means she's going to give it to me without me knowing.

I want to give Dot something in return, but I've got nothing so I decide to confess a nicety. "Sometimes I tell your mother that you're like a sister to me," I say. "Because I think I want your mother to think of me as a daughter."

"Mrs. Fuoco?" she says. "Evelyn, take her. I swear to God, she's yours." And then Dot mumbles something under her breath.

"What was that?"

"You heard me."

"No, I didn't."

"You're better than a sister, Evelyn, because you're like a sister I got to choose. You were not thrust upon me by birth, like, you know, feudalism."

This makes me very happy. "One day I'm going to hug you, Dot Fuoco. I am. You have been warned."

She shakes her head. "Let's not get carried away."

"Do you think there's a hole in me that can't ever be filled?" I ask.

She thinks about this a moment. "I think our souls are always being hole-punched, like old train tickets. In the end, we're all perforated. If we were buckets, we wouldn't hold water."

"Like that song about the hole in the bucket, dear Liza, dear Liza."

"Exactly."

That's when we hear a tap on the window. We both turn around and look at the window. It sounded like a big bug flew into the panel, but there aren't any bugs in Baltimore in February.

Then another tap.

"Did you hear something?" Dot says.

"I think so."

Dot sets her glass of wine on the floor and log-rolls out of bed. She moves to the window, spreading apart the blinds with two fingers. "You're not going to believe this shit," she says.

"What?" I say.

"Come look for yourself," she says.

I sigh, log-roll out of bed, and walk to the window.

Dot still has part of the blinds spread apart. "Look."

"What am I looking for?" I say. "It's all just darkness."

"To the left," Dot whispers, "then down just a bit—guy throwing pebbles at your window, all Romeo and shit?"

I want to tell her there's no need to whisper. But then I see him. Godfrey Burkes.

"Holy shit," I say. I step back from the window. "Holy shit, holy shit."

"You just said that."

I look at Dot. "But holy shit."

"Do you know who that is?"

"Godfrey Burkes, that son of a bitch."

"And to think Mark Standing shot him and he's back already."

"I am not understanding what is happening right now." Now I'm the one whispering. "I can't believe he found me."

"I'm sure it wasn't that hard. You know, with the Internet and everything."

I'm smiling, but I know I shouldn't be smiling. "This is real, right? This window isn't a video screen?"

"We're not at Dr. Chin's."

"Godfrey Burkes."

We both turn back to the window. Dot parts the blinds again, and we peer through it. "Look at him shake," she says. "It's got to be, what, fifteen with the windchill?"

"Maybe less. He's not even wearing a hat."

Dot grabs the cord and gives it a tug. The blinds shoot up.

"What are you doing? He's going to see us," I say.

She looks at me, genuinely confused. "Isn't that the point? Why else would he be standing outside *your* window throwing stuff."

Dot's right, obviously. She turns back to the window and slides it open, letting February into my bedroom.

I take the comforter off the bed and wrap it around myself.

The weather doesn't seem to faze Dot.

"You're creepy," she calls down to Godfrey.

I lean against the wall out of sight.

"Who are you?" Godfrey says back.

"I'm Dot."

"Oh," he says, like that makes perfect sense. He shuffles his feet a bit while he looks at his hands before looking back up at the window. He had to be the cutest fucking kid in the world. "Dot? Dot," he says. "I'm sorry you end up in jail and all that. I'm sure you're not guilty."

Dot puts her head back inside my bedroom and looks at me. "Does everyone know?"

"I keep saying you need to stop stealing shit."

Dot ignores me and sticks her head back out the window.

"I'm glad you opened the window when you did," Godfrey says. "That was my last pebble."

"Where are your gloves and hat?"

"In my apartment."

"You didn't think this through very well."

Godfrey considers this for a moment. "My heart was beating very fast at the time."

Dot looks at me and smiles before turning her head back toward Godfrey. "Evelyn is scared to talk to you because she wants to make babies with you."

"Dot!" I scream, shooting up in front of the window.

"Evelyn!" Godfrey shouts.

I shout down to him. "Who are you, just showing up here like this, Godfrey Burkes!"

"And you, Evelyn Shriner, you're always ready for rain, Evelyn Shriner! I really like saying your name, Evelyn Shriner! I would like to chew gum with you, Evelyn Shriner," Godfrey calls wildly.

"I can't get away from you, Godfrey Burkes. You're everywhere." I don't wait for a response. I stick my head back inside the apartment. I should still be cold, but I feel like I'm running a fever. I take off the comforter and toss it back onto the bed. I look over to where Dot was standing, but she's not there anymore.

I call her name.

Nothing.

"Dot?" A little louder this time.

"In here." Her voice is coming from the living room.

I walk into the living room. I'm on fire. "I might be running a fever," I tell her.

Dot's putting on her boots. I'm paying too much attention to things I shouldn't be paying attention to: how meticulous Dot dresses herself—she ties the left boot, then the right one. Then it's the ticking of the wall clock hanging over the couch, the blinking of the smoke detector.

Dot has her coat on. She zips it up.

"Where are you going?" I say, but I already know. I'd be doing the same thing if it were Adam Greenberg outside of Dot's place.

"You'll thank me," she says, opening the front door. She turns to me. "You don't need to check my pockets this time. I didn't steal anything." She grins.

Dot is halfway down the hallway when she turns back around. "Let the poor boy in. He's going to freeze himself dead. Then he'll be dead for real, and who will die in your envisioning sessions?"

"You, obviously," I call down the hall, but Dot has already turned the corner. I whisper, "'Constant use had not worn ragged the fabric of their friendship.'" Dorothy Parker again. But it's even better than that. We're like sisters, nonfeudalism sisters. We're capitalistic, democratic sisters.

And then I realize I'm alone with a freezing Godfrey Burkes outside my window.

I walk back to the open bedroom window. When I get there, Godfrey is still in the same spot he was before.

"Someone stole my message. I had a message to give you," he calls. "It was about having lunch. It sounded like a job application. I'm kind of cold."

"Why didn't you take a cab? It's freezing out."

"I don't have my wallet." He pats his pockets for effect. Godfrey smiles. It's dark, but holy shit. This is why birds make noise and music sounds like music.

A window from the apartment directly to the left of mine slides open. It's Mr. Carlos, a widower, who is always grumpy unless it's spring and I'm wearing a sundress. He leans out of the window, looks at both of us for a second, then yells, "Invite him up already! It's late!"

If I wasn't on fire before, I am now. Then I say, "Sorry, Mr. Carlos! We're just finishing up here."

He slams his window down hard.

Below, Godfrey is talking to Dot. I can't make out anything they're saying, and even though it's freezing, I lean out the window a little farther. What could Dot be saying to him? Even more so, what could Godfrey be saying to Dot? And I realize I'm leaning so far out the window I might fall. I grip the window frame. Dot hugs Godfrey and looks up at me and blows a kiss.

And then it's just Godfrey. Staring back at my window. I know he can't see my red ears, but he's looking at me like he can see my red ears, so I give him a nod.

"YOU'RE IN THE PHONE book," Godfrey tells me. He smells like frost, like those first fifteen minutes when you're sitting in your car, waiting for it to warm up and the windshield to defrost. It is easy to look at him; his midtwenties are being kind to him. His voice is deep but tender, sensual, and briefly, I imagine him spreading me out in bed, his mouth over my ear, telling me exactly what he's going to do to me while he's doing it. I can't look away.

We're each holding cups of hot cocoa in my living room. I lean against the wall that separates the living room from the kitchen because every thirty seconds or so I think it's the only way I can keep myself upright. I find myself squeezing my legs together, imagining how hard he'd grip under my thigh, if he'd bite my lower lip.

Godfrey looks around the apartment like it's a museum, but I'm staring straight at him—his face and his arms and the white oxford under his coat before returning to his face again while Godfrey just keeps talking. "The white pages—not the yellow ones, because you're not a business."

"Are you warming up?" I ask him, finally finding my mouth again. "You should drink the cocoa."

He nods, but he doesn't bring the mug to his lips. He's listening to the record that's started over again. I listen to him listening. The record player is an automatic, so when the side finishes, it flips the record itself. "There's always music, but this is the good kind," he says.

"You should sit down," I tell him. "You look flushed."

"I'm probably drunk." He finally brings the cocoa to his lips, but I'm not sure if he actually takes a sip. "Which I am."

He finds the height markings in the doorjamb. "What's this?"

"I take people's heights when they come over," I explain. "My mother didn't believe in writing on doorjambs, so it was a childhood ritual I missed out on."

He notices the name at the very bottom. "Who's Fipps Fuoco?"

"My friend Dot, who you just met, has a bichon frise."

"You measured her dog?"

"The bottom is pretty empty. Do you want me to measure you?"

"My childhood doorjambs were properly cluttered."

"Oh, I should have known."

"What?"

"You had a happy childhood." I lean in a little closer to him, touch his eyebrow, his cheek. "Now I see it."

"See what?"

"The years of being steeped in safe happiness."

"Imperfect, but yes, safe and happy." He smiles. "Do I stink of a happy childhood? Do you think it'll scrub off?"

"If there were a scented candle called 'happy childhood,' it would smell like you."

He tilts his head. "Are you sure?"

"I'm really, really sure." He hasn't touched me yet, but it feels like we've played house for twenty years.

"And what would your scented childhood candle smell like?"

"Quiet permanent loss." It's the closest I've come to telling someone the truth. I can still feel the cold coming off him. "And libraries." I regret not turning up the heat while I was making the cocoa, but I don't want to do it now—I'm worried he might not be here when I get back. Our legs aren't touching, though I'm tempted. I want to tell him that we have a strange future together—wild and bright, the bunnies, the sky, the pool . . . He's about to ask another question, but I say, "I can't swim."

"You can't?"

I shake my head.

We're staring and staring and staring and then he says, "I want to be lost in a human Habitrail with you."

"Really?"

"Did you know your friend's name is Dot? As in Dotty?"

"Sometimes I call her Dotty Dot Dot."

"Hey, let me ask you a question." He doesn't wait for me to respond. "How do you feel about yachts?"

"I don't feel anything about them. I've never been on a yacht. I couldn't even tell you the last time I thought about a yacht."

"Bart wore boat shoes," he says. "In the winter. In Baltimore. Can you believe that?"

"Who's Bart?"

"How are you in so many places at once?" he asks me.

"I don't know what that means," I tell him.

"Do the rain boots grow the flowers, or do they come that way?"

"I make them that way."

"You're a gardener," he says. "You're everything."

"You're drunk," I say.

He ignores the accusation or maybe just accepts it. "I'm not scared to be alone again, you know."

I reach up and run my hand through his hair. I can feel the cold leaving. I can feel the heat from my fingers and the steadying of his breath. My body feels drunk but my mind is very, very still. "Who said anything about being alone?" I say. I can feel the night in his hair. "This is the least alone I've felt in years. In fact, I feel kind of thawed out, heart-wise. You know?"

And then in one fluid motion, Godfrey sets his mug of cocoa on the floor and then reaches up and cups my face and kisses me. A kiss that means we're just getting started.

Godfrey
MORNING

The air is different. That's what I realize before I even open my eyes—like there's a window slightly ajar somewhere, letting in little bursts of cold, fresh air. Madge likes to keep the apartment stuffy with heat.

I open my eyes to see if Madge is trying to fumigate the apartment or something, when I'm suddenly, brutally aware of my skull—the avalanche of pain inside of it.

I'm lying in a bed in a bedroom with crown molding.

That's not my crown molding. Madge and I don't have crown molding. Madge is envious of crown molding. I can't watch HGTV when Madge is around or she'll grip the remote too tightly when a newly married couple references the perfect curves in the crown molding of the house that's just slightly above their budget but still probably manageable if they don't eat out so many times a week.

And then I remember that Madge hates me.

I jerk my head around and see a pillow covered in tendrils.

Evelyn Shriner's tendrils, to be exact.

I sit up, delicately—my head pounding—and peer over her head to see if I'm right.

I'm right.

And there I find her beautiful lips, the smudges of mascara around her eyes, her jaw, her cheek . . . and Evelyn Shriner's nude shoulder.

Evelyn lets out a short sigh. I freeze and hold my breath, but she doesn't open her eyes. I feel a twinge and I try to talk myself out of the morning wood I was too hungover to wake up with. But I can't stop staring at Evelyn. She has freckles. I must have missed them last night. They're light. They dot the left side of her nose. Where do they go? I hope I get the chance to find out. I want to thank whoever put them there.

I decide this is my favorite part of her neck—the left side—but if someone were to ask me tomorrow, I might say, *No, no, it was the right all along.* Or *I never said it was her neck—why do you think I always walk behind her at grocery stores and strip malls?* But this neck! Men don armor for this kind of neck. Break oaths to God. Discover continents and cut off their ears.

The most obvious fact here is that she's real. Evelyn Shriner isn't an image on a screen. She isn't just flowered rain boots and legs pumping an old bike. She is actual. And this terrifies me.

I try to keep myself calm, brave, confident, but there are heartbeats in my fingers. I feel brutally alive. I slide closer to Evelyn, cautious not to wake her. Or maybe I'm cautious not to wake myself.

This trance—even with the ache between my temples compounded with my imminent ax murder by the hands of Madge—is something I want to nest in. The air is clearer here.

Last night comes back in patches, with each patch being really fucking bright. Briefly, the Velvet Underground gets stuck in my head: *White light, White light goin' messin' up my brain / White light, Aww white light it's gonna drive me insane.*

The painting therapy went badly. I remember that much. I was overly contentious about boat shoes. I got drunk. I made a toast. I was a winner. I found a phone book. I got drunker. I walked for miles because I had to see Evelyn, real, in person. There was a window. Pebbles. The window opened. A strange girl was framed within it, and then Evelyn. I was in her apartment. Evelyn's. And I loved her immediately. I think she loved me, too. Is that possible, so fast?

There was kissing, bungling, a couch too small to fit the two of us, and we landed here. The sheets are a mess, ruffled and uneven and mostly bundled around her. Evelyn must have stolen most of the sheet and blanket in the middle of the night.

The sleeve of my button-down has been shoved over the hook of a hanger that hangs on a closet doorknob. The sleeve has been buttoned up, so it looks like the hook of the hanger is a goose and the sleeve is a stuffy collar. I remember that we thought this was hilarious.

My pants are staring at me—the top of them has been shut into a dresser drawer so they're upright—zipped and all. My cell phone number is written on the mirror in lipstick—my handwriting, undeniably; the numbers have kept a blocky fourth-grader feel. And I remember her telling me how bad my handwriting is. Her eyes squinting as if she's astonished that a grown man could be so incredibly bad at something so basic.

My boxers? I look on the floor, next to the bed. There's an old Liz Phair record, a tin of Altoids, some plastic flowers, but no boxers. I look for any remnants of condom wrappers—or used condoms, for that matter—but don't see anything. I reach under the sheet below my abdomen. I'm still in my boxers. And thank God. Why am I glad to still be in my boxers?

Well, it makes me just a little less detestable. Even though Madge doesn't wear the ring, I'm still maybe-engaged, for shit's sake.

Also, if I have sex with Evelyn Shriner, by God, I want to remember it—in exact detail. How else will I keep the image on a continuous loop?

I look back at Evelyn. I want to bite her shoulder like a piece of fruit. I'd like to have sex with her now in this bed.

Because this is it—after all these years—my animal nature, the one my mother warned me about at the age of eleven and telling me that my real father is not Aldo Burkes, but this other man named Mart Thigpen—the beast, the animal! I believe my mother told me all of this in hopes that I could curb my animal tendencies. People tried talking me out of it, but my mother was right all along. Here is my predisposed animal nature, finally out in its natural habitat. Maybe it only needed a night of shitty beer and an open phone book to set it off.

I'm my father, Mart Thigpen—my animalistic, biological father.

But Madge would kill me. There's no segue in my head. No transition. Just this image: yellow police tape, no chalk outline because the detectives won't find my body—just my head in the freezer. The medical examiner will have to use my dental records to identify what's left of me. She won't make it a murder-suicide. No, that's not Madge's style. She'll want to take full credit.

But damn it. I'm lying beside Evelyn Shriner. I should drink this in. I know what I want more than anything: to go back to sleep and wake up like I belong here.

I shift slowly, trying not to wake her. This is a *huge* bed. It's like sleeping in an ocean of bed. Who has a bed like this?

And then Evelyn Shriner's completely all-nude shoulder rises and falls, working her ribs under the blanket; a quick sigh moves through her beautiful lips. She turns on her shoulder. As she does, the sheet slips farther down her body. I catch a thin strip of fabric, then a clasp. It must be a bra. With each breath, Evelyn shows a little more of herself. Her spine, arched back like the middle of a parenthesis. She leans forward; her back arches. I imagine my tongue tracing her awake, rolling down the outline of her backbone. I imagine doing this every morning until dementia sets in, until . . .

I'm alive. This might be the first time I've ever really been alive in my whole fucking miserable life. This moment is what causes wars to start. The only books worth reading have been written about those lips.

Evelyn turns and stares at me. She's a little stunned, too. She tugs the blanket up. "Godfrey Burkes," she says. And then she smiles. The smile is inexplicable. I mean, she has an animal in her bed. She should be reaching for a tranquilizer gun.

"I'm so sorry," I say.

"What? Why?"

"I'm Mart Thigpen. Jesus." I try to sit up, but my head feels like a piano dropped from a seventeenth floor window.

Evelyn doesn't blink. "Wait. You're Godfrey Burkes. I know you are. I said your name in an envisioning session and you showed up and last night . . . and well . . ."

"You envisioned me?" It's incredible how quickly I can go from loathing myself to an inflated sense of self. Should I confess I envisioned her, too?

"Who's Mart Thigpen?"

"No one. Just a family thing. And not the kind of family thing you really talk about."

"I have one of those."

"You do?"

Evelyn relaxes a bit. She lets the sheet slide down below her collarbone. She bites her lip and nods. And I think, that lip biting might turn me on more than anything in the world. That lip biting. Goddamn.

I'm aware that I'm shirtless and haven't been working out the way I should. I'm no prison-Godfrey, that's for sure. The Iron Gym that I ordered so I could do regular pull-ups made black indentations on the doorjamb and Madge told me to just stop already.

I sit up in bed. Madge. My head in the freezer. I think I might throw up.

"Godfrey," Evelyn says.

"What?"

"I don't know you all that well, but I'm pretty sure you're freaking out."

"I am."

"Why don't you lie down for a second? You're breathing really hard, and I think if you stand up, you might pass out."

I am breathing like a bull. My head settles on the soft pillow. I say, "There are a lot of feathers in this pillow."

"I haven't opened it up and counted, but I bet there are thousands. Are you feeling any better?"

My breathing has started to slow. "You have a huge bed," I tell her.

"I spend a lot of hours here every night." She turns and faces me, up on her elbows.

"Why are my pants clipped in the drawer like that?" I would point, but I don't need to. It's right there, directly in front of us. "And my shirt looks like a goose."

"Actually a duck," she says. "Don't you remember?"

It's coming back to me, piece by piece, and thank God because it's glorious. "But we didn't . . ." I look over at her.

"No," she says. "But it was sexy." She pulls back the covers and she's wearing a red, white, and blue retro-looking swimsuit. "For some reason, I put on my vintage 1976 bicentennial two-piece. We sang the national anthem."

I smile. "I usually only mouth that song at ball games. I'm not a strong singer."

"We did it à la Barry Gibb."

"I see." I remember the feel of that swimsuit against my skin. I remember kissing her, too, running my hands up her ribs.

"So why are you freaking out, Godfrey? Tell me that."

"Shouldn't I save that for my therapist?" I try to crack a smile.

"Don't get coy with me now. What happened to the boy throwing pebbles at my window?"

I start to sigh, but Evelyn cuts me off.

"Don't sigh at me, Godfrey Burkes."

"Okay," I say. "How about we make a deal?"

"I'm listening."

"I'll tell you my family story if you tell me yours."

Evelyn looks startled, like I've asked her to put on a bicentennial bikini and sing the national anthem à la Barry Gibb. She flops backward and rubs her temples with both hands, considering very carefully. "Okay," she says finally. "Okay, fine. But you go first."

"I'm a bastard, Evelyn."

She turns on her side, so she's facing my right cheek. "Don't be so hard on yourself. I obviously didn't mind that you came over the way you did." She points to her bikini. She points to my pants. "Like I said, it was sexy."

"You're not understanding me. I'm legitimately illegitimate—a bastard. The Merriam-Webster version of the word."

"Oh."

"Mart Thigpen is my biological father."

"Mart Thigpen?"

"The man who knocked up my mother and then left her."

"Have you ever met him?"

I shake my head. "My mother sat me down one day after school and said, 'That man who watches *Jeopardy!* every night in his underwear isn't really your father.'"

"So your father is actually your stepfather."

"Technically."

"And Mart Thigpen is . . ."

"Probably the man who helped us cross the seven-billion population mark faster than we were supposed to."

Evelyn shifts herself closer to me. I can feel the heat from her mouth, from the tops of her breasts not covered by the bikini, even from her neck and the smoothness of her thighs. "So we can solely blame him for global warming?" she says.

"My father, the Great Mart Thigpen."

"'Fathers are biological necessities, but social accidents.' Margaret Mead said that."

"And I always thought I was the accident," Godfrey says.

"You seem handcrafted to me."

"Well, I hope Margaret Mead is wrong. I'd like to be a nonaccidental father one day."

She looks at me and smiles—just the corners of her mouth. "I want to mother some kids like crazy." And there's something about the way she says that makes me feel like she has a huge vast capacity for love. Her love could stretch on unconditionally and endlessly, like it's a universe within her. I'm drawn to the edge of that universe. I'd like to fall into a black hole of it somehow. I just whisper, "God."

"What?"

I shake my head. I feel like I'm going to get in a fight one day about the validity of falling in love so fast. Not a heated one because why would I give a shit if some other person gets it or not? Right now, it's no longer the big flooding rush like when I saw her naked shoulder. It's just this honest, frank truth. I love Evelyn Shriner. Love doesn't start with need. Love meets love and just fucking recognizes itself. I'm supposed to be scared to death. Modern man isn't built for these kinds of things. But I feel good.

"What kind of animal did your mother say Thigpen was?" she asks.

I have no fucking clue. All of these years—how did I never ask such an obvious question? "I never asked," I finally say.

"You know, penguins are monogamous. Lassie was based on a true story."

"Is that right?"

"Everything in black and white is true," she says. "Besides, you're not supposed to argue with a girl in a bikini. A girl in a bikini *in bed* with you, no less."

"Are you just going to always be mostly naked so I can never really argue with you?"

"Whatever works."

"That's not fair."

I'll never forget what Evelyn Shriner looks like in a 1976 bicentennial bikini. "Cats will eat their dead owner's face once they run out of food."

Evelyn sighs. "Really?"

"I only know where half of me came from. I guess it's dumb, but sometimes it's hard to rest myself."

"Have you ever tried to find out about your dad?"

"I looked him up in high school. He was living in Burlington, probably trying to raise the census level of Vermont. It's really low, you know."

"What did you do?"

"I wrote a letter. Even included pictures. I rewrote it three times because I wanted it to look neat. I was on my way to the mailbox when I saw my father . . . well, my stepfather, and he smiled at me. I couldn't do it."

"Maybe you should consider doing it again," she says. "Instead of stamps, there's science now; the future could tell you a lot about the past."

"Chin? I thought he only did romantic futures."

"You could at least ask him. I mean, for a few bucks extra, he'd probably try to find a loophole. Plus, love is love."

"He does seem financially motivated."

"Imagine finding out what your future would be like if you and your father knew each other."

"That's exactly what I'm afraid of."

"You have penguins on your goddamn boxers, and you held on to me as we fell asleep last night. But what if there *is* some animal in you? Would that be all bad? It can't be because it makes you *you*, and I like Godfrey Burkes—animal, Thigpen, and all."

This has never dawned on me—not once, not ever. How is *that* possible?

"Let me put it this way." Evelyn traces circles around the same piece of skin right above my collarbone. "Thigpen and all, you're the boy girls want to marry. It's why Dr. Chin has a job. It's why his envisioning service is more lucrative than a Chinese restaurant."

If she really knew the truth. The boy girls want to marry! I think about where Madge might be right now—maybe at work, maybe at an envisioning session, picking someone who understands abstract art and realizes the importance of having friends who will own a yacht.

"So I'm a boost on the economy?" I say.

"Chin should write you a thank-you card."

I close my eyes. Evelyn is still tracing circles on my shoulder. "It's your turn." I spread one of my hands on my chest.

Evelyn's finger stops tracing. She puts her hand on mine.

"My sister would be thirty-eight this October," she says.

Would be.

"She was hit by a car when she was twelve," she says.

"I'm so sorry."

"I never met her. My parents had me after the accident. The next best thing, I guess. I'm Dolly the sheep."

"You're way prettier than a sheep," I say.

"That might just be the sweetest thing anyone has ever said to me in bed," she says.

"I am part Thigpen. I hear he was charming."

"You know what's fucked up? If my sister never died, none of this would be happening right now. It was either me or my sister. Part of me feels grateful that she's dead. I've never told anyone that before."

"Not even your best friend?"

Evelyn shakes her head. She wipes tears from her cheeks. I brush a piece of loose hair behind her ear.

And then I kiss her. It's a surprise to both of us.

Evelyn rolls back over to me and slides her leg inside mine. She takes the sheet and pulls it over our heads.

"I like how cloudy it feels under here," she says.

"Can we stay for a while?" The white sheets make it feel like we're in an illuminated tent.

"Please."

This time she kisses me.

She kisses the middle of my chest, letting her lips sit on my sternum. "Do bunnies mean anything to you?"

"Not really. I mean, I grew up with them. My mom rescues them. Someone has to."

"When I envisioned you, there were bunnies everywhere. As if they were growing out of the ground. And birds the color of pastels. It was beautiful, but overwhelming and sad."

"Well, my mother does collect them like a boy collects baseball cards. She'd never let them loose."

"She wasn't there. It was fifteen years from now. We jump into a pool completely dressed. I'm wearing a dress and you're in a suit."

"You were in my parents' backyard." Suddenly Evelyn's giant bed seems very small. I pull the sheet from our heads. "Was my suit black?"

She nods.

"And were you wearing black, too?"

"Yes."

"I think you envisioned my mother's funeral."

"Would we have jumped into a pool?"

"Were we okay?" I ask her. "Tell me we looked all right."

"It was crazy. Otherworldly. The bunnies, the sky, the pastel colors. Your fingertips were tinged like you'd been finger-painting."

"I always wanted to work with kids."

"Teaching?"

I nod.

"I think you'd be good at that." She looks down at her hand then and says, "I felt your hand through a video screen fifteen years away. We were both sad and happy. We were together." This is comforting. "I have to tell you something, Godfrey."

"What is it?" I say.

"I was really scared. It was all of these emotions at once, but mostly love and fear and I couldn't tell the difference between the two."

"I envisioned you once, too," I say.

"You did?"

I nod. "We were in a Habitrail built for children and we'd lost our daughter and then you found her. You slapped me and gave me a speech about how this was proof we'd endure. And I think I fell in love with you."

"Well, you were already in love with me. You'd married me, and we'd had a kid together."

"I mean, current-me fell in love with you."

Her eyes are fixed on mine. She says in a quick rush, "When we jumped in the pool, I just kept thinking, 'I don't know how to swim, I don't know how to swim.'"

And it just comes out of me. "You should learn."

"I should?"

"Yes." And this feels like a promise—maybe even a proposal—the natural kind, not the popping of the question, the getting down on one knee, the ring. No. This feels right.

"You should learn how to swim," I say again.

And then she kisses me softly.

"Work!" she says. "I should go to work!"

"Where do you work? What do you do?"

"I'm a librarian. Can't you tell?"

I tilt my head and think, *Yes, sexy librarian, I can see that.* "Yes, completely. Which library?"

"The grand old biggie."

"With the skylights and the intimidating dead patrons of yore in the entryway?"

"That's the one!" Evelyn hops out of bed. She tugs the edge of the bikini bottom on one cheek as she walks out of the bedroom. I'm in awe of that. Moments later, she comes back into the room with a bottle of water and Advil.

"Thank you." I untwist the cap, pop three Advil, and take a sip. "Can I ask you a question and you promise not to think it's weird?" I screw the cap back on the water bottle.

"Look at your clothes pinned to the dresser," she says. "Look at the penguins on your boxers." Evelyn lifts up the sheet and looks at them. She smiles and bites her lip again, *again*!

"How do you feel about abstract art?" I say.

Evelyn scratches behind her neck. She flips her hair to the right side of her face. I smell fruit. Mangoes. "Dots on a canvas, right? Streaks of mixed color simulating emotion?"

"Right."

"Yeah," she says, "I've got nothing."

It dawns on me that I'm not trying to guess the right answers to the conversation. I'm not trying to think of something interesting to say. I'm not second-guessing what I've just said. I'm just talking. And in one fell swoop, I realize that I've never felt anything quite like this—talking about the heart of things, words and then more words. With Madge, there's always been a voice in the back of my mind, a shaky voice, like a guy on a game show holding a buzzer but never quite knowing the answer, just sure that if he doesn't ever press the buzzer, he'll never accidentally say the right thing and get some points on the scoreboard.

With Evelyn, I want to be known and I feel like she can know me. I want to know her, and as soon as she says something, I feel like I get it. If, for some reason, this never works out and I never get any more than this one morning with her, I'll always remember what it's like: feeling understood. God, it feels good. It feels like the kind of thing that could take two people a long way in life.

She pauses and looks at me. "You know, I was really addicted to envisioning. Chin has threatened to blacklist me. Maybe I'm done with it now. Maybe I've finally caught up to it."

"Caught up to what?"

"The future."

"You're even prettier in the morning."

"You're less drunk in the morning."

"And we're both more naked." I look at the pieces of her that are pretending to be from 1976, and under the sheet, penguins shift slightly every time I breathe.

There's kissing. Lots of kissing and then she pries herself loose. She really actually has to go to work.

And then she's gone.

I call a cab and wait in her apartment alone.

This is her home. This is where she dwells. I don't want to pry. I don't even touch anything. I just admire the fact that she's breathed this air. The real her.

Finally, the cab pulls up. I grab my coat and rush past the doorway to the kitchen. That's when I see the heights in the doorjamb. She didn't take my measurement. I grab a pencil off the counter, stand tall against the jamb, and scribble a mark. I turn and jot: Godfrey Burkes, in all caps.

I was here.

WHEN I GET OUTSIDE, the cab's waiting for me at the curb. The cabbie has a thick paperback propped on the wheel. I get in, give the cabbie my address, and stare out the window as the car begins to pick up speed. I finger the twenty-dollar bill Evelyn stuck in my right coat pocket as she lightly kissed me good-bye. I want to text her something smart and funny but I don't have my phone, of course, and I feel suddenly like a man without hands or the ability to speak. It's a momentary flush of panic. My phone, my keys, my wallet—Madge has them all! She'll give them back, right? *Right*?

My eyes are wide with fear and I tell myself to relax my face. *It's going to be okay,* I say to myself even though myself disagrees.

To make matters worse, I realize I left my cell phone number on the mirror but didn't get hers in return. Of course I'm wearing the same pants as last night so I quickly rummage through my pockets and pull out the white page I tore out of the phone book at Fontana's. There's her name, address, and home phone number. At least I've got this much. If nothing else, a little proof that the whole night happened, that she's real.

At the first stoplight, I ask the cabbie, "What do you think about love?"

The cabbie looks at me through the rearview mirror. "You know, people think cabdrivers are oracles, that we speak the truth in moments of crisis. We're not. We drive cabs."

It's true, I do expect certain people to be more oracle-like: bartenders, small children, old people with dementia, maybe even the blind and Jedis, but seriously, I'm pretty sure the cabbie is goading me, which is very oracle-like. "What were you reading before I got in?"

"Tolstoy."

"Well, that's just my luck."

"You've got a problem with Tolstoy?"

"I've got the one cabbie in all of Baltimore reading dead Russians and refusing to be an oracle."

"Okay, okay," he says. "Ask me again."

I'm thinking this might be a trick but what do I have to lose? "What do you think about love?"

"It's rare."

"What else?"

"That's enough, isn't it?"

Maybe he's right. Maybe he means it might only come once in a lifetime. It's rare so it's precious. It's rare so it shouldn't be squandered. It's rare so you should fight for it. "How many times a day do you say that stuff about not being an oracle?"

"About four or five. Night shifts call for it a little more than mornings. You must have had one of those nights that fucks with your worldview."

"I think I did." I grip the twenty-dollar bill. It's the last tangible thing I have that proves last night actually happened.

He looks at me through the rearview again. "People are pretty committed to their particular worldviews, especially certain types. It can be disorienting when one gets fucked with. This girl must have shook you up good."

"She sure did."

He pulls up outside my apartment building. I pay and let myself out. There's a blast of wind. I look up the six steps to the front door. After the six steps, it's three stories and a brown chipped door. I don't have the first guess about what could be behind that brown chipped door.

The cabbie rolls down his window. I walk back to the cab and put my elbows on the open window. The Tolstoy paperback is on the passenger's seat.

"Stay shook," he says.

"It's kind of terrifying."

"That's all your tip gets you," he says.

"Fair enough."

I take my elbows off the open window. The cabbie puts the cab into drive and slowly pulls away. About a half block down the street, he honks three times.

• • •

AS I'M WALKING UP the third flight of stairs in my apartment building, I think about how I left the apartment last night with nothing. If my wallet symbolizes an identity crisis, then does forgetting my keys symbolize not wanting to come back home again?

It doesn't matter—I can still taste Evelyn. I'll sleep on a park bench if I have to; it's worth it.

I walk down the hall to my door and see my wallet and my key ring, sitting there on the doormat.

My wallet and my key ring—except it only has my car key on it. The key to the apartment has been confiscated. There they are, all by their lonesomes. Unguarded in the hall.

I'm stunned they haven't gotten stolen. One of our neighbors enjoys the company of bondagey-type women. Not that I think bondagey-type women are thieves; it's just that he has a lot of them. Sheer numbers is what I'm saying.

Madge has left the wallet and car key out for me; this is as a half kindness, a small warming. No cell phone, though. Not even a little SIM card action. This isn't good. I feel sweaty. I need my phone. Without my phone, how can I text Evelyn something smart and funny? Unlike the last time I lost my phone, which offered a little rebellious feeling of freedom, this time I feel lost and sick and dizzy. How will I know where I'm going? How will I know when I'm supposed to be there or what time it is?

I pick up my wallet and key ring, shove them into my pocket, and can't believe how light my pockets feel without my phone. It's like I'm weightless. Without the phone, I could just lift right off the face of the earth. Do I even exist if my cell phone isn't tracking me?

I knock on the door. Normally I freeze up at confrontations.

Godfrey, the boy who always rolls over, whose dormant animal nature is a joke, the little shit who still wears mittens.

But I kissed Evelyn Shriner last night and this morning. A lot. I rolled around animalistically with her in her giant bed this morning. We might even be engaged. Now I just have to end the other engagement.

No one comes to the door.

I knock again. "Madge!" I shout. "Madge! Come to the door! We have to talk!" And then I'm kind of pissed. Madge's fiancé, missing all night long. I could be dead in a ditch somewhere. Didn't Poe famously die in a Baltimore ditch, or is that a myth? I make a mental note to Google "death of Poe Baltimore ditch" and tape my findings to the refrigerator door so Madge can feel appropriately guilty. And then I realize—my mind clearing like smoke dissipating after a rocket launch—*I don't care.*

"Madge! Please! This is important! It's about us! We have to talk!" I pound until my knuckles are bruised and then I press my forehead to the door and clunk my head against it a few times. "Madge." I sound really plaintive now. "Madge, please!"

And then the neighbor's door squeaks open and I'm expecting a bondage girl, but it's the neighbor, the hefty, broad-shouldered, bare-chested masochist. "Jesus! You're killing me! Could you please shut the hell up? She's obviously not home!"

There's something damning about being yelled at by a masochist. "Sorry." I apologize. "I'm really sorry."

He grunts at me with disgust and slams the door.

I charge back down the stairs, and that's when it hits me: Madge has my cell phone in her possession for her own purposes.

I slow down on the stairs.

I grip the railing and come to a complete stop.

And Evelyn has my number—written in lipstick on her bedroom mirror, in my own stupid, dumb-ass, fourth-grade handwriting.

At this very moment, I can feel the collision course. Madge will receive a text or a call. Probably a text. And she will put two and two together.

And she'll text back. Yes, she will. She most definitely will. And it won't be simple with Madge. No, she'll take her time and really think it through. There's no telling what she will do, but I know one thing: she will ruin this.

Evelyn
SWIMMING LESSONS

On a break, I call Dot and fill her in on my night with Godfrey Burkes. She doesn't comment much, but finally she says, "Okay, I'll teach you to swim," as if that's what I've been getting at all along.

"Do you belong to a gym with a pool or something?" I ask her.

"Pool?" she says. "I don't need a pool to teach someone to swim. In fact, I find water generally gets in the way." I don't know what this means exactly, but I trust Dot. What do I know about swimming? Dot says to meet her around four at the picnic tables under the pavilion just north of where the dogs are allowed to shit at Robert E. Lee Park.

I take a late lunch and bike to the park.

When I pull up to the pavilion, Dot's already there, sitting on top of a picnic table. She's dressed top to bottom in matching blue Adidas sweats. A whistle hangs loosely around her neck. And if

I'm not mistaken, there's a pooch over Dot's midsection that wasn't there yesterday.

"I see you've grown four months pregnant overnight." I lean my bike against one of the four poles holding the pavilion in place and wrap my bike lock around it. I spin the numbers until I hear a click.

"It's a throw pillow," she says. "I was getting into the role."

"Swim teachers are pregnant?"

"It's a potbelly. What gym teacher isn't overweight? And I figured a swim teacher is the same as a gym teacher, just one capable of doing even less." Dot rubs her belly. "That Krispy Kreme sign is always flashing when I happen to be driving by."

Luckily, the park is mostly desolate except for a few kids on skateboards. Dot points them out. "I don't trust emo skateboarders," she says. "I think they're criminals in disguise."

"How do you know they're emo and not Goth or scene?"

"With that head bop, you can just tell that they're piping screamo into their ear buds."

"I think they're kind of sad."

"Just keep your pocketbook close. It takes a thief to know a thief."

On the floor next to the picnic table is a large bag from Dick's Sporting Goods; I'm scared to ask what's in it. But I give in to the afternoon. There's no wind, but it's overcast. The sky looks like it's aching. The trees are naked. I find myself embarrassed for them.

I realize how tired I am. I've been running on pure adrenaline since a handful of pebbles hit my window late last night. It's amazing how much has happened today. One day. Twenty-five years and everything happens in one day. I started seeing Dr. Chin for a hint, a cheat sheet, but somehow everything still seems like a complete surprise.

I had told Dot about Godfrey's mother's funeral, the pool, the half-naked conversation where Godfrey told me I should learn how to swim. But I couldn't tell her that it felt like a proposal. She knew I was holding back, but she didn't push for more.

"So what exactly is going to happen here?" I ask.

"We're here to teach you how to swim, obviously."

Obviously.

I consider telling her that this was a mistake. *Let's go waste a few hours at Café Honeybun. I won't even make you give back whatever you swipe.* But then I think of Godfrey's lips, the fullness of them. And then I think of Godfrey's lips again—still the fullness of them. I think about the necessity of his entire face, how everything is put exactly where it's supposed to be. His penguin boxers. His eyebrows. So I take a breath and ask, "What does a park have to do with me calling you for a swim lesson?"

"I might be good at stealing things, but I haven't learned how to steal a pool," she says, looking at me out of the corner of her eye. It feels like she's smiling, but she's not. "Not yet anyway."

And I believe her. One day Dot will steal a swimming pool.

Dot puts the whistle in her mouth and blows hard. The ringing is shrill, and it stays in my ears—still ringing, still shrill—even after the whistle leaves Dot's mouth and is hanging quietly around her neck.

"Was that necessary?" I tug on my earlobes.

"I was getting into character." Dot puts her hands on her hips, but the inside of the throw pillow has started to slide down the bottom of her track jacket. She fixes herself quickly. "Now stop giving me lip and get on the bench. I want to see you doing the back float, Shriner!"

Dot wants me to get on a park bench and float in my puffy coat.

This is fucking ridiculous. But water is the exact thing that seems to have always thrown me off. It crosses my mind that Dot's a genius, and this is the only way I'll learn how to swim.

I climb onto the picnic table. I lie on my back. The wood is hard and cold, but I could probably fall asleep if I let the top of my eyes fall into themselves. The table creaks slightly.

Dot reaches into the shopping bag and pulls out a pair of orange floaties. "Every swim teacher is prepared." She hands me the floaties. "Put these on."

"You're kidding," I say. But I take the floaties. I have to push hard to get them over my coat. I know there's more in the bag. It's a big bag.

She grips something in her right hand. They look like iPod ear buds, but the buds are too close together. She tosses them to me. They land on my chest. They're knotted. By the time I've untwisted them, I realize they don't go in your ears. They're nose plugs.

"So you don't take on water and get waterlogged," she says.

"You need water to get waterlogged."

"I'll blow the whistle again."

"Okay, okay." I plug my nostrils. "They're tight," I say.

"That's the point."

"Of course."

"One more thing." Dot rustles through the bag before handing me a pair of goggles. "Now," Dot says, trying her best not to sound like Dot, "on your stomach, Shriner!"

"Will you stop calling me that?"

Dot brings the whistle to her lips.

I turn over slowly. On my stomach, I can see through the bench's cracks.

Dot adjusts my body so my head hangs off the end of the picnic table. "So you can turn your head with every stroke," she says. I can feel all the blood rushing to my head. She stands in front of me. I have to stretch my neck out like a turtle to see her.

"It's going to be stroke, breath, stroke, breath," she says, inhaling and exhaling with each word.

"That sounds simple enough." I'd like to get this right.

"Try to be as smooth as possible," Dot's saying. "Like you're in the shower shaving your legs. You have to move your face to the opposite side of the arm you're using to stroke. Just glide."

In my puffy jacket, it's hard to move my arms in any motion that resembles a glide. I'm sweating. I'm trying to pay attention, but I'm getting dizzier and dizzier. Everything is fuzz, white noise. Who stuck me in a blender? I don't want to drown in a pool at the age of forty. I practice holding my breath. I close my eyes so the chlorine won't sting them. I then remember the goggles. I open my eyes.

Within minutes of my stroke, breath, stroke, and breath, there are worms dancing over my eyes. I let my arms drop to my sides, and slide down until my forehead rests against the picnic table.

"Stroke and stroke and stroke! God damn it!" Dot blows her whistle. "I said to stroke. Left arm. Right arm. Left arm. Don't quit on me now, Shriner!"

A couple walking their German shepherd where the dogs are permitted to shit turn and look at us. Dot blows the whistle again and waves. She motions with her hand for them to keep moving. "Jesus Christ," she says. "I don't know what's worse—your effort in the pool or those assholes rubbernecking."

"It's not a pool, Dot. It's a goddamn picnic table." The sweat is drying, and I'm shivering. "And it's like twenty degrees out here."

"I checked the weather after you called this morning. It hasn't dropped below forty all day."

"Well, it's gray out."

"*It's winter.* It's supposed to be gray." Dot puts the whistle back in her mouth. It hangs loosely from her lips like a cigarette about to be lit. "Congratulations, Ev, you're the first sober forty-year-old to drown in a swimming pool right after her mother-in-law's funeral."

"Fuck." I roll onto my back. My throat is stinging like it's been stung by an entire wasp nest.

I take off the goggles and hang them around my neck. I pull off the nose plugs and toss them on the grass in front of me. I'm still wearing the orange floaties. "He kissed me with his whole mouth. I forgot how to stand." I don't tell Dot that it made me feel safe, that even when Godfrey was just looking at me, I felt like I just came home. I'm keeping that for myself.

Dot sits next to me on the picnic table. She tugs on the whistle wrapped around her neck. "Oprah brought back the book club." She pulls two bottles of water out of the Dick's shopping bag and hands me one.

"It looks like Adam Greenberg will never leave you."

"You're nuts," she says. She takes a sip of water. "But at least you're going for it."

Across the way, the couple with the German shepherd has doubled back. They're not even pretending not to stare.

"Fucktards," Dot says. She starts to bring the whistle to her lips when I stop her.

"Let me," I say. I take the whistle from Dot's hand and blow it as hard as I can. My ears ring. I keep blowing. Shrill, just shrill, but I can't stop. It's liberating. The German shepherd is barking. Dot's laughing. The couple looks slightly frantic. I let the whistle drop and hang around Dot's neck.

"The student becomes the teacher," Dot says.

"And the teacher becomes a mother." I rub Dot's puffed belly.

"I hope it looks like Adam," she says.

"He'll probably pop out with glasses and an argyle sweater vest already on."

Dot doesn't say anything. She's pushed my hand away and is now rubbing her own belly. "Did you text Godfrey?"

I nod.

"Has he texted back yet?"

"Not yet."

"Maybe he's the thoughtful type."

"I think he is," I say, and then I ask Dot what people eat after swimming.

"Peanut butter sandwiches." Dot hands me a paper lunch bag and pulls a beach towel out of the Dick's shopping bag. "Put this around your neck," she says.

"Why?" I say, taking the towel from her.

"It just feels right."

I put the beach towel around my neck. It's white with blue stripes. "Will I really have to wear a nose guard when we finally get to a pool?"

She looks at me. "Wipe the chlorine off your face and give me a quote from Churchill, God damn it."

"'Success is not final, failure is not fatal; it is the courage to continue that counts.'"

"Then that's what we will do. Continue!"

Godfrey
THE SMELL OF PETTY TYRANNY

I get to work as fast as I can, mainly so I can use the phone. It hits me as soon as the elevator doors open—the smell of the Department of Unclaimed Goods. I can't stand it. Now I don't smell so good either, but that's not it. This is the smell of . . . what? I don't know, but it's awful.

I walk to my cubicle. Bart isn't there. His computer isn't on. He hasn't come in yet. Or has Madge taken him hostage? Was he in the apartment, duct tape over his mouth, when I knocked on the door? I need Bart. I need him to tell me Madge's location so I can retrieve my cell phone or make him a double agent so he can steal my phone back for me.

Where is he? Huh? In my hour of need?

Gunston isn't here either, but that's not unusual. Gunston is the Reigning King of Dead Aunts and Uncles, of Minor Surgeries, of Communicable Infections That Entail Bed Rest.

I'm not supposed to be here either. In Evelyn's envisioning session, I had multicolored fingertips. In the right future, the one I want more than anything, I'm teaching kids to apply finger paint to rolls of newsprint.

And then I see the little note: *Godfrey—We need you in Lost Cell Phones again. —C.*

Chapman.

I've mentioned that I hate Chapman, the idiot prick, haven't I?

I sit in my seat, refusing to go to Lost Cell Phones. Evelyn's the kind of girl to text something brilliant and tender right out of the gate, especially after an irreversibly fantastic night—and morning. And, in response, Madge will intercept that text. I could call Evelyn's home number. I've got the white page torn from the phone book in my pocket still. But she's at work. I could call her at work and have her paged. But, in either scenario, what would I say? My fiancée might be in possession of my cell phone and therefore ignore all texts and calls from my number?

Shit. No. Of course not. God, I wish I'd explained it all last night or even this morning. We were being honest. I should have come clean.

Okay, okay. I promise that I will come clean as soon as I see Evelyn in person. You have to be looking someone in the eye when you explain about hooking up with them while you are almost engaged.

But, for right now, I have to stop the panic. There's the rational possibility that Madge found my phone and shoved it in the junk drawer. There's the rational possibility that she spiked it and its splintered parts have been swept up and now sit in the kitchen garbage.

I just have to get to Madge, break things off as quickly and cleanly as possible, and then find Evelyn, explain everything.

Why not be an optimist? Why not put a little faith in love?

I think: What would Thigpen do? That ladies' man. That Casanova. That animal. Evelyn spoke the truth, I've got him in me—why does that have to be a bad thing? Thigpen wouldn't do something wussified like having her paged in a library. Do they even page people in libraries? No. He'd do something big.

I look up ways to send messages. And there—in five or six quick links—I'm at a singing telegram service. Yes. I will send her a singing telegram—something so big and old world that, as a gesture, it will blot out all other forms of communication.

I call up and order a duck.

"What kind?" the receptionist asks.

"What kinds are there?"

"Daffy, Donald, or something more generic."

"I'll take the generic duck." I don't want this to be commercialized.

"And what's the occasion?"

"Nothing, really. It should be romantic."

"Not a birthday or anything?"

"No, but do your singing telegrams know anything by, like, Iron and Wine?"

"No, sir. Our ducks sing 'Happy Birthday.' Also available in Spanish."

This goes on for a while. The woman is dying to get off the phone with me. Finally, it hits me. "The national anthem. Tell the duck to sing the national anthem. In falsetto—for extra points. How about that?"

I give her my name and Evelyn's name. Just saying her name makes me happy, like full-body happiness.

"Address?" the woman says.

I give the library's name. I know this won't go over well in a library, but surely there's a back room somewhere in which singing's okay. We settle on the financials, and I get off the phone, feeling triumphant. What if I could become a triumphant type of person with Evelyn in my life?

I hold out my hands. They're shaking a little. I'm hungover and hungry and jacked up. And I think to myself. Why not start being that triumphant type?

Step 1 seems clear: *No more, Chapman. No more pushing around Godfrey Burkes, you petty tyrant!*

I walk down the hall, past the water cooler and straight into Chapman's office without knocking.

Chapman is drinking Red Bull. He puts down the can and says, "What?"

"I'm not going to Lost Cell Phones again today. Tell Garrett to do it. He's new. He needs to pay his dues."

"I'll make a note of your suggestion," Chapman says, and for effect, he lifts a pencil and licks the tip and makes a checkmark in the air.

"Do you smell that smell?" I ask.

"What smell?" Chapman says.

"It's the smell of petty tyranny. It's the smell of dying souls. It's the stench of unlived lives!"

"What the fuck are you talking about?" Chapman says.

"I quit." I can't believe I've just said these words.

"What?"

"Listen you fuck-wagon, you ass-dangle, you prick-wad, you douche-hopper!" I call him a few more names, a blur from my mouth.

"Those aren't real curse words!" Chapman says, though he's clearly stung by them.

"I quit because I have another life to lead." And with that, I turn around and walk out of this office and down the hall. I can hear Chapman yelling at my back, "*You're* a douche-hopper! You are! You hear me? Douche-hopper! You're fired, too, so don't come back!"

I open the back door of the office building, and the parking lot stretches out before me. I start running. I can't help it. I'm not running away from my shitty job. I'm running toward the future—the one future I really want.

"Godfrey!"

I turn.

Five cars away, Gunston hits the button on his car lock and his car beeps twice. "What are you doing?"

"Can I borrow your phone?"

He's wearing a puffy blue down jacket that is snug on his wide hips and one of those wool wrap-around ear-warmers, the kind that look like a girl's headband. His hair is puffed up on top of his head. "Tell me what you're doing first. You look different . . . and weird."

"I'm free, Gunston. That look you don't recognize, that weird-ness—it's freedom!"

"Really? Because it looks kind of shroomy."

"Give me your phone, okay?"

I want to call Evelyn, but I'm a man of honor. I can't call her until I'm completely free of Madge. I can only hope a giant patriotic duck gets to her before Madge does.

Right now, I want to tell *someone*. Why? Because I'm becoming myself—for the first time in my life. I feel like I'm becoming Godfrey Burkes.

I decide to call my parents. I feel like they should know. I push in the numbers of my mother's cell. It's midmorning. She's often out in the yard with the bunnies at this hour.

"Godfrey?" she says. "Where are you?"

"I quit!" I tell her. "I quit my job!"

Gunston says, "You what? You quit?" He's incredulous.

"You quit your job?" my mother says again.

"It's okay!" I tell her. "In fact, it's really good!"

Gunston paces a small circle. With his mouth open, he slightly wags his head in awe.

My mother muffles the mouthpiece and says something, probably to my father. And then it's my father's voice on speakerphone. "Are you coming or not?"

"What are you talking about?" I ask.

Gunston has started flapping his puffed arms like he's going to try to fly away. "You really quit?"

I nod to Gunston.

"Lunch!" my father says. "We're waiting for you. We're at Sal's on Calhoun. You and Madge were supposed to be here twenty minutes ago."

Lunch with my parents. How could I forget lunch with my mother? "I'm sorry. I'm so sorry," I say. "And Madge isn't there?"

Gunston starts jumping now, and he's still flapping. A small bark emits from his mouth. Is he trying to yawp? Is he hoping to get a promotion or something? Or is he weirdly joyful? It dawns on me I've never seen Gunston express joy before.

"Isn't Madge with *you*?" my father asks.

"You quit!" Gunston cries out so loudly that his voice bounces across the parking lot and rings up in the open air.

"Quiet down, Gunston." I turn back to the phone. "No. I don't think she's coming." It terrifies me that I have no idea where she is or what she's doing.

"Is she mad you quit your job?" my mother asks with a disapproving tone. Madge is only allowed to have one emotion about me: joy, utter joy.

"I think she's mad, yes."

"But you have another job, don't you?" my father asks.

"I have a plan." I could get my degree in early education. I could grow into those finger-paint-stained fingers that Evelyn saw in her envisioning session. It's possible.

My father says, "You'd better get your ass down here. This is important."

"Important?"

"Your mother has already cried twice."

"Over what?"

"Never you mind. Get here."

"Go ahead and order," I say, but my father's already hung up. My mother's cried? Twice?

I turn around and there's Gunston. He's taken a knee and seems to be praying on the pavement. "I quit," I say again aloud. It's just dawning on me in a new way.

"Why?" Gunston says. "How?"

"In the end, it was the smell of petty tyranny. I got to the end of it."

Gunston nods. "I get it. I understand."

"Follow me, Gunston." I hold out my hand to help him up. "You can get out, too."

Gunston shakes his head. "I wish I could," he says, tearing up. "I wish I could."

I can only save myself.

Evelyn
AMNESIA

I step into my apartment, talking to Dot on my phone. I pull off my coat, gloves, hat.

"Maybe you should call him," Dot says.

"I've already texted." I unwind the scarf around my neck and stare at the sofa. Godfrey and I kissed on that sofa.

"It doesn't mean you can't call."

"It does, actually." I walk to the kitchen, grab a bottled water, and start drinking.

"Maybe his phone doesn't get texts," Dot says.

"I'm now pretending that you're talking about Ryan Gosling, even with the full beard, because I can no longer think about why Godfrey's not texting." In the sink, there are two coffee mugs that previously held hot cocoa—and empty wine bottles.

"I mean, maybe his phone doesn't get texts?"

"Maybe," I say. But that's dumb. "What phone doesn't get text messages?" I imagine my grandmother's rotary phone, next to the cuckoo clock.

"Maybe he lost his phone?" Dot says.

"Maybe." I walk slowly to the bedroom.

"Maybe after he left your apartment that morning, he got mugged, and now he's floating down the Potomac."

"Dot!"

"Maybe he fell down a flight of stairs or out of a second- or third-story window and hit his head. Days from now, he will wake up in a hospital room, not knowing who he is. So it's not his fault, you know? He'd love you if he could only *remember* you. He sees you sometimes in his dreams. Amnesia is a bitch."

I appreciate Dot for trying, but it's not helping. "I'd rather pretend to hate him than be worried that he's hurt." His clothes are gone, of course. He's gone. Did I half expect him to still be here? I stare at his cell phone number written sloppily in lipstick on my mirror.

I pace back to the kitchen. "I'm sorry," she says. "He might just be a prick." I lean against the doorjamb all etched with measurements.

And then I see a new scribble on the doorjamb.

I nudge Dot out of the way. "Wait," I say, and there's his height, his name written next to the mark. It seems like such a thoughtful, sweet thing. And yet I'm not sure what I should be feeling. It's still completely possible that Godfrey Burkes has one-night-standed me?

And then I see his incoming text.

Godfrey
THERE, THEIR, AND THEY'RE

I see my parents as soon as I walk into the restaurant. Their steaming entrees—both of which look like dollops from large vague casseroles—sit on their plates. And my parents look freshly steamed, too. Both are red-cheeked and dewy. Why has my mother been crying? Has she gotten bad news—the first signs of the disease that will kill her? My throat cinches up. My God, is this the beginning of the end?

The hostess wants to seat me, but I wave her off. "I see my people," I tell her, and it hits me that these two people are my people. Thigpen doesn't matter. I'm Godfrey Burkes and this is my sweet, ailing mother and my sober, loyal father.

As I walk up and take a seat across from them—the hostess handing me my laminated menu—I realize what I must look like. Mussy, bloodshot, bleary-eyed, euphoric, but also spent. I'm unshaven and stinky, and I might start crying.

"Godfrey," my father says, glancing around the restaurant. "You okay?"

"I'm better than I've ever been in my life, to be honest. I mean, I've got some things to attend to . . ." Madge. Lordy, Madge . . . "But I'm really, really good. How are you?" I look at my mother. "Are you feeling all right?"

"We're feeling fine," my father says. "The point is . . ." He looks at my mother who clasps her hands and lowers them to her lap. She looks down at her brick of casserole. "Your mother wanted to talk to you."

"About what?" I say. "Have you been to the doctor? You should go to the doctor—EKG, complete blood work, cancer screening. Are you on top of all this? You know that Guy Lombardi died because he refused to get a colonoscopy? This is no time for rash pride."

"*Vince* Lombardi," my father says. "Godfrey! He's the patron saint of the Green Bay Packers!"

"Sorry," I say. "You know I'm no good at sports trivia."

"There's nothing trivial about Vince Lombardi!" my father says sternly.

"And it's Guy *Lombardo* anyway," my mother says.

"I think we've gotten off topic," I say.

"We're fine, Godfrey," my mother says. "Medically. If that's what you're talking about."

"For how long?" I say. "You've moved into a new demographic. Your risk factors are higher."

My mother rummages through her pocketbook and whips out an envelope.

"Test results," I whisper, and I push back in my chair.

"Test results?" my father says. "What the hell are you talking about, Godfrey? It's a letter. It's a goddamn letter—"

"From your father," my mother says. She shoves the envelope at me. "Mart Thigpen."

"Thigpen?" I take the letter. The envelope has my name on it: Godfrey. Nothing else. No Burkes. No address. No stamp. This thing was hand-delivered—from Mart Thigpen to my mother?

The handwriting on the envelope is large and has a little fanfare to it—small flourishes. It's almost girly. I think, *This is a forgery.*

The envelope is old, faded. I flip it over and nudge the seal. It's brittle and pops open easily. *Old spit kept it together all these years,* I think to myself. How old? "What's it say?" I ask.

"You'll have to read it yourself," my mother says.

"Have you read it?" I ask both of my parents.

My father looks at my mother. She says, "Mart read it to me once and then gave it to me to give to you, sealed."

"He read it to you *in person*?" This seems completely absurd—the idea of Mart and my mother sitting on a sofa somewhere while he reads a letter he wrote himself, and she sits there—pregnant? Am I already born? Am I in a crib nearby? "How?" I ask.

"What do you mean *how*? He *read* it!" my father says, and then he looks at my mother. "*How?* What's he saying *how* for? Does he think Thigpen read it in an accent or something?"

Thigpen can't read or write. He's an animalistic womanizer. He's a heathen lover. He's a biological necessity, but a social accident.

My mother leans forward. She touches my hand. "The other night on the phone, you said you wanted us to know each other better as adults. I've been waiting for you to say—in some way—that you were ready for this, that you are now *finally* an adult."

Her stress on "finally" is a little insulting, but I let it go. On some level, I am the little shit who wears mittens. I've been slow to mature. Granted. And right now, I have the deep desire to backpedal, to reframe my comments. I start to say, "I kind of meant that maybe we would . . ." What? Debate politics together? Did I just want my parents to trust me to be able to follow a discussion of interest rates?

I'm still holding the unsealed envelope. I can see a triangle of the stationery, which is as yellowed as the envelope.

"Read it, Godfrey," my mother says. "It's time."

I gently pull out the letter. I unfold it. My hands are shaking so badly that the paper trembles, so I lower it to the table.

The letter—in more of that flourishy handwriting—goes like this:

Dear Godfrey,
One day you'll be old enough for your mother to read this to you.

This means that my mother is way overdue. This was supposed to be read to me before I was able to read myself.

I want you to know that despite the fact that your mother and I can never be together as a couple, I love you.

Mart Thigpen loves me? By those words *as a couple,* does he mean that he could be with my mother as a lover, sure, but as a couple meant something publicly acknowledged. So this was a reminder pointed at Gloria: Mart was a married man.

Their will always be times when you need a father figure. I don't know if I'll be able to be there for you. I hope I'm allowed.

But, if I'm not, I want you to know that I want to be there and it's killing me that I'm not.

Well, now I know that Mart Thigpen does not have mastery of the correct usages of *there, their,* and probably *they're,* too; I hate him for this. Really, I feel actual grammatical rage, something I've never felt before. But I know that my emotions might be misdirected. He sounds sincere—not being there for me is "killing him." For whatever reasons, I believe this. Maybe because I imagine having my own kid one day. I want to be there. Did my mother not allow Mart Thigpen to see me?

If you ever want to come to me for anything, I'm here. Count me in!

Love,

And then there's a large space. Maybe it is there to suggest the passage of time—the time that Mart is trying to decide how to sign the letter. Can he write *Dad* in all fairness when he's just confessed he probably won't be much of a father?

No.

He opts for *Mart Thigpen* because, I guess, if this is one day read aloud to me, at least I'll have a full name to go with when I decide to come to him for anything.

I look up at my parents.

Their eyes stare back at me—expectant and glassy.

"And?" my father says.

My mother remains speechless.

"He misused *their.*"

My mother nods, waiting for me.

My father says, "Is there a little more you want to share with us?"

I look back at the letter and then up at them. This is a moment that I will never forget as long as I live. This restaurant will be the restaurant where I read the letter from my biological father. These clothes will be the clothes I was wearing when I read the letter from my biological father. This feeling in my chest—hot and fiery—is the feeling I'll always associate with reading the letter from my biological father. Maybe I should be mad at my mother for not allowing Mart to be there for me, but that feels like ancient history. There's a more pressing realization.

I say, "He's not an animal."

"Who said he was an animal?" my father says.

I look at my mother. She shakes her head. She means *Let's not go back over it. Ancient history.*

"I have to go," I say, standing up. "I love you and now I have to get up and breathe air."

"Okay," my father says. "Okay there. Steady!"

My mother says, "This will take processing time. I know, I know. It's going to be okay . . ."

I start to walk out of the restaurant like I'm not so much walking as much as I am gliding leglessly. *Thigpen, Thigpen, Thigpen,* my heart beats in my head. And just as I'm moving toward the front door, I pass the ladies' room. The door opens and I nearly run into Dr. A. Plotnik. "Dr. A. Plotnik!" I say, startled.

She looks awful. Her nose is red, her eyes puffed. She's gripping her pocketbook and a bag from Bed Bath & Beyond with such desperation that I'm afraid of what might be in them.

"Who are you?" she says. "What do you want?"

"I'm Godfrey Burkes. You said Madge and I had great potential.

You said you rarely see couples with as much potential as we had. But guess what? We did one of your exercises and it all exploded!"

"Burkes," she says, narrowing her eyes, "you, with that crack about the dead moles. Were you one of the ones to turn us in?"

I feel dizzy, flush with adrenaline. Am I hearing Dr. A. Plotnik right? "Turn you in? No, I'm thankful we exploded, Dr. A. Plotnik. What do you mean—turn you in?"

She looks around, as if afraid someone's following her, and then she whispers, "Madge put in more effort than you, coming in on her own, you know, seeking extra counsel. In fact, I saw that she called earlier today, probably about this explosion. I just haven't had time . . ." Again, she peers around, eyes the hostess, and glares through the glass door to the street.

"Are you okay?" I ask her. I don't feel so good myself. Am I just projecting, or is Dr. A. Plotnik shaken by something big that's just happened to her?

"Of course I'm not okay!" She sighs with exhaustion. "In retrospect, we all realize that a lasting relationship is work, Godfrey, no matter which one you choose! Work, work, work!"

"You're wrong," I tell her. I'm not an animal. I'm a man who uses words. I might even come from sensitive stock. "A lasting relationship isn't work, Dr. A. Plotnik. It's home."

Evelyn Shriner is home. I just have to find my way back.

Evelyn
PSYCHOSIS

Text 1: Squeee. How great are you? I love your boobs.
Text 2: I'm in the mall with my mother buying bath salts.
I don't know if we'll bathe in them or smoke 'em!
Wish you were here!
Text 3: I really really really love my mother. You will too. ☺
Text 4: I'm not gay. I swear. Pinky swear!!!!
Text 5: Did I mention I'm still on parole? BTW: Do you
have any clean pee?
Text 6: Never mind re: pee issue. I found an 8-year-old. All's
cool.
Text 7: Oh, and it's okay. I didn't kill that guy. It was
accidental.

Conversation in my head:
He's joking. Right?

Of course!
He's spoofing weird post-first-date texts.
It's funny. It's funny!
He's being funny.
He's just really funny.

I excuse myself from the Youth Services desk. "I'll just be a second," I say to Jill, who's an overly earnest intern. "Family emergency." I point to the phone.

As I head back behind circulation to find a private spot, there's Fadra walking in through the main doors. Her hair is a little less red than when I saw it last. She's limping.

"Are you okay?" I ask.

"I'm going home!" she says, pure joy in her voice.

"You have a home?" I know I shouldn't have said it, but it's already out.

"I'm from Ohio."

I feel completely turned around. I hear myself saying in my head, *Right, of course! Ohio! Where else?*

"Where you were a taxidermist?"

"My whole family's made of taxidermists."

She's walking toward the elevators and I find myself following her. "Can I ask why you left in the first place?"

"I don't remember," she says, her eyebrows lifting.

"And why are you going back now?"

"Because I finally forgot why I left."

We step into the elevator together. She presses the third-floor button, where she'll presumably collect her things.

We ascend in silence. She steps out and says, "Thanks for everything!"

"You're welcome."

The doors start to close but I shove my arm in and stop them. I reach out and hug her. I don't know why, except I don't know if I'll ever see her again—or maybe I'll see her tomorrow, but still. I say, "Keep in touch! Send postcards!"

She hugs me and says, "There are only two choices in life: to open up or shut down."

I step back. "And you've chosen . . ."

"I keep opening up. It's kept me alive so far." She turns then and walks off past the rows of shelves.

I step back into the elevator, ride it back down, and quickly slip into an empty office—one that's small and filled with boxes—and I stare out of the window out at the street. Fadra's going home. Just like that. Anything can happen. Open up or shut down. Isn't there one other option? Just one?

My phone buzzes like a convulsing hive in my hand—texts 8, 9, 10. I try to take deep breaths. I fog the glass and close my eyes.

Don't be a murderer, Godfrey Burkes, I whisper to myself. *Don't be a creepy freaking murderer. Please.*

I open my eyes, and as if walking out of the fog on the window, there's a human-sized duck. A person in a white duck costume, holding an American flag in one duck mitt and a pocketbook in the other duck mitt. The duck looks up at the library, as if unsure of its decision to borrow books today or not.

And then a teenager glides by on a skateboard—one of those emo kids, looking really skinny and emotive—in from the other direction and snatches the duck's purse. Dot was right about those skateboarders!

The duck spikes the flag and starts running after the kid, but there are giant webbed feet strapped onto the duck's shoes and she can't really run.

The duck pulls the duck head off, drops it, and screams obscenities at the kid on the skateboard. Then, in an act of pure rage and desperation, the duck grips handfuls of feathers from her own costume and rips them out, shaking them in her fists over her head, and screams, falling dramatically to her knees.

Under my breath, I say, "We've got a duck down. A good duck down."

I turn and start running. "Chuck!" I shout, running to the entrance. "Chuck!" When I get to the bright airy entranceway, he's already through the doors and darting through traffic running down the marble steps toward the distraught duck.

A few customers are staring at me. I raise my hands. "No need for alarm! Go about your business!" And I turn on my heel and half jog, half fast walk to Gupta's office.

I knock on his door. "Mr. Gupta! A duck just got robbed! In broad daylight!"

What's the world coming to?

Godfrey
GODFREY IN LOVE

I knock at Bart and Amy's door and no one answers. I'm about to walk away, but then I hear Bart arguing with Amy through their door, which is thick—the kind that can support three heavy bolt locks, so I know the argument is loud. I think again about leaving. I could crawl back to my parents' house, but that just seems even more pathetic than this. I could sleep in the hallway. But aren't nights like these exactly what best friends are for?

I finally hear a deadbolt unlocking, then the slight turn of the handle. The door doesn't open all the way. I'm not surprised. I can still hear Amy yelling in the background. "That shit-turd" rings loudly.

Bart pops his head out of the half-open door. "This isn't really a good time," he says, clearing his throat, trying to mask the noise that's going on behind him.

I want to tell him, *Save your throat. I could hear the two of you bitch for the last five minutes.* He's not wearing the boat shoes, but he's still decked out in pleated chinos and a white linen button-down that's only buttoned up halfway. The strands of his chest hair make him look like a little boy dressing up as a sexy Ernst & Young accountant for Halloween.

"Madge locked me out," I tell him.

"I know," he says. "She went hysterical after you stormed out last night. DEFCON 5." His voice hushes, which only magnifies Amy in the background. She's dropping plates in the sink.

"You mean DEFCON 1," I tell him.

"No," Bart says, "she's got the crazy eyes."

"Exactly. One is like nuclear fucking explosion. Five is Switzerland."

"Whatever, Godfrey, I'm too tired to argue about stupid stuff." Bart quickly glances behind himself before turning back to me. He opens the front door a little farther. A pan hits the floor. "That was probably what was left of the lasagna."

Bart lets his head fall against the doorframe. He looks exhausted. In moments I go from slight contempt to heavy pity. I don't even know my best friend anymore. In a year or two would I even be able to recognize him in a police lineup? *That's my friend!* I'll tell the cop, and the cop will say, *No, that's a war lord being burned in effigy,* and I'll go, *Oh.* "You've aged like ten years," I tell him. "Like those before and after pictures of two-term presidents."

"Dude, I have aged. It's crazy."

I wonder how long it's been since I've lost Bart. Was it my fault? Was Bart this way last week? Last month? "Have I just been too self-absorbed to notice anything around me?"

"Well, you noticed the boat shoes."

"Sorry about that. What's wrong?"

"I think I'm dying inside." He looks over his shoulder. "I can't talk about it now."

I ruffle through the pockets of my wrinkled khakis and run my fingers around the winning receipt from Fontana's, then the Thigpen letter, given to me just hours ago by my mother. Will she still die? "Everyone dies. I just happen to want to live a little first." I want my fingers to be ruffling Evelyn's hair, wringing the chlorine out of her dress after we jump into the pool. My mother would be buried by then, but we will survive the grief caused by the cycle of life and death and life. Everything really is like *The Lion King*.

"No philosophy lessons now, okay? What do you want, Godfrey?"

"A shower. A pillow. Maybe some clothes." I smell myself. "Hell, we can look like a GAP ad together."

"You're an asshole," he says, "And it's Banana Republic, not GAP." He's smiling some—not a lot but enough.

I recognize *that* Bart! The one with the smile—my old roommate. Hi, Bart.

"Look Bart, where is she?"

"Madge? I wouldn't rush in."

"I have to rush in. For one thing, she has my phone. I'm nothing without a phone. I'm standing before you completely amputated by a lack of technology—amputated, Bart! Also, she could be sabotaging me with my own phone at this very moment. I could be hoisted by my own petard, here, Bart. And no man wants that!"

"I don't know what that means. Hoisted by your petard? Is that a dick reference?"

"No! God, no! Look." I growl a little with frustration. "I'm trying to mitigate the damage with a grand gesture." I'm kind of rambling now, full-head-of-steam variety. "Maybe you can steal the phone back for me. If you can get Amy to let you talk to Madge, you know, on my behalf or something, and then you can get in close and you can steal the phone back. You know? It's not really stealing because the phone is actually mine to begin with and—"

"I'm not stealing your phone back! My God, Madge could bite my arm off! Amy would amputate me somehow, too—for real!"

"Okay, okay, just let me spend the night. You can dust off the PlayStation," I say. "We can be in college again, even if it's just for a night."

Behind Bart, another pan hits the floor. We both cringe.

I continue. "Or forever. I found a time machine in a Dumpster behind Fontana's." Another loud clang. We don't cringe this time; we were ready for it. "I'll take us there right now."

"You really fucked up, man." Bart's voice is lower than a whisper. "And now I'm paying for it. She's been so pissed off; everything got burned to shit. Half of it is still stuck to the pan that's now on the floor."

"I didn't do anything to Amy."

"That speech! That comment about her ass getting fat?"

"I incriminated all of our asses," I say, wagging my head. "That was democratic."

"You screwed up the abstract art lesson," he says. "We weren't there to celebrate. Madge called and told us before we showed up that you'd fucked it up."

"If you weren't there to celebrate, then what were you there for?"

"Moral support!"

"For me?"

He wiggles the knob.

"Wait. Moral support is for someone who has to do something hard. Were you there to support Madge? Was she going to break up with me?"

Bart just keeps fiddling.

"Bart."

Was Madge really going to end this first? I can't decide if I'm offended or relieved. On one hand, it makes everything easier. With Madge gone, and by her choice, things with Evelyn can fall into place. It'll be like I did nothing wrong. Everything wiped clean—a Windex relationship moment. I think about Evelyn's envisioning, the hand-holding, the proposal. Still, something sinks inside of me.

I take his nonanswer as confirmation, but I still need to hear him say it. "Bart," I say again.

"She said the art session was your last shot. But you can't say anything. Seriously, forget I mentioned anything. She might not want to break up with you now. She might want to . . ."

"What? Torture me?"

"I've heard some talk," he says ominously. "Look, Godfrey, I'm not fucking around. If Amy finds out I even mentioned this, she'll smother me in my sleep. I'm serious. The rhetoric in this house has gotten really dark."

"Bart," I say. "I just need a place to crash tonight."

"Give me a sec," he tells me, holding his hand out before shutting the door in my face.

Madge was going to break up with me? Is that possible? Maybe we can broker a clean breakup. Something mutual. I mean, she won't want to torture me forever, right? That's heat-of-the-moment talk. I'm feeling almost free—almost.

When he opens the front door this time, he opens it all the way and gestures me inside. We stop in the hallway.

"The rules," he says.

"Rules?"

"You have to sleep on the couch."

"But you have a guest room, and it's so aptly named."

"We keep things in there," he says.

"Things?"

"Yes, things."

"What kind of things?"

"I don't know, Godfrey. We have things. We keep them in the guest room. The things."

"Yes, you said that. The things."

"Yes or no?" Bart says.

"Okay," I say. "The couch. I'll sleep on the fucking couch. Do I get a pillow?"

Bart actually has to think about this, like I'm asking for a kidney or a wife swap. "I didn't ask."

"You're not kidding, are you?"

"No." He looks at me like I just asked to fuck his sister. "Kidding? I'm not kidding. This is no joke, Godfrey. Nothing about this is funny."

"You said rules. Plural. That was only one."

"You're not allowed to eat anything. Amy threatened to lock the pantry. I guess we have locks; I didn't know we have locks, but I assure you, we do. And if you want some water, it has to come from the tap. Amy says you can't use the Brita pitcher."

Baltimore tap water. Jesus. "You're really not kidding, are you?"

"Don't. I already said no."

We're still in the hallway. Amy drops one more plate in the sink before finally huffing off into the bedroom.

Bart exhales. "You know I'm not getting laid tonight because of this," he says.

"Were you anyway?"

"If I did the dishes . . ." His voice trails off. He pauses. "Maybe."

"I'm sorry for cock-blocking you," I say. And I mean it. I feel bad. He seems so stressed, so wound up.

"It's okay," Bart says, and then we're just standing there. This quiet awkward—the pregnant pause of our voices, the slight hum of the heater, the lack of pans and dishes banging.

Finally I say, "Are there any rules stipulating whether I can borrow some clean, dry clothes?"

"Maybe I can have some say over that. They're my clothes. I'll see."

"I really appreciate this, and I'm sorry about what I said last night. All of that shit about your shoes and all."

"Godfrey." His eyes get nervous. He glances back over his shoulder. "Don't worry about it. I'm on your side."

"What?"

"I can't talk about it now. Just know that I'm with you, man."

BART WON THE CLOTHING argument and he lent me a pair of pajamas. Since I've got almost four inches over him, his pajama pants fall short of my ankles. But they're flannel and warm, so I can't complain. My old clothes are balled into a clump next to my bed, the couch. The letter from my father is still in my chinos. I pull it out.

Once I start reading it, I can't stop. I read well past complete memorization, but it still feels fresh each time. I want to tell Bart about the letter, how most of my life has been a lie and how I've accepted the love I've accepted because of that lie. But it's time to say, *I'm a Thigpen and it is okay that I'm a Thigpen. It has been written. And on the seventh day God did not rest. He made the Thigpens and He was pleased.*

Bart walks in and says, "You all right?"

"I'm fine. You don't understand the urgency of this situation. I really need to talk to Madge."

"What's there to understand? You want to win her back and you've got to let it breathe a little."

"I don't want to win her back."

"What?"

"I'm in love with someone else." I can't believe I've said this out loud.

"Are you insane?"

"I have to break up with Madge. I have to."

"Ho, God. Ho, God," Bart says. "This is bad. This is so much worse than I thought." Bart sits down on the arm of the couch closest to the hallway. He props one foot on one knee and cradles his head, rocking. Then he pops his head up. "Who is she? Tell me."

"Evelyn Shriner."

"I don't know that name."

"No, you do not."

"Godfrey, this is ape shit."

"I know."

Bart slides off the arm and into the chair itself. His body is now slack. "I don't like change. I have a hard time with it. You know that."

I prop myself on one elbow. "What did you mean you're on my side?"

"Shhh," Bart says. "Jesus."

"Okay, settle down," I say. "How long have we known each other, Bart?"

He thinks about this for a minute. "Twelve years," he finally says.

"Since eighth grade."

"Ms. Maloney's class."

Algebra. Honors, I think, but it's hard to remember exact logistics from that long ago. What I do remember: the size of Evelyn's bed. Her ass in her bikini bottoms when she got of her giant bed. "We both sat in the front row because we didn't want to wear our glasses because we thought the girls wouldn't like us if they knew we had to wear glasses."

"The girls didn't like us anyway."

"Took us a while to figure that out."

"Too long," he says. "We were never the smartest."

"Actually I don't know how we got into Honors Algebra."

"Everything works out," Bart says. "Eventually."

"Is this working out, Bart? I mean it, is this part of your definition of working out?"

"Look, man," he whispers. "I'm worried. Deeply worried."

"About what?"

"I think seeing my future messed me up."

"How?"

"I'm old."

"You don't look any older."

He points to his sternum. "Inside. I aged. I can't explain, but I think I'm headed for a midlife crisis." He kneels beside me and grabs my arm. "I'm about to have some kind of fucking crisis."

I sit up. I'm a little scared he's going to start crying or throw up.

I'm not sure which scares me more. "It's okay, Bart. It's okay. I'm here. You're going to be okay. Okay?"

"Am I?"

"We all are," I say, though I don't really believe myself.

"I'm sorry I told Amy that story about you getting lost and being too embarrassed to call that girl back."

"It wasn't meant to be, you know?"

"I'm going to be okay," he says. "Okay." He stands up and starts to skulk off. But then he stops and says, "You should try to slip out in the morning before we're up. It's not going to be pretty." It's too dark to watch him walk away, but I can hear his feet plodding against the hardwood floor as he makes his way down the hall.

Evelyn
MRS. FUOCO

I'm sleeping at Dot's place. She insisted. "What if that effer's a real psycho? I feel bad about letting you invite him up. I mean, that stuff he texted you about Kristen Stewart and his *Twilight* paraphernalia was just so wrong. It was some twisted shit."

I agreed.

DOT'S MOTHER'S IN TOWN, so I'm sharing a futon with her and Dot's bichon frise, Fipps, an adorable dog with labored breathing, currently dressed in a hand-knit Irish fisherman's sweater. Mrs. Fuoco is wearing a yoga outfit to bed and I'm dressed in an old-fashioned flannel nightgown. I stare up at Dot's ceiling. Her mother says, "They're all nut jobs, Evelyn. You just got to ask yourself, would I be better off as a lesbian? Think about it. I think you're a really good influence on my little girl."

"I think we're just not lesbians, Mrs. Fuoco."

"I don't know why she steals stuff like that, you know?"

"You've done your best, Mrs. Fuoco," I say, trying to console her. This day has been so shitty. I need someone to tell me everything's going to be okay and I haven't just spent the night with a psycho. "I'm for tighter gun control laws. I worry about sociopaths, don't you?"

"What in the hell are you talking about?" Mrs. Fuoco shifts on the futon, and I realize I'm no longer making sense.

"I'm sorry," I say. "Never mind."

"You should absolutely take this the wrong way," Mrs. Fuoco says. "You're a really unusual person, Evelyn. Good heart. Weird head."

"It's just been one of those days, you know?" Mrs. Fuoco doesn't say anything. I bet she's had a lot of days like this. I press on. "I had to give a witness account of an emo skateboarder robbing a duck. I don't know what to think about anything anymore. And, well—"

"Just spit it out."

"I need a hug," I say. I worry I'm being too forward. I backtrack. "But I'll settle for a hand through my hair or a pat on the back."

"I thought we were talking about me and my daughter issues."

"Right," I say, but I'm thinking maybe I should become a lesbian and marry Dot in a gazebo on the edge of a lake. We'll have a small service—just the extended family. We'll write our own vows. Creepy Godfrey will stand on the other side of the lake, staring.

And then I think of Mrs. Fuoco. I mean, we were, in fact, talking about her and her daughter issues. I say, "Well, Mrs. Fuoco, you could play charades in a nicer manner."

"Are you saying I don't play charades nice?"

"You can be a little aggressive," I say, "while playing charades."

I wonder if Mrs. Fuoco's going to get vicious and make mean comments about my hair. But I just hear her breathing. Fipps gets up, turns a few circles, scratches at the comforter, and flops down again.

Mrs. Fuoco says, "See, honesty. That's what I look for in a person. Just don't rush the nonlesbian thing. These people can get married now in the state of Maryland, you know? Free Belgian waffle makers. You get my point."

"I do." But I'm in love with Godfrey Burkes, a person I thought I knew, deep down and immediately, like a sudden recognition of someone you know will be with you forever. The *ah!* of *Hey, you finally showed up; I've been missing you.* How could I be so wrong? "Do you think there are only two options to living, Mrs. Fuoco? Either opening up or shutting down?"

"I'm Italian. Shutting down isn't an option. So we've got just the one." And then I feel this little pat-pat on my arm. "You're going to be okay, Evie," she says.

Evie. My parents never nicknamed me. I like Evie. But part of me knows that not so long ago, I'd have read more into it. I'd have tried to allow the nickname of Evie to fill the hole inside of me that Adrian says I can't fill. It's not enough—this nickname, this pat-pat. And it shouldn't be. Still, I appreciate it. "Thank you, Mrs. Fuoco," I whisper.

"For what?" she says, the moment having passed.

Then my phone buzzes and buzzes—more and more deranged texts.

"Can you turn that thing off?" Mrs. Fuoco says.

"Sorry, Mrs. Fuoco. I've started to pretend it's the sound of peepers," I say. "You know, those little frogs that chirp at night." As if one of the texts will be the right text and I'll be able to tell by the quality of its buzz.

"Well, it's annoying as shit. Who can sleep with that crap-noise?"

I turn it off.

Godfrey
INTO THE SEA

The sun wakes me up and I slip out of Bart and Amy's apartment as quickly as I can. I'm so quiet it's as if I ghosted through the front door, down the two flights of circular stairs, and into my frost-covered car. I've got shit to do.

I put the key into the ignition and let the car warm up. I turn up the defroster. I count to sixty. Twice. I pull away from the curb. I take a left and head toward the suburban sprawl of the outskirts of Baltimore. I'm going to Chin's.

Evelyn was right. I should see my future with my father. Mart Thigpen.

I wonder if Evelyn has gotten the singing telegram yet. It's bolder, more romantic, more clever than any text message could ever be. I remind myself to stay positive, to show a little bravado, to hope for the best. I'm making decisions from the heart here. That should count for something.

Dr. Chin's is packed. This early? Why? Not a single chair is available. Patients are glued against the two far walls like wallpaper. The office is hot, not from the heating system as much as the amount of skin in such a cramped space. Can all of these people have appointments?

I make my way to the receptionist window. Lisa is behind the glass. She's always here, behind the glass. Briefly, I feel very sorry for her. Her bangs are damp, clumped against her forehead from sweat. I'm the sixth person in line.

I think of Evelyn. This is where we first met. I look down at my feet. Maybe this exact spot. No, it was closer. We were at the window because she was talking to Lisa. Evelyn held her driver's license between her teeth. I should've kissed her then, in line. I should've taken the driver's license out of her mouth with my teeth, and followed her home to her giant bed and shelves stacked with Modest Mouse and Cat Power records. I should have known.

Soon enough I'm standing directly in front of Lisa. Only the glass is between us. I never noticed how thick the glass was. It looks bulletproof, which wouldn't surprise me. Desperate patients who haven't been able to get appointments are bound to raise hell. And for the first time I notice that the chairs have mismatched upholstery and some of the legs are chipped and the walls are pocked with small dents. Is this the result of patients losing it, throwing chairs and chucking them into the walls? If so, I get it. I look at Lisa. "I need an appointment today," I say. "Yesterday would've been better, but today will have to do."

"You're kidding, right?" Lisa actually guffaws. "You've seen the waiting room, right?" She points to a group of hopeful patients in the far corner. Some of them are holding white cone paper cups in their hands, sipping slowly, while others just sway back and forth. If I strain my ears, I can hear teeth chatter.

I turn back around. I nod. "They're the Desperates," Lisa says. She leans forward in her swivel chair. It creaks. Her voice drops to a hush. I have to strain to hear her. She shakes her head. "Poor bastards." She leans back in the swivel chair.

The teeth chattering. The swaying. Those white cone cups that aren't thick enough for the cold water so they melt in your hands. Aren't I better than they are? I press my hands against the bullet-proof glass that separates her from the rest of us. "I need this," I say. It comes out as a hiss.

Lisa wags her finger before reaching for something under her desk. She pulls out a sign, handwritten on orange construction paper: DO NOT TOUCH GLASS. I drop my hands to my sides. I can feel my voice start to rise, which is awkward, because my hands are still at my sides. I want to be animated, but I'm not allowed. "Can you smell me?" I say. "I'm probably the only thing that can cut through the shitty scent of egg rolls and dirty woks. Go ahead, ask me the last time I brushed my teeth. Things are not going well—at all!"

"Twenty bucks," Lisa whispers.

"What?" I have to blink to focus on her.

"Idiot, I'm asking for a bribe."

I reach into my back pocket and pull out my wallet. I don't expect there to be any money when I open it, but there's one bill. I don't know how it got there. Maybe Bart slipped it in when I wasn't looking. God bless that poor bastard. It's a twenty. I pinch Andrew Jackson's face between my index finger and thumb.

"Now slide it to me," she says. "Slowly and carefully."

I do.

Lisa folds it up into four tiny squares and sticks it in her bra. Her hands find the keyboard on her desk and she starts typing. "Have a seat, Mr. Burkes," she says, not looking at me. Her fingers are still moving. "A nurse will be with you shortly."

I turn away from the glass window and look around the waiting room. I lean against a wall with the rest of the patients until my name is called. I follow a nurse all the way to the end of the hallway. There's a back door, which is a fire exit. EMERGENCY USE ONLY, the sign says. I didn't know that Chin's office went this far back. The nurse stops. I stop with her. I look at the number above the room: 19. Maybe this is where the deep fryer was when this was a Chinese restaurant. She sets a paper gown on the chair before leaving. Even though it's stuffy in Chin's, I'm cold. I change quickly.

Moments later, two knocks on the door before Dr. Chin lets himself in. "An emergency envisioning," he says, and he looks like his night was hellish, too. He's bleary-eyed, rushed, distracted.

"I'm on a mission," I tell him. "I'm broke, I smell, and my fiancée might be telling my girlfriend that I have a fiancée. I don't have time for idle conversation."

Dr. Chin says, "It's bad all around, Godfrey. No one is spared their personal grief." My hands are folded in my lap. My face is staring straight at the blank screen.

"I'm here for my father," I say. "I know it's not a romantic request, but I've heard that maybe you can find a loophole, and love is love and—"

Chin cuts me off. "Do you know what I sell?"

"Um, the future?"

"I sell a comfort. There's one fear that most people want allayed. It comes from a simple question: 'Is it always going to be like this?'"

"Like what?"

"Like whatever fearful, anxious, vulnerable, specific lives they find themselves in. And it doesn't matter what future I show them because all they really want to hear is, 'No, it's not always going to be like this.' Anyone who's the least bit unhappy wants to hear this, Godfrey. And that's what I sell. Not futures and surely not *better* futures. I just sell an answer: 'No, it's not always going to be like this.'" Chin squeezes his eyes shut and shakes his big head. "Is that so wrong?"

"No?" I say.

"That's right!" Chin says. "That's not wrong at all!" It seems like I've said the right thing because Chin walks to the computer. "I can try to swing it. It'll be a moment that still has to do with your romantic future, though. That's locked in, but I'll have it circle around your father."

"Perfect," I say. "Thank you."

"I need Mr. Burkes's first name."

"No, my real father. Mart Thigpen. Ten years into the future. I don't want him to be dead, you know?" I think of my mother—the rabbits, the pool. Evelyn. It's easy to think of Evelyn.

"Thigpen," Chin says. "Thigpen, the animal." He's leaning over the keyboard, typing Mart Thigpen's name into the computer. I watch each letter of my father's name fill the screen.

"I'm surprised you remembered." I put on the helmet. I pretend to be in a spaceship. I pretend this is all a game—it's easier that way, nothing to let you down.

"A doctor never forgets," Chin says, and then he types in thirty years even though I told him only ten, which casts doubt on Chin's theory on the steel-trap memories of doctors. He slides the tray of pills over to where I'm sitting. I think about correcting him. Thirty years is a long time. The world could be dead in thirty years. I haven't seen the Al Gore documentary, but I think that's what he says in it. He hands me the pills. "You know I was training on the better equipment. I wanted to make it more surgical. When to enter the future to give you the answer to an exact question . . . Oh well."

"You'd have to know the right question, though, right?" I pop the pills.

"The right question is always more important than the answer."

"Then why even get the new technology?"

"I'll miss you, Godfrey," he says.

"I'm not going anywhere."

"I know," Chin says, and with a sad mysterious smile, he walks out.

As the medication rolls the fog in over my eyes, I think of the Pixies' song: *If man is five . . . the devil is six.* Out loud I finish the line, "Then God is seven."

I stare at the screen. The camera opens on future-me. I'm sitting on a bench. In thirty years, my hands still aren't pruned. My face isn't too sagged. I'm quite handsome. I take this as a good sign—I'm taking care of myself, which means I'm probably happy. The camera slowly pans out. An old man is sitting next to future-me on the bench. A walker rests in front of him. The old man is Mart Thigpen. His face is smeared, but his body is the shape of a retired mobster. Or maybe a linebacker from a Division III college team. The years have hunched his shoulders. Gravity's constant pull has shortened him. Baldness found him. I find his lack of hair disconcerting. I wonder when it started. I instinctively start to reach up to touch my hair, but it hits the helmet. I always forget the helmet. I focus back on the screen. The bench is outside, but it's not at a park. I can't pinpoint the location until I hear waves crash into themselves. I look at the bottom of the screen. There's sand around our shoes. It's caked onto the rusted legs of the bench, years of salty air eroding the metal.

I study my father. Mart Thigpen rubs his thinned out ankles. He's wearing thin white tube socks with black loafers, a pair of shorts and a T-shirt with a small rectangular pocket. The camera pans out and I can see the coastline, the roughness of the waves. I think it's the Atlantic.

My father uses the walker for support as he slowly pushes himself off the bench. But even with the walker, he still wobbles. Future-me grabs his right elbow to steady him. When future-me curls his hand around my father's thin bicep, I catch a glimpse of a silver wedding band on my left ring finger.

In thirty years, I'm married. Does this mean things work out with Evelyn? Do I get to her before Madge does? Or maybe I've been freaking out about nothing, and Madge doesn't even have my phone. Maybe I lucked out and a bondagey woman stole it but left my wallet out of kindness. Right now she could be prank-calling parts of Canada and Argentina and Sweden, running up my phone bill before selling the phone for scraps on eBay. I can live with that. I mean, I'm married! And my father is still alive in thirty years! I am feeling optimistically petrified.

Still, nothing has been said. I wonder where we're going. Is my father deaf? If so, why wouldn't I learn sign language to talk with him?

The way the two of us walk down the paved path horizontal to the ocean looks rehearsed, like this is a normal thing. Maybe a Sunday morning ritual, before or after bagels and the *New York Times*—if newspapers somehow still exist—at the corner deli, sitting in the same booth—the one in the corner closest to the bathroom because Mart has to pee *all the time.*

Abruptly, the two of us turn left and head straight for the ocean. I find this surprising. I'm in slacks and Mart's in shorts and socks. Are we going in?

We can't be going into the water, can we? I help him take off his shoes and then take off my own.

My father's gripping the walker with both hands. Future-me is right by his side—my hand is curled again around my father's bicep. He pushes the walker awkwardly but with determination through the sand.

Is future-me taking my father into the ocean to drown him? Is that why we aren't talking—a quiet understanding that it's time to go? Is Mart Thigpen sick? Is this a tepid excuse for family to get together? Am I about to shout out, *Hey, kids, come to the ocean! We're drowning Grandpa!* The optimism is gone. I could vomit.

We are *definitely* going into the ocean. The waves roll up to our knees. My pants are soaked. We have both forgotten how to speak. The camera is in shaky-cam mode now as it follows future-me and my father as he pushes his walker slowly into the tide.

Can someone this old swim? Their bellies are often bigger than when they're young, so maybe they float, like citrus. The camera cuts. Now the view is from the ocean shore, with the lens of the camera pointing up. My father and future-me look like giants. Maybe slow giant sloths. Mart Thigpen in his eighties, pushing a walker through bleached sand. Mild grunts. Slowly trudging into the ocean.

Every few seconds a wave crashes up over the lens. Each time, I want to hit the side of the TV, as if it's a static issue from the 1960s. But I don't get out of my chair. The helmet wouldn't let me if I tried.

Is this the moment of precipice?

And then the session is interrupted by a short commercial from Earl Chin, Esquire. "He'll stand up for *you*!" Earl smiles with his hands crossed, looking tough but smart and stern.

Then a jellyfish washes up with the tide. In thirty years, there are still jellyfish. Finally future-me stops. He's up to his hips in the ocean. My father hands him the walker. Future-me reaches out and grabs it.

My father says, "What do you think happened?"

"The girls grew up," I say. "The house was suddenly too empty." Am I talking about Evelyn? Did something go wrong with us? "Now that we aren't parents to the girls, who are we? Do we even need each other?"

"Now more than ever," my father says, the waves pushing both of us, relentlessly.

Future-me says, "Are you going to tell me what to do?"

"I regret so much in my life," my father says. "I should've fought for you. If I had, I wouldn't have felt so weighted down." And then, with a final heave forward, my father is buoyant. He moves slowly like a sea turtle. "Go home and fight for her!" he shouts over the waves. "Fight like hell!"

And with that, he glides through the water, bobs over a wave, and keeps swimming. He's got a very smooth breaststroke.

A wave crests my chest, and I look back to the shore. My father wishes he'd fought for me. I didn't know it, but it's what I've been waiting to hear. My father, Mart Thigpen, regrets letting me go. I'm not my father. I'll learn from his mistakes.

If I marry Evelyn, it won't always be perfect, but I'll fight for her. I'll fight like hell.

Evelyn
THE DATE

"Fuck text messages," I say.

"Fuck phones," Dot says.

"Fuck learning to swim."

"Fuck guys who show up freezing, throwing pebbles at your window. But you should still learn to swim."

"Fuck Godfrey Fucking Burkes," I say too loudly. Two high-school students camped out by the periodicals turn around and look at us. Dot flips them off. Luckily, Gupta isn't around. Dot's still working through her "trial basis." "From now on, we will not speak his name."

"Like Voldemort," Dot says.

"Which we're also not supposed to say."

What's strange is that I know I read Godfrey all wrong. All wrong. But really? *That* wrong? Some part of me doesn't want to talk about him because I still hold out hope that he's going to come back to me—the Godfrey of that night. And when I think of that night, I feel like I'm letting myself fall through a hole, spinning in circles, like during the opening credits of *The X-Files*. Would Godfrey's rabbits be at the other end of the carpet hole?

"Fuck Godfrey's rabbits," I say, already breaking the rule of silence. "And that kiss on *The X-Files* was less than inspiring. We waited seven years for Mulder to finally do it, and we got *that*?"

"No kidding," Dot says, no segue necessary.

I check my phone again. The texts have stopped. Mercifully. Still, I keep checking it.

"Stop looking at that," Dot says.

"It's like a drug," I say, "that my parents pay for every month."

"Your parents still pay for your phone?"

"I'm on their plan. It's a small thing that they've forgotten they give me. I take it."

With her free hand, Dot grabs the phone from me.

"What are you doing?"

"Saving you," she says, shutting the phone off and putting it in her back pocket.

And I let her. Is this opening up or shutting down?

A flyer at the edge of the desk catches the corner of my eye. There's always a new flyer at the corner of the desk—WEEKEND BLOOD DRIVE: SAVE A LIFE AND GET A FREE MOVIE TICKET!, CHLAMYDIA IS NOT A FLOWER, CAR WASH FOR FOOTBALL JERSEYS, CAR WASH FOR JESUS—but nothing that's ever looked like *this*.

This being an old printing press in the center of the flyer and next to it is a hand—God's hand?—on the lever, cranking the machine. Pages of babies fall from the printing press and litter the floor. You can't see the floor. Above the printing press and maybe

God's hand, typed in all caps and bolded: THE BABYMAKERS LIVE AT CLUB Q. FRIDAY. 7 P.M.

"Have you seen this?" I say. I'm a little impressed. They've upgraded to a full sheet this time. And it's the best looking artwork that's ever graced the front of a Babymakers flyer. It's apparent that life can easily go on without me.

Dot clears her throat. I look up from the stack of flyers. She's not looking at me. I follow her eyes to Adam Greenberg. He just came out of one of the fiction aisles and has made a beeline for us.

"Shit," Dot says. Then, after a balloon deflates from her chest: "It's not even Friday." There's a book cart in front of her, and she's started packing books from the return bin onto it.

"Spoiler alert: it is Friday. If you didn't take my phone, I'd show you."

Dot glances at me for a second. She raises her eyebrows.

"Friday." I nod.

"Well, he's *early.*"

I look at the clock on the wall. Dot's right, Adam is early. Exactly four minutes early.

"You really, really should stay," I say.

Dot stops.

Adam is closer. He's picked up his casual pace of sweater vest ambivalence. His legs have built a purpose. I look back at Dot. She still hasn't said anything. It's like a split-screen movie scene: Adam holding the book for—presumably—his mother against his chest like it's the only thing keeping his insides inside him. Dot not doing anything. Adam getting closer, the argyle pattern on his sweater vest becoming visible, how the striped colors curl and fold into themselves like a magical act. Dot still not doing anything. And then both screens blend into one with Adam standing in front of the check-out desk.

"Hi!" I say.

"Hi," Adam says, but he's not looking at me. His eyes are focused on Dot. I'm too nervous to look over at her. It's Dot's turn to talk. I pinch her leg behind the desk, out of view of Adam Greenberg.

"It's Friday," Dot says finally.

"Yes," Adam says. He's still smiling. "It's been that way since I woke up."

"I thought it was Thursday," she says. "But then Evelyn said it was Friday . . . I didn't know."

I cut in. "Is that the next one?"

Adam looks at me, confused. He starts to open his mouth, but I save him by pointing to the book cemented to his chest. He looks down at it and blushes a little.

"Yes." He sets the book on the desk and slides it over. "My mother loved the last one."

"That Oprah sure knows how to pick 'em. Am I right, Dot?"

Adam and I both look at Dot. She's looking between us. And for a few moments we stay this way, an awkward tripod not holding anything up.

I shift first, taking *The Reader* out of his hands and putting its barcode under the scanner. I could light the book on fire, and neither Adam nor Dot would notice the library burning down around them. It would be a pretty great music video for a Babymakers single. I reach for my phone in my back pocket. My pocket is empty. I forgot that Dot took it. I slide *The Reader* back across the counter to Adam.

"So," I say. "Any big plans for the weekend?"

"I'm volunteering with The Boys & Girls Club this Saturday," he says. "The Lyric Opera Baltimore is doing a children's benefit concert this Saturday at the Lyric."

"That is so sweet of you," Dot says. "Children are good. *I mean,* they're like the future."

"Yes," I say. "Children. Are. Good." This is painful. I wish I weren't a witness to it.

"I'm free tonight, though." Adam's eyes are back at Dot. Dot's eyes are back at Adam, if they ever left.

I pinch Dot again. She shifts violently. Her upper lip is gleaming. "Well, Evelyn and I are going to a show tonight."

"Really?" Adam and I say simultaneously.

Dot looks at me in mock surprise. "You remember, Evelyn." She picks up one of Adrian's flyers. "We've been planning on going for *weeks.*" She turns back to Adam and hands him the flyer. "The Babymakers. You should come; they're pretty great."

My heart gets on a treadmill. Dot can't be serious. I place my palms on the counter.

"I'd love to go," Adam says. "If it's okay with Evelyn."

I can feel them both looking at me. In a twisted way, this is all my fault. I prodded Dot to stay, basically forced her to ask Adam out. I haven't seen Adrian since he went through his box of shit in the middle of my living room. I was actually hoping to never see him again.

"Evelyn would love if you came," Dot says, this time pinching my leg behind the information desk. "Isn't that right, Ev?"

"Yes. Yes, of course. It'd be perfect."

Adam folds up the flyer and puts it in his back pocket. "This is great," he says, still smiling.

What I wouldn't give to be Charlie from *Firestarter*. Watch Adam's sweater vest light up in flames. Watch him flail around the library. I wouldn't let him die, obviously—Dot would be crushed, hopelessly chained to a life of stolen forks and an impending prison sentence—but he'd have to spend the night in the hospital. And that would mean no concert. No Adrian.

"I'll see you two tonight." He's still smiling, backing away from the information desk slowly, as if we might disappear, before finally turning around and walking out of the library with *The Reader* tucked under his arm.

It's been years since I've taken drugs, but that's how I feel right now, stoned on my old friend Jared's green shag rug, an orange soda stain the shape of a moon in the center of it, and Jared trying to count how many Aderall can fit in a Pez dispenser.

I still feel dazed. "Really? I mean, really? Adrian's band's concert?"

"I freaked out!" Dot throws her hands up like the Feds just busted a three-year deal she was planning with the Columbian cartel. "I think one-half of my brain stole the other half of my brain! You have to come with me. I can't do this alone. I can't. Please, God. You have to come, too. This means everything to me. You know I hate begging. You know that!"

I look at the stack of flyers. I pick one up. Beneath the printing press churning out baby pages is the tiny line, YOUR EX-GIRLFRIEND WILL NOT LIKE THIS. I want to crawl back to my empty apartment with its single wineglass in the sink and a Cat Power record just below the needle. I feel safest there.

"Your ex-girlfriend will *not* like this," I mutter.

"At least you won't be going in with any expectations."

Godfrey
LIVE AT CLUB Q

Hunched behind one of the two green Dumpsters in the alley between Club Q and a Western Union, I wonder if maybe this is all a setup. That these last two months of my life—the whole idea of an envisioning session—never actually existed. That someone like Evelyn could breathe outside of a television set. Do beds that big even exist? When was the last time a woman wore a bikini to bed and didn't wake up still drunk off Jäger? It's not spring break. This isn't Panama City. Did Madge hire a call girl to get in bed with me just to get out of an engagement she never seemed to want in the first place? If so, did Evelyn—if that's even her real name—at least enjoy it? Even a little? Is Bart in on the plan? Amy would be, for sure. She's always hated me. But Bart? He could be like a brother I'm sometimes embarrassed of. Is he just a pawn? Jesus, I can see him right now at the end of the alley, standing guard, pacing with his hands in his pockets. No, Bart's innocent; his only sin is being oblivious.

I'm going bat shit. I'm seeing the wrong kind of doctor. Nobody could think up anything this crazy. This is my reality: I'm half naked behind a Dumpster in the tail end of a Baltimore winter, changing into a fresh set of Bart's clothes.

His chinos sag around my waist—I didn't realize he'd put on the chubby midsection weight. He forgot to bring an extra belt, which means I have to use my belt, which is frozen stiff like a riding crop. My two-day-old pants are on the ground next to my shirt and coat. My cock is shriveled from the frozen wind. I feel like I haven't hit puberty yet. The chinos are four inches too short, exposing my bare ankles. Bart forgot socks.

He did bring Speed Stick and his cologne, Obsession by Calvin Klein. I go liberal with it on my neck. It runs down my chest. At least the club will be smoky, and I doubt most of the patrons showered today. Or yesterday, for that matter.

I get Bart's pink linen Oxford buttoned up when two girls slide out of the back entrance of the club. The light is bright, and I think, *Deer.* But they're already drunk, loud, holding hands and giggling—both wearing boots up past their knees and black tights that do nothing but cover what their skirts don't. And they pass on by. I'm thankful for my ability to be overlooked by women.

I toss my clothes into the Dumpster—screw it—and make my way to Bart. We stand and stare at Club Q.

"This stress is making me swirl," Bart says. He reaches into his pocket and pulls out a package of Tums. He takes two and offers them to me. My stomach feels deflated, but I take one anyway. It's the closest I've come to brushing my teeth in two days.

We both chew the Tums slowly, trying to put off what we're about to do for as long as possible. The new clothes feel like a half shower.

I'm glad Bart's with me. I need the support, not to mention the clothes.

And this is why we're here.

First off, Amy told him to "get his face away from her face for a while," and she's never said anything like that before. That was four hours ago. At the time, I was in a diner, panic-stricken that my time was running out. The quick breakup with Madge wasn't going to happen and I was trying to devise a new plan to track down Evelyn again and ease her into the truth—without scaring her off. The waitress, a motherly type I'd confessed my problems to, cut me off from coffee I'd been downing like shots and lent me her cell phone. "Call someone to come pick you up, hon. Trust me on this." I called Bart. His voice was shaky. He said he'd be there as soon as possible. When I got in the car, he spilled it.

"Madge knows about the other woman," he said dramatically. "She's had your phone the entire time and has been texting with Evelyn, pretending to be you. Madge hates you, but she doesn't care that much because she had sex last night with this guy in a band called the Babymakers."

I was plenty pissed—I've yet to see the asshole, but I can imagine their future children—half Madge, half Sid Vicious. It's not attractive. I can't really be that mad at Madge for cheating on me—I don't have much of a leg to stand on there—but I'm fucking pissed I was subjected to that music for an entire afternoon.

The most important intel that Bart got was that Madge would be at Club Q tonight. I will finally be able to end this.

And now, standing outside the club, the chalky remnants of Tums on my tongue, I ask Bart, "Does Madge know I'm going to be here?"

"Sometimes I think Amy's a genius. I mean, who knows whether she let it slip in front of me that Madge was coming here tonight just so you would come here tonight. Honestly . . ." He rubs his wrist. "I can feel the strings being pulled by the puppeteer."

"It doesn't matter. We are where we have to be."

THE INSIDE OF CLUB Q smells like an Urban Outfitters fitting room. Three guys walk by in tank tops. You can tell they're cold—their nipples poke through the cotton. We stand in the least populated corner. Everyone is white, skinny, and chain-smoking. They all look like they'd rather be somewhere else. A skinny girl in leopard-print tights is pressed against a skinny guy. I hear moans coming from their direction, but I'm not sure which one is doing the moaning. I feel self-conscious.

"You couldn't have brought jeans?" I say.

"Amy threw out all of my jeans while I was at work the day after our envisioning session." Bart pauses. "I miss them."

"I need a drink," I say. "How much money do you have?"

Bart takes out his wallet out and flips it open. "None," he says, "but I have a credit card, which is like money but better. Amy figures one day we'll pay it all off—lump sum."

The inside of the club is no bigger than an oversized Starbucks. But as small as the club is, it's efficient. There are two bars, one on each end, maybe twenty-five feet apart. Both bars are about half full, but the club isn't near capacity yet. It's about thirty minutes until the first band goes on. Bart follows me to the bar on the east end.

I scan the club for Madge while Bart orders two Heinekens. "I don't see her." He starts a tab and hands me a beer.

"What are you going to say?"

"I'm going to walk up to her and say things I haven't thought of yet." I set my beer back down on the counter. "They'll be damn good things, though."

There are three bands on the bill, and I don't know which is set to go on first. But I'm sure all of them are here by now. We drink and scan and drink. I point at Bart's Heineken bottle. "Another beer?"

Bart looks at his beer bottle. He nods. "But make it a light. Amy's been all 'Those pleats look like they're pinching your waistline . . .'"

"Two Heineken Lights," I tell the bartender. Bart's staring at Leopard Tights and the guy she's with. They're still pressed against the wall. Someone's scribbled THE BABYMAKERS STOLE YOUR GIRL-FRIEND in permanent marker and in all capital letters on the wall behind them. It had to be Adrian or someone else from the band—I can't imagine them having any fans, especially any willing to graffiti in the name of their art.

Still, this is starting to feel so hopeless. I should've come clean that morning in Evelyn's bed. I was too busy falling in love and too chicken shit that I'd screw it up.

And then—apropos of nothing—I see Dot. She's at the other bar. She's holding a mixed drink. Next to her is a guy in an argyle sweater vest. He looks like a barista or an accountant, depending on the city. He sips from a bottled water. Dot laughs every few seconds, like an alarm.

Bart follows my eyes.

"That's Dot. Evelyn's friend. You don't think . . ."

The lights dim and the house music gets louder. I'm not familiar with the preshow music. It's fuzzed out from the shitty equipment and what seems to be equally, if not more so, shitty acoustics, but it sounds like Passion Pit or maybe of Montreal—a repeated bass line with a half-dozen synths and a unisex falsetto. I'm scanning the crowd now for Evelyn.

And then: past the bouncer banding everyone over twenty-one, not ten feet away from Leopard Tights and her boyfriend still going at it against the wall, is *Evelyn.* Just standing there. Right there!

Evelyn looks like she was cut out of a magazine ad. She's in a navy polka-dot dress under a tan trench coat. I almost choke. I think about telling Bart, but I worry if I look away and then back, Evelyn will disappear.

Evelyn doesn't look around the club. She's obviously not a tourist. There is still no sign of Madge. Bart is still watching the couple dry-humping against the wall. I have formulated my plan: there is no plan.

Evelyn is now heading toward Dot and Sweater Vest. This is my one chance.

"Hold this," I tell Bart, pushing my beer in his direction. He reaches out to grab it, but I drop the bottle too soon, and the Heineken Light falls on the floor, spilling all over Bart's boat shoes. We both look at his shoes for a second. "You'll thank me for that," I tell him. I'm already backing away before I turn around and head straight for Evelyn.

I catch her in the middle of the club. It's pretty smooth, actually. It looks rehearsed. In a stroke, I slide my hand into hers and guide her to the most desolate part of the club, which ends up being the wall space between the men's and women's restrooms.

Evelyn's not shocked, which momentarily shocks me. She seems annoyed. I'm glad she doesn't have a drink yet. She has nothing to throw in my face. I'm worried what Madge said to her when she was pretending to be me. A few strands of Evelyn's bangs have fallen over her forehead. She pushes them to the side. She leans against the wall as casually as possible.

There's a steady flow of people going in and out of the bathrooms.

"What are you doing?" Evelyn says.

"Hi," I say.

"What are you doing?" she says again. "Godfrey, let go of my hand." We look at my hand together. I didn't even realize I was still holding hers. "Now," she says.

I let my hand fall to my side. It feels awkward. I stuff it into my pocket. I do the same with the other. I like to feel evened out.

"What the hell has gotten into you?"

"I found my father," I say. "He's been keeping himself seaside."

"What? I'm talking about the text messages. The bath salts, the clean pee, all that *Twilight* stuff."

Damn. Madge has had some sick field day. "Okay," I say. "The truth. I didn't send those texts. I still don't have my phone." I raise my hands as proof of my obvious phonelessness. "It was my fiancée. My *ex*-fiancée." But since I can't honestly fully claim the ex part, I say, "Well, technically—"

"I'm walking away. Right now. Don't talk to me. Or look at me with that face."

"What face?"

"*That* face."

"But it's my face. How can I look at you with someone else's face?"

Evelyn pushes herself off the wall. I'm losing her, and there's nothing I can do. I'm about to give up when I catch Madge out of the corner of my eye. There's no meandering in her steps—she's on a straight march. I look back at Evelyn. Fuck it. I put my hand on her cheek. There's a light gasp. I see the light freckles under her eyes.

I know that I don't have much time with her. "If you ever find a brooch," I say, "a specific brooch . . ."

"What?" Her face is still flushed.

"Just promise me you'll think of me and wear it. A pear brooch . . ."

"A pear brooch," she says, astonished. "You want me to wear it . . ."

"In some future, any future at all!"

And I don't know why, but Evelyn softens into me. I slide my hands around her waist. I pull her to me. And I kiss her. We fall in place. Evelyn's eyes were closed before my lips touched hers and I don't want to feel left out, so I close mine and imagine everything that will probably not happen: days feeling like amusement parks, burying my mother together, following our kids into tubes, dying together in a bed the size of the moon.

And for a few moments, Madge ceases to exist. For a few moments, I understand why we have lips. We give escalators of light a reason to wrap around our heads. I discover a new part of mouth and teach it to French. I study every movement like a history lesson.

A tap on my shoulder jars me away from Evelyn's lips. When I finally open my eyes, Madge is standing next to us, smiling like she just bought a winning lottery ticket and stuck it into her bra for safe keeping. My eyes go from Madge back to Evelyn. Evelyn looks confused. Madge looks disconcertingly confident, and I can tell by the infinitesimal droop of one eyelid that she's already had a drink or two.

Madge is about to win, and she knows it. It's obvious she's not going to speak first. She's wearing the engagement ring, twirling it with her thumb like this was her wish all along.

I feel like I'm fading. I want to find a backseat with Evelyn, melt into her until morning. I'll explain everything when we wake up. All news is taken better in daylight, right?

I could grab Evelyn's hand right now and make a run for it. We'll push right through Madge. I'll high-five Bart on our way out of the club. Hell, there's already a sound track going. The lighting is damp. Outside of the club, I'll hold up a map. *Close your eyes and point,* I'll tell her. *This is an anywhere feeling.*

Evelyn speaks up first. "Since Godfrey isn't going to introduce us," she says, extending her hand to Madge, "I'm Evelyn."

Madge takes Evelyn's hand. Madge's face is a portrait at Sears. She got that smile surgically planted to her face. "That's so Godfrey," Madge says. "Always aloof. I'm surprised he remembered the ring when he got on his knee." I'm sweating. Madge wraps her arm through mine and kisses my cheek. Madge's voice jumps an octave. "Isn't that right, honey?"

I can see my future shape-shift right in front of me. In fifteen years my mom is still dead, I'm wearing middle management pants with an elastic waist, balding, in a basement jerking off. There's no Evelyn. I'm holding air.

"I'm sorry," Evelyn says. "You said something about a ring?"

"Oh, honey, you didn't think?" Madge points to Evelyn and then me. She laughs. "Oh, sweetheart. The wedding's in June. I know, I know what you're thinking. Summer wedding, hot, probably rainy, but my grandmother's sick. Don't worry, you look worried. It's not cancer or anything; she's just really old, and we don't know how long. Godfrey here just adores her so much. He couldn't imagine having the wedding without her. Isn't he just the cutest?" Her grandmother is a real wise-cracker, but that's the only truth here.

"This isn't true, Evelyn. Let me tell you everything from the very beginning. It'll all make sense."

"Is she your fiancée or not?" Evelyn asks.

"I want to start this over," I say again, extricating my arm from Madge's grip. "From the beginning. I'd like to start at birth, but I can speed it all up to this very moment in time."

The house music seems louder now. I feel dizzy. The bass line is a metronome. I wonder why we aren't all talking in rhythm. Evelyn is breathing heavily.

"Godfrey," Madge says in her very calm voice. "Aren't we engaged?"

"You know it's not that simple, Madge."

"I think it's very simple!" Madge yells.

"Are you engaged or not?" Evelyn says again, but this time softly, almost inaudibly. She's beginning to shift from foot to foot, like she could bolt at any moment. She pulls a scarf out of the pocket of her trench coat and starts winding it around her neck. Her hands are shaking. She looks like she's trying not to cry.

"Tell her!" Madge says. "Tell her the truth!"

"You slept with the Babymakers' lead singer," I say. "That doesn't feel very engaged."

"You had sex with Adrian?" Evelyn says at first looking stung, but then she raises her hands close to her ears as if she's overloaded.

"Wait," I say. "You know Adrian?"

She nods her head ever so slightly.

"You're *that* Evelyn? The one who was obsessed about some future where you two fought over *cheese*? Small, small world," Madge says.

"You dated Adrian?" I'm the last to catch on here.

"Yes," Evelyn says. "But before I even met you. We were already broken up. See how that's supposed to work?"

"Wait." I'm trying to figure out what went wrong. What happened to all of my decisions being made from the heart—that counting for something? "But I sent you the singing telegram, the duck. Didn't you get it?"

"The duck was for me?"

"Of course! It sang the national anthem. Who else would it be for?"

"The duck got robbed, Godfrey."

"Before or after the national anthem?"

"It doesn't matter now. Does it? I mean, is that your definition of meaningful communication?" Evelyn fumbles with the scarf at her neck and that's when I see the brooch. A pear-shaped brooch.

I say, "Wickham Purdy!" just like that because, my God, somehow that brooch already made it to Evelyn!

"Wicked what? What are you talking about?" Madge laughs loudly. "Is that a New England thing or a Southern thing?"

Evelyn looks down at the brooch. "Dot," she says. "She reverse-stole it back to me. Did you plan this?" She stares at me angrily. "Did you set me up somehow? And all you have to say to me is 'wicked purdy'?"

"No, I didn't set you up. Why would I do that?"

"Why didn't you tell me about her?" Evelyn says, motioning to Madge, but she's not looking at me. She staring at the floor. "You were engaged. You must have loved her—at some point, in some way. You can't just pretend that someone doesn't exist."

Everything's swirling around so insanely that I can't grab hold of any part of the conversation.

Evelyn taps her fingers on her forehead and says quickly, as if trying to cast a spell, "It's all bullshit! It's all bullshit! It's all bullshit!" She shakes her head. "It's not working!" She points at Madge. "You wrote those texts. You said he overly loves his mother and *Twilight* and that he smokes bath salts and . . . wait." She swings back to me. "Are you on parole?"

"I'm not any of those things! Though I care about my mother deeply and what asshole doesn't love his mother?"

Madge laughs. "You want the truth?" she says. "He lisped as a child, which his mother was very worried about because she was convinced that was a sign he was going to grow up gay."

"Did my mother tell you that?" I say because my mother has never told me that.

Madge charges on and it feels like some horrible nightmare. "He sometimes hums while having sex. He's part of a longstanding D and D group, like they've met for *decades*. And, and, the worst part of Godfrey Burkes." She swings around and gestures at me sarcastically like I'm a game-show prize. "The saddest fucking part about him . . . is his potential. He could be *amazing* and he isn't. And how can you be with someone like that day after day?"

Madge reaches out and touches Evelyn's arm. "Adrian and I met at our envisionist's office. He told me he'd have never gone if it weren't for you." Madge then turns to me. "He handed me an ad for his band in the lobby, and after you took off, I tracked him down."

"You met at Plotnik's?" I say as if this matters at all, but still, I'm pissed at Dr. A. Plotnik. She could have been more forthright in the restaurant, but she probably was on Madge's side all along.

"As if any of it matters. I mean, what with the news," Madge says.

"What news?" Evelyn says.

"CNN's breaking the story. Didn't you hear? All that envisioning is bullshit. The FCC is coming down on all of them hard. I never believed it anyway. I mean, why wouldn't someone just use it to fix the stock exchange, right?"

"That's what I said!" I tell Madge.

She just stares at me. "What?"

This explains why everyone had flocked to Chin's—one last chance—and why Chin said he'd miss me. And why Dr. A. Plotnik accused me of being one of the people who turned them in. It's not bullshit. There are all the things I saw and Evelyn showing up again and again and the brooch . . . Still, there's a tide of relief—my mother might not die so young.

"Too bad about Amy and Bart," Madge says. "I guess they're not going to end up rich after all!"

Evelyn glances between me and Madge, sharp glares. "Chin is closing? I've got to go back before it all gets shut down." And then she turns and starts to push through the crowd, which has gotten dense.

"Evelyn!" I shout.

"Don't follow her," Madge says, and then, with a flicker of compassion, she adds, "Give her time."

And maybe Madge is right. I'm not sure what to do. I can feel the distance between Evelyn and me stretching out. She's past the woman in leopard tights and her boyfriend—dry-humping now with intensity. I know that I should maybe let Evelyn go, but I can't. I have to follow her. I really have no other choice.

I start to head after her, but Madge grabs my arm and says, "I loved you." For a second her eyes flash with tears and the real Madge is there—the one I fell in love with. She exists. Madge's chin bobs once and then she's angry again, but she manages to say, "I don't regret it. Don't . . ." And then she stops and takes in a sharp breath. "Don't regret loving me either."

I can't look at Madge now. She's become real and vulnerable when I least expected it. I feel sorry for us—all that time together not being real and vulnerable. I say, "I wasted a lot of time just trying to guess what you wanted me to say."

And then there's a figure behind Madge—a man wearing a deep purple V-neck. He has just enough stubble on his face that it looks like he didn't have time to shave this morning because he was up all night fucking and missed the alarm. He smiles at Madge and she smiles back, like two people seeing each other in the wild for the first time after having sex. "Hey you," he says, and he gives Madge's shoulder a friendly punch. "You showed up!"

"Godfrey, this is Adrian," Madge says, beaming. "Adrian, Godfrey."

"Hey." Adrian—lead singer of the Babymakers, former boyfriend of Evelyn, current lover of Madge, creator of the line "You are only aware of love when your lips are drenched in sun" and now wearer of purple V-necks. "You're going to love this set tonight. It's rank with broken hearts." I'm not sure if this means Adrian knows that I'm the ex or if Adrian is a salesman who thinks broken hearts sell?

"Whether envisioning is real or not, I'll still bet that in ten years the Babymakers will be selling songs to Volkswagen commercials," Madge says, and then her viciousness is back. "And you'll still be in a basement touching yourself."

Adrian puffs a little and says, "Hey, thanks," to Madge.

I turn to go, but then stop. And I realize as I'm turning around that, all this time with Madge, I've been terrified of her. From the first moment when she called my doodling vaginalia to this very moment now. From the moment she looked at me and seemed to see a better me, I've not wanted to lose that better me. But that better me is not me.

"Give me the ring back," I tell her.

Without looking at me, she slides the engagement ring off her finger and shoves it into my open palm. I'm confused by its lightness. Shouldn't something so important be heavier?

"You know what? You brought me to Adrian," Madge says happily. "There are no accidents, right?"

I'm not afraid of Madge anymore. She's just this human being in a bar who had sex with the guy standing next to her. I imagine that I should have to screw up all my courage to say what I have to say, but I don't. "Adrian," I say. "It was a pleasure meeting you." I look at Madge, and the smile is easy and free. "Screw you."

I run back to the east bar. Bart has a new light beer. He's crying.

"Bart, what the hell? Jesus, I don't have time for this. Pull yourself together."

"It's been debunked by scientists," Bart says, blubbering. "I'm not going to be rich! I'm going to be just me but old! The bartender told me. Did you hear?"

"You need to get this guy out of here," the bartender says.

"Stop crying!" I say to Bart.

"No, no, no," Bart says. "These are happy tears, Godfrey. I'm going to stay me."

"I'm happy for you, Bart. Listen, I need your keys!" Evelyn has a head start, but I know where she's going.

Evelyn
FUTURES

The strip mall parking lot is completely empty. I'm standing in front of Chin's, jagged with nerves. I want to lift a car, metaphorically, to save someone pinned beneath it. I think the person pinned beneath it, metaphorically, is also me. What happened in the bar? Who is Godfrey Burkes? Is Godfrey Burkes a liar? How did he know about the brooch? I asked Dot before I left; she had no idea and didn't want me to leave, but I told her she had to let me be alone—that's something Dot respects. The hardest thing is that he didn't tell me anything about Madge—nothing at all. And then, poof, this woman and a ring and Godfrey standing there, his feet glued to the floor. I swam on a goddamn park bench for him. I was planning for a future with Godfrey while Godfrey was planning for a future with . . . Madge. Pathetic. I've dealt with closed eyes long enough. He pretended she didn't exist. Like my parents with my sister. It's too much. We all have closets, but he should have emptied his out before he threw rocks at my window.

What happened in the bar doesn't matter anymore. None of that matters. It's already the past and the past is dead. It's a shed skin. The present is worthless. It's just a thin membrane between the death of the past and the endless offerings for living in the future. I pick the future.

"'People can foresee the future only when it coincides with their own wishes, and the most grossly obvious facts can be ignored when they are unwelcome,'" I whisper. That's some George Orwell. Was I only duping myself? Was any of my envisioning real? It felt so real.

I want the future only. Is this what Fadra would call shutting down? Maybe. But it's opening up to something else—trading in reality for possibility, right?

I prop up my bike with its kickstand but don't take the time to lock it. Let some emo skate punk steal it. I no longer care. I walk to Chin's front door. There, dead center, is an official sign. DO NOT ENTER. CRIME SCENE. The address and date are scribbled in pen and signed by an investigator.

I need more futures. Just enough to restart my life. Tomorrow it might all be gone. Tomorrow I might not have another chance.

I am going to break into Dr. Chin's. I find a sizable rock in a fake garden outside the nail salon.

I played softball in high school, but I was stuck in right field. I was referred to as the Girl Least Likely to Ever Touch the Ball. I can see the faded paint chips of the red dragon that was painted on the glass of Chin's front door. How hard do you throw a rock at a glass door to break it?

I cock my arm back and the rock goes. It hits the glass door and falls to the ground. It barely makes a sound—just a slight thud, like a firework with a bad fuse.

I walk to the front door and pick up the rock again. I take ten steps back. I imagine Godfrey's fiancée's face at the door.

I cock my arm back. *It's all in the follow-through.* That's what the sports movies tell you. *Follow. Through.*

I do. I keep my arm stretched out even as the rock hits Godfrey's fiancée's face and bounces off the glass. It hits the ground with the same muted thud as before. I pick up the rock, grip it, knowing it's not going to work a third time.

I know this is crazy. This buzzing in my limbs isn't good. My heart feels like a hyper-gong. My breath is ragged in my throat. None of this stops me. I can't stop. "Desperation is the raw material of drastic change." Who said that? My mind is a blank.

I put the rock in the pocket of my trench coat and scan the entire strip mall. There are two benches on opposite sides of the double doors, potted plants covered in week-old snow. The benches have bars in the middle of them so the bums can't sleep there. The entire strip mall is bare. Really, the only two things standing are me and the trash can down by the curb.

The trash can. It's settled in a steel bin so it won't blow away, but the trash can itself isn't secured to anything. I try to lift it. It's heavy and my mittens don't have any gripping. I get it halfway out when I lose my hold.

"Fuck!"

I look ridiculous. Me, in a dress and tan trench coat, mascara bleeding down my cheeks, frozen, trying to yank out a trash can. I'm also wearing the scarf—one that Dot pinned a stolen pear brooch to without my consent—one that made me believe, for

a brief moment, that Godfrey and I were meant to be together. A
brooch. I put that much into a brooch.

I take off my mittens and stick them in the right pocket of
my coat. I lift the trash can from its sides and breathe out of my
mouth. I dump the remainder of the trash on the ground. The
trash can is light now, and I'm able to lift it above my head. I feel
invincible. This is a story I will tell my future children during a
future envisioning session. I walk to the door, grunt while I throw
the trash can at the glass door. It bounces right off the glass and
begins to roll down the walkway. It's coming straight for me. I step
out of the way and the trash can keeps going down the walkway,
over the curb, and right into the parking lot. It stops right in the
middle of the lot.

And then I figure, why not? I came this far. I walk right up to
the front door and give it a push. It swings open and I'm hit with
a blast of heat. Of course the door is unlocked. How could it not
be? This is Dr. Chin's—probably the shittiest envisioning center in
all of Baltimore.

I don't waste any time.

To avoid memories of past envisionings, I walk to an examination room I've never been in before. In fact, I've never been this far
down the hall before. I lock the door. In case that's not enough, I
drag a chair across the room, and prop it on its hind legs. I shove
the back of the chair under the doorknob. I've seen this in movies.

The pills are locked in a glass cabinet. Then I remember the rock
in the pocket of my trench coat.

This time the rock goes through the glass like a punch.

The pills are in a large, clear container. It's nondescript—no label
or anything. This shit is shady. The FCC *should* be on Chin's ass.

I unscrew the lid and dump half of the bottle onto the tray. I feel strangely calm, resolute.

I pour a cup of water from the water cooler. I roll the tray over to the examination table. No gown for me, thanks. Why were they ever necessary?

I type my name, date of birth, and Social Security number into the computer. The system starts. The machine knows it's me. "Hello," I tell it. "It's just the two of us now."

The welcome screen I've seen dozens of times before appears. This time, though, it's a little different. On the bottom right-hand corner of the screen is a tab labeled Hypotheticals. I've never seen this before. Has Chin upgraded his software since the last time I've been here? I move the cursor down and click on it. The computer grumbles. One of those swirling beach balls spins in the center of the screen while I wait for the information to load. It feels like I'm on hold. The only sounds are the on and off spasms of the modem. Chin is cheap. This Dell is aged.

The computer finishes loading. The screen is white. At the top, in all caps: WARNING! THIS IS A BETA TESTER! USE OF THE SYSTEM MAY CAUSE SEIZURES AND/OR INDIFFERENCE!

The interface looks like Google's homepage—a tiny box to type your question into. If I understand correctly, this program will allow me to ask it a question and it will play the scenario out. I could ask it anything: What if every book had a happy ending? What if the votes in Florida were counted correctly? What if Godfrey Burkes goes off and marries his fiancée?

But there's only one question I am interested in asking. There's only one question I've ever really wanted to know the answer to. And it has nothing to do with Godfrey Burkes.

My hands are shaking. It takes four tries before I spell everything correctly. *What would have happened if my sister lived?* Next to the box where you type the hypothetical question is a link: Go! I swallow a pill and then one more for good measure, sip some water and click Go!

Everything on the screen is crisp—beyond high definition, the realest real ever. Brand names aren't fuzzed out. You can almost see the air move.

The scene opens in a middle-class suburban neighborhood. The camera goes from the row of houses and manicured lawns to the street. I know this street. It's my childhood neighborhood. Cars drive by, but there is no noise. It's eerily quiet. I guess the beta version doesn't have sound yet. The muted world gives me a chill; I shudder. The camera is pointed at an intersection, halted by a stop sign. I look at the names of the streets on the green signs crisscrossed above the stop sign. It's the intersection of Maple and Bellington. I used to live right down this block, and I know exactly what day it is.

Right on cue, there's the bike. The camera starts at the spokes. Then a quick cut to the pedals—a little girl's feet in loosely laced red Keds. My sister's face. She's breathing, her cheeks puffing, over and over again—like little bellows on her face, and I stare at her face. Her hair is longer than I remember from the photographs—her bangs are bouncing off her forehead. She's flying down the sidewalk. She's almost to the intersection.

I grip my legs. She rounds the intersection. I want to close my eyes, but I can't.

There's no car this time.

My sister makes a sharp turn down Maple and takes her first

breath from her second life. And she keeps going, keeps breathing. She stops pedaling and coasts up the driveway to the house I grew up in. She hops off the bike and lets it fall in the yard. The grass looks like it was cut yesterday. The camera follows her through the front door. My father is on the couch, reading the paper. My mother is in the kitchen, dropping berries into a blender. They're so young! So vivid! They look at my sister. My father puts down his paper and motions for her to come to him. He opens his mouth.

The screen skips in five-year intervals. Now, my sister, at seventeen, is in the back of a truck. She has breasts. Her bangs are tucked to the left. She's with a boy. They're lying in the bed of the truck, wrapped up in a sleeping bag. I guess it's cold—their breaths crisscross. It's dark, but you can see three constellations I can't name. My sister laughs into them.

The screen cuts again. A large auditorium. It's a college graduation. My sister walks across the stage in a red robe. The tassel, the fake diploma, the real handshake with the dean—it's all there. The camera pans around and up, into the balcony. My father is pointing a video camera toward the stage. There's an empty seat next to my mother. She rests her purse on it. I've never seen them smile so purely. I look at the empty seat, my mother's purse. I'm not here. I was never supposed to be.

And then a shrill ringing. I think it's the fire alarm, but it's coming from the screen. The screen goes black and then back to the auditorium. The ringing gets louder. The screen keeps flickering, like the power can't decide if it should go out or not.

I'm not there. The camera focuses on the empty seat. It's taunting me. Everything blurs. My cheeks sting. I wipe my eyes. I'm crying. I didn't even know. How long have I been crying? The screen stops cutting in and out. The image starts to bubble and darken as if it's being cauterized.

I hit the panic button on the joystick. Nothing happens. I press the button and hold. The ringing stops. The screen goes black. I'm still crying. A second later it's back to the main page. The Hypotheticals tab is back on the bottom right corner of the screen.

I've known that if my sister hadn't died, I wouldn't be here. I've known since I was in middle school and pieced it together. So why do I feel like I've been gutted? My parents were so happy. It has been confirmed and for some reason I can't bear it. I wouldn't even have been a thought. Living in an alternate future feels right. It's my destiny.

The blinking cursor on the screen. Whom do I want to spend my future with? Now is the time. The future can swallow me whole. A lifetime of infinite futures . . .

What about twenty-five years from now. The fifties are the new thirties, right?

I take another pill. Maybe the extra pills will make things better. I bring the cup of water to my mouth, but it's empty. I chew the pill and feel dizzy and lost and hungry and sad.

I grip the joystick tightly until my knuckles turn white.

It should've been me, not my sister.

I hit Enter.

Godfrey
NOW

I turn into Chin's parking lot too fast, and there—lit up in the headlights—is a metal trash can. I swerve, but I'm not fast enough and I clip it, hard, with the corner of Bart's grill. The garbage can rolls and then spins to a stop. I pull into a spot, crooked, and jump out of the car, but I don't look at the grill of Bart's car. I know it's whacked. I know this will go on my permanent record with Amy: shit Godfrey's done. And I don't care.

I see Evelyn's bike, propped on its kickstand but unlocked.

The building is quiet and dark. An official notice hangs on the door—CRIME SCENE.

To my right, I catch a light coming from one of the examination room windows. Colors flicker. It's the envisioning screen. Evelyn. She's already started.

I run the length of the building to the lit window. I wipe mist from the glass and look inside.

The screen flickers—people I can't make out, voices talking. Evelyn is lying on the examination table, curled on her side. She's still wearing the dress and trench coat. The tray is dotted with loose pills. Her water glass is tipped and empty.

Is she asleep?

I bang on the glass. "Evelyn!" I shout.

She's asleep, my brain tells me, but I'm also jolted with fear. "She's asleep," I say aloud. I shout her name and she doesn't move. *She is asleep. She is.* I tell myself this, but I'm covering my fist with the sleeve of my jacket, and I punch the window, breaking it. Glass shatters and litters the tiles inside the room. I knock loose the jagged edges of glass with my elbow and climb through the window.

"Evelyn!" I grab hold of her arm. "Evelyn. Talk to me."

She murmurs, but I can't hear what she's saying.

I feel like crying. "You're not dead," I say. "You're not at all dead."

But she's not fully awake either. She whispers words I can't understand. A small language of its own passes through her beautiful lips. I say, "I'm not engaged to someone else. I'm in love with you. The first time I saw you I should have taken your license out of your mouth and kissed you. Do you hear me?"

I look at the screen. The camera is following an older Evelyn as she walks the aisles of a grocery store. She's wearing a nicely tailored suit jacket, a skirt, and modest heels. The fluorescent lights are glaring. Her stockings have a shine to them. Her legs are still beautiful. She's not dressed like a librarian; this is the outfit of someone who holds court—in a boardroom or something?

She picks out a can of soup and tosses it into the cart.

Why is she in this future alone?

And then it's as if the Evelyn on the screen hears me. She whips around and glares at the camera. She's wearing makeup. Her hair is beautifully whipped up on top of her head. She seems to see me—the real me, sitting before the screen—and her expression softens. She says, "I know you. I remember you."

She's older, much older, but glamorous in a way that seems foreign to the Evelyn I know though she's still beautiful.

I look down at Evelyn on the examination table. Her lips tremble. She isn't here, I think. She simply is not here. She's there—in the future.

In the grocery store, Evelyn looks directly into the screen. She says, "I know it's you."

She's not supposed to know I'm here. She's not supposed to be aware at all. The rules are breaking down. I remember what Dr. Chin said about science and the mysteries of true love—they can only exist for so long before weird shit occurs. *In the case of true love, there can be system failures.* This is one hell of a system failure.

"Godfrey," Evelyn in the grocery store whispers. Her full lips lightly chapped. "Godfrey, Godfrey, Godfrey. It's me," she says, and then she tears up. She says, "I want it all back." She smiles and shakes her head, wiping tears from her cheeks as if she's not sure whether she's happy or devastated, or both. Is this what life offers each of us in its own way—moments of happy devastation and devastated happiness? "All of it," she whispers urgently, her eyes bright with tears.

Evelyn's lost her grip on the joystick. It's fallen to the floor. I pick it up, my hands shaking, and press the button. The lights in the grocery store flicker. Evelyn grips the shopping cart's handle, glances beyond the camera, speaking to someone unseen. "I'm sorry," she says. "I shouldn't have. I know the rules." She looks into the camera, fleetingly—at me, I'm sure of it. The real me. Right here. And then she pushes her cart down the aisle and disappears.

The screen is black.

If she's not here but instead somewhere *in there,* I have to go in!

Shit, I need a helmet. I try to open the door but then see that there's a broken chair propped under the doorknob. I kick it out of the way and race down the hall to the next examination room, unplug the helmet, shove it on my head, run back into our examination room, and plug it into the back of machine.

I pluck a pill and swallow it. I type in my name and Evelyn's. I pick a date that's only a year from now. Start small. I'll take what I can get. I climb onto the examination table and pull her up. She's groggy. Her eyes flutter. I say, "Evelyn, I'm here."

She says, "Mmmm," but nothing more. She reaches around my neck but doesn't open her eyes. She rests her helmet on my shoulder and I cradle her.

And then the screen flickers. A new image rises as if from colored ink stains. We're in a kitchen. The windows are sunstruck. But then they go dark as if it's suddenly dusk, then night. I grab Evelyn's hand, and I can feel her hand in mine. I've broken through in some way. I'm not here looking in. I'm in that future with her; we're together.

We move to a patio door and the yard is sunny, the grass a brilliant green. The trees then burn to a bright orange as if it's instantly autumn. I yank open the sliding door. And we walk out into the yard as it starts to flurry. The air is suddenly gusting and the snow covers our shoes.

"Evelyn!" I say. "What is this?"

She looks at me, wide-eyed. "It's moving too fast," she says.

And then the snow melts. Grass muscles up from the ground. There's rain. I feel it on my skin. There's sun. I feel the sudden warmth on my skin.

Evelyn's stomach broadens through another season and another.

And then there's a baby in my arms—beautiful and fat-cheeked. My God! A baby! Evelyn and I stare at the baby, mesmerized, and then the baby is gone. She's tottering around us—a little girl.

The seasons roll, one to the next—the sun, the chill, the snow, the sun . . . And the girl grows and then Evelyn's stomach broadens again. Another baby! She holds the baby for the length of one deep breath. And then there are two girls.

In a heartbeat or two, they're chasing each other until they're older. They seem distracted and grown up and beautiful and then they wander from the yard, as a garden of flowers sprout, flare into blooms, then die, flare and die, flare and die and flare.

"Wait!" Evelyn says—her face older now—beautiful and weathered. "Make it slow down, Godfrey!"

I look around in a panic. "I can't."

And then with no children we both wander the yard. We touch the leaves that wither and fall to nothingness. I'm scared and we're quiet. I walk away and away. There are rolling hills. I crest a dune. There's an ocean.

Evelyn isn't with me. I miss her. Is this how it ends?

The sea is calm and then roiling, beaten with sun then cold and gray. I remember my father, Mart Thigpen, before he pushed his old, heavy body into the waves, telling me to fight for Evelyn. I run back and she's in the yard still. I walk up to her and she touches my face. "There's too much between us to let go." I'm old now but still strong enough to lift her up off her feet, and I hold her as the seasons come and go.

One of my knees gives. I kneel. Evelyn kneels, too. She's crying and I am, too. We hug each other tightly. Our daughters, now older themselves, hover and circle and cry.

Evelyn looks at me. Her breath is rattled. My head is shaking, ever so slightly. We're scared. I grab my chest. I can tell that it aches, deep inside of me. I say, "It goes too fast. How can anyone accept this?" I shake my head. "I can't take it."

But Evelyn says, "I'll take it." Winter melts around us. Spring shoots up. "Because I'm with you."

"And I'm with you," I say.

Summer gives to fall.

Winter is back.

Evelyn presses her ear to my chest, her grip tightens—snowflakes collect on her lashes then melt—and her hold goes slack. Her eyes stare blankly, and I know she's gone. I rock her as the snow and sun whip around us and then the dusk turns to night. And the night lasts.

The screen is blank.

I'm sitting in the examination room, cradling Evelyn.

She draws in a breath so quick I feel her ribs expand against my chest. "Godfrey!" she says, staring up at me.

"It's that quick," I say. "Our lives. That fucking quick and then it's over."

"It's that quick," she says. "But we never stop yearning. We don't give that up."

"I'm not on parole. I don't smoke bath salts. I love my mother but not too much. I really haven't followed *Twilight*. I'm not any of those things you thought. And I'm not engaged to someone else. I'm not perfect. But love's rare," I tell her. "The true lifetime kind. Someone told me that once. And we can endure. *You're* the one who said that—or you will one day, I hope."

"I have a hole inside of me that's never going to be completely filled. It's not possible. I felt it even when I was holding the children. I felt it even in the end when you were holding me."

"I love that about you," I say. "It draws me to you."

"We could really build a family," she says. "And it's not perfect and even though we saw it, that's not how it's going to happen. It can't."

"We can't know," I say. "Whether you think you know the future or not, it's all a leap of faith. You've got to be willing."

"I'd like to try some *now* with you," she says. "One *now* after the next."

"Let's make it so they add up after a while," I say.

"I think that's the way it is with good *nows*."

"Like this one," I tell her.

"And this one."

Author's Note

The original idea for *The Future for Curious People* came from Julianna Baggott. I was sleeping on an air mattress in my childhood bedroom when Julianna approached me to write this book with her. At the time I was thinking about my own future—not in any curious way, mind you, but more of a *I'm twenty-seven sleeping on an air mattress in my childhood bedroom, this will probably be me at forty with a widow's peak and a penchant for microwavable Salisbury steak, holy shit* kind of way. But then I looked at the world Julianna had begun to create, and was immediately consumed. I saw pieces of myself in all of the characters—Godfrey and Evelyn and Bart and Madge and Adrian—and I grew curious. I groped over past romances. What if the one who got away didn't? What if she just stayed? What if I was cooler in high school and girls actually noticed me, and instead of eating lunch in Ms. McNeely's classroom I was outside by the bike rack, making out with Carey Henderson? These were characters to love, to dream about, and eventually, to learn from. I had to be a part of it.

It would be an understatement to say that this book you are holding wouldn't exist without Julianna. For those who don't know Julianna, she's a bestselling, critically acclaimed author who's published twenty books under her own name—most notably The Pure Trilogy—as well as two pen names, Bridget Asher and N.E. Bode. (You can find out more about her at www.juliannabaggott.com.) A mentor of mine for eight years now, Julianna has not only cultivated my voice, but she has also become a friend and someone whom I love dearly. Creating this book was a ride that I didn't want to end. From the moment I agreed to take on this project, we shared the same vision of what this book should, could, and eventually did become. I can't tell you how excited I am to share The Future for Curious People with you. Thank you for picking it up. Take it home with you. This book is ready for a good home.

Acknowledgments

Thank you to my agent, Nat Sobel, as well as Judith Weber, Julie Stevenson, and Kirsten Carleton. I am in constant awe of your brilliance.

Thank you to my editor, Andra Miller. You fell in love with the novel before you even finished it, and if that's not foreshadowing, then I don't know what is. You're kind of amazing.

Thank you to Justin Manask for being the novel's West Coast lifeline. You were one of the earliest champions of the book, and your constant persistence has meant so much.

Thank you to Gregory Greenberg and Megan Laurel for your promotional help before the novel even went to auction. Your likeness is not just in the art and music you put together, but it's on every page. Your friendship has made me a better person.

Thank you to David Scott for typing in edits and keeping all of the paperwork in order. Also, for loving Julianna (which is way more important than typing in edits).

Thank you to my early readers Dario Sulzman, Abigail Cory, Lorin Drinkard, Ashley Harris Paul, Alise Hamilton, Ariell Cacciola, and Mindy Friddle.

Thank you to Julianna Baggott, for everything I've already said. There are not enough words to thank you, so I will make up some of my own. Look for that email soon.

And never the last, thank you to my parents for keeping me going these last eight years. I know it hasn't been easy; I'm sorry for all of the premature wrinkles and gray hairs I've given you.

MIKE STANTON

Gregory Sherl is the author of three collections of poetry, including *The Oregon Trail Is the Oregon Trail,* shortlisted for the *Believer* magazine's 2012 Poetry Award. He currently lives in Oxford, Mississippi. His website is www.gregorysherl.net.